Patch Town
A novel based on the true story of the town that united against corporate power
J.A. Stein

J.A. Stein

Copyright © 2025 by J.A. Stein

All rights reserved.

No part of this publication may be reproduced, distributed, or transmitted in any form or by any means, including photocopying, recording, or other electronic or mechanical methods, without the prior written permission of the publisher, except as permitted by U.S. copyright law. For permission requests, contact J.A. Stein at authorjastein@gmail.com.

The story, all names, characters, and incidents portrayed in this production are fictitious. No identification with actual persons (living or deceased), places, buildings, and products is intended or should be inferred.

Book Cover by Venom Co.

Edited by Gail Delaney

ISBN (paperback): 979-8-9864908-6-1

ISBN (ebook): 979-8-9864908-7-8

For Granny, Poppy, and all my Mary D family members

Author's Note

This novel is based on a true story. The main events described within as they pertain to the coal company of Maryd and bootlegging are as accurate as I could reconstruct. That said, since a great many of the current residents of Maryd are descendants of those involved in the real 1938 event, I have chosen to make all of my characters and their families purely fictional. Any similarities in name or actions are purely coincidental. The one exception to this is Sheriff Fred Holman, who I kept in name only.

Note the modern-day spelling of the town is Mary D. I chose to keep the spelling as Maryd, which is how the newspapers and other records printed it in the 1930s.

For a detailed historical note that further separates fact and fiction, please see the end of the book. Any mistakes are my own.

Prologue

As bootleg coal miners, the 500 residents of the town of Maryd, Pa., did not like it when the new Maryd Mining Co. began legal digging in the hill under their town. When the company tunneled back 100 feet into the hill and its shafts threated to undermine Maryd's homes, Maryd took action. One night last week, Maryd's menfolk marched down the hillside to the mine opening, dragged out the watchman, machinery, tools. As Maryd's womenfolk stood back looking on, they set off 36 sticks of dynamite, blew the new mine clean out to the sky. Maryd shook slightly, settled down. Maryd Mining Co. had nothing left but a big hole. "If we arrest anybody," shrugged Sheriff Fred Holman, "we'll have to arrest the whole community."

"Under Maryd"
TIME Magazine, June 27, 1938

CHAPTER 1

Monday, May 30, 1938

His gaze caught that of the lanky, shirtless boy. He was perhaps ten, with messy hair and a streak of dirt across one cheek. His pants—at least two sizes too big—were held up with a frayed piece of twine. He padded by in his bare feet, meeting the stranger's gaze with a fearless challenge, and then he was past. Though the boy carried on, the man stopped in his tracks, turning back to look over his shoulder at the boy's bony back.

Strange, this town. The children ran free like wild things. The women watched from porches and small yards as they washed and hung laundry. And the men—what men? The stranger knew they worked below.

As if to confirm his thought, the steam whistle at the mine down the road let loose. He was just in time for the end of the shift. He straightened his worn fedora, hefted his rucksack higher on his shoulder, and headed down the small rise where Main Street fell into a V between the hills to the mine office, a block building outside an old breaker and the mine outbuildings. The black coal tailings crunched underfoot. As he got closer to the looming steel-clad breaker, the hair on the back of his neck prickled. It was too quiet. The giant machine that took up a building as large as a factory warehouse was still. It wasn't the first coal town he'd been in that was living in the shadow of closed mines and shuttered breakers. But he'd come here because the mine was supposed to be open. And hiring.

Nearby, an arched tunnel into the side of the mountain disappeared like the yawning mouth of a monster. From there came the noise, and Patrick relaxed the tension within himself. The mine train, four cars long and led by a small engine only as high as Patrick's waist, returned to daylight, laden with men as black-faced as the hole they emerged from. One by one, they turned off the sandwich-box-sized battery packs of their headlamps, removed helmets, shook out dusty clothes, and wiped sweat from their brows. With a nod to each other, they swung their empty lunch tins and headed to town, sparing the stranger only a glance or a courteous nod. It was a good sign. They must be used to new blood in this town. He wouldn't be the outsider for long.

He headed into the mine office, where the clerk, partially buried behind a pile of paperwork, seemed to be in a hurry to go home. Judging by the stack before him, he likely would still be a while. Without looking up from his work, the clerk asked, "Yes?"

He cleared his throat, shifted his rucksack, and straightened. "Patrick Kane, sir. I heard you were looking for more miners."

"Position's been filled."

Patrick frowned and shifted his weight slightly. He didn't let the man's brusque manner deter him. He knew what it was like to work a job you hated. "I need a job, sir."

"Well, you didn't spend money on a ticket from wherever you came from just to work here. Go about your business. Try the collieries down Middleport or Tamaqua."

Patrick didn't move. He kept his gaze steady on the clerk, letting his presence put the pressure on the man.

It worked, as it always did if he was patient enough. Eventually, the clerk sighed and looked up from his ledger. "If you took the train here, you can take the train back out. Plenty of other mines to try."

Patrick shrugged. "I like the area. Can't afford a ticket without a job anyway."

The clerk leaned back in his chair. "Let me guess, you didn't buy a ticket in the first place? You hopped a train like the rest of the hobos, and this is where you've ended up. And I bet you've already inquired at the other mines, and they told you the same thing I'm telling you. We can only hire so many men. Roster's full till the next one quits."

"I'm a good mechanic, sir."

"*Mechanic*? I need *miners*. I need men who know something about anthracite. How it moves like hard black water through the mountain. I need men who can sniff it out and blast it from that mountain like gophers. Can you do that?"

"I learn fast, sir." When the clerk still appeared unconvinced, Patrick tried a different track. "Well, I'm clean out of money until I can work for enough to move on. There someplace I can stay in town until you have an opening? I don't mind camping out."

"Not sure when that'll be."

"With all due respect, sir, it's mining." Patrick met the man's eye. He'd been in coal country long enough to know that mining was a dangerous business. Men got hurt. "Something will open up. I just ask you consider me first."

The clerk studied him up and down. Patrick didn't flinch. He knew the man would gauge his size, slightly less than average, but advantageous for navigating narrow, low tunnels. He wasn't old, but he was old enough to have the work ethic and experience of a man, not a boy. He was wiry, too, not that the clerk could see that. He *would* see there wasn't much extra weight to fill out his clothes. He needed work to feed his belly.

The door to the mine office opened then, and both men watched as a dirt-encrusted miner limped in. His eyes were glazed with pain, and Patrick quickly noted the bandanas wrapped around a grotesquely swollen knee that strained at the cloth of his pants. Had they been able to see under the layer of coal dirt that darkened the man's face, Patrick was willing to wager the man was as pale as a ghost.

"I smashed my knee on the coal car. Made it through the day, but now it's throbbing. Might be bad. I gotta take some time off. Hopefully only a few days."

The clerk looked from the miner to Patrick, then shook his head in exasperation. "Take all the time you need. Just found your replacement. Mr. Kane, it's your lucky day."

The miner looked warily at Patrick. "But I'll have my job back as soon as the leg is healed, right?"

"Sure, Roger." The clerk looked dubiously at the man's knee. "Better fill out an accident report." He opened a binder and spun it around on his desk for the miner to fill out. His information only took up one line in a grided list of other accidents. Patrick looked away from the binder before it could shake his resolve. The clerk was watching, his lips a thin line.

After a brief second of evaluation, he said to Patrick, "You start at 7 a.m. tomorrow. You can get appropriate clothes from the town store." His eyes raked over Patrick's tidy attire. Perhaps it had been the wrong decision to wear a light-colored shirt to this kind of job inquiry. "You need to supply your own helmet and headlamp. We pay every Friday. You can start at twelve dollars a week. Any questions?"

"Thank you, sir."

The miner watched this exchange with no small degree of distrust.

The clerk spun another piece of paper towards Patrick, which he quickly filled out with his vital information, leaving the address line blank. When both men had set down their pens, the clerk turned back to his ledgers, ignoring them both.

Sensing their dismissal, Patrick followed the miner out of the office, and they paused on the step.

"You new to Maryd?" Roger asked.

He'd have to ask where the town got a name like that later. "Yes." Patrick held out his hand. "Patrick Kane."

The miner shook it firmly, his grip iron. "Roger Clemens. Been here my whole life. You a miner?"

"Steel worker." Patrick hesitated, uncertain how much to reveal, then decided he was far enough away to be safe. "Out of Pittsburgh."

"You come to anthracite country for a change of scenery?"

"You could say that."

"Humph." Roger started limping up the hill towards town, and Patrick followed. "Well, I want my job back. Need it for the family. Soon as this knee has had some time to heal. Dang coal car brakes didn't hold and it pinned me. Ain't looking good."

"Rest should help."

"I sure hope so." He winced. Something in the hard man seemed to soften. "Where you stayin'?"

"Not sure yet. Any boarding houses? Need somewhere cheap."

"Just saw that Ruth Flannigan's got a bed for rent. House is at the top of North Main. White siding, red shutters."

"Thank you."

"Good luck to ya." Roger hobbled off up the south side of Main Street, while Patrick turned north. The town may be hardly more than one central street with a few rowhomes in the back alleys, but he passed two bars on his way to the top of North Main, which overlooked the entire little town, including the dusty breaker down the bottom of the hill. The bars could wait until later. Right now, he wanted nothing more than a place to drop his knapsack and pull off his boots. He'd spent most of the last day walking, hoping that the old, crinkled newspaper ad was a job lead. Luckily, his timing was just right.

The only identifier for the boarding house, other than the rust-red shutters, was a small cardboard sign tacked to the porch railing, "Bed for rent." It looked just like all the rest, a half-a-double townhome with a wooden porch and peeling white paint. Interesting that the sign only mentioned a bed, not a whole room. But that was okay;

hopefully it was cheaper. Hopefully, his roommate wasn't some grouchy, filthy slob. He'd had enough of those.

As his eyes caught those of the rugged yet beautiful woman on the porch, he felt a glimmer of hope that maybe this was one of those scandalous establishments that small towns tried to pretend didn't exist. At the very least, his landlady was a looker. He allowed his lips to show a wry smile.

CHAPTER 2

Ruth straightened, a protective hand over the belly that had just started to strain the fabric of her dress. Her eyes narrowed at the stranger, natural defenses heightened beyond the usual. He was clean—too clean—thus not a miner. His light brown hair was neatly trimmed, his chin clean-shaven. His trousers and cream-colored shirt weren't anything fancy, but they certainly weren't caked in coal dirt. There was no automobile full of luggage, so he wasn't a businessman come to deal with the mine company either. He strode with a straight, easy-going gait towards the house, a worn military-green rucksack tossed over his shoulder with casual grace. The muscles in his forearms bulged beneath the shirtsleeves that were rolled neatly to the elbow.

Maybe he *was* a miner then.

He lifted his chiseled jaw, and she noted the dimple in his chin. His gaze fell into hers. A smile played at his lips, as if he thought he shouldn't be smiling but couldn't help it. There was a hesitation, and then he walked on. His boots thumped loudly on the porch stairs, and then he stood before her, one step down, yet a few inches taller. He had the ideal build for a miner. Short, broad, and likely solid muscle.

He cleared his throat, then held out his hand. "Patrick Kane, ma'am." His brown eyes sparkled.

Warning flared through her nerves. Perhaps it was the appraisal—approval—in his eyes. She should send him on his way. And yet she needed to pay their mortgage for another month. She squinted at him, then slowly proffered a hand. His hands were calloused, his grip gentle but strong enough to promise more strength. She let out a tired breath. Another miner. Well, miners she could handle. It could work.

"How long you be needing a room for, Mr. Kane?"

"Long as I last, I suppose." He flashed a toothy grin, one that the old Ruth would have found handsome.

The baby kicked, a pinching sensation forcing her to withdraw her hand to rub her belly. His eyes followed her hand, lingered for a moment, then met her eye with a shine of recognition. She didn't acknowledge it. "Well, there's a bed available, board included. Room's a decent size. You'll have one roommate. You got a trunk?"

He shook his head, shrugging off his rucksack.

She eyed it, then turned her back, holding the screen door open to him with one hand.

"Supper is at six, just after the shift change. Breakfast at six during the work week, seven on weekends." She stopped and shot a glare at his boots. "I expect clean boots in my house. And I don't do laundry. Mrs. Krajnak down the street does good work, good price. Lord knows I've enough of my own children's clothes to launder." There, she'd said it. The mere mention of children should keep his appraising eyes solidly in his head.

The sound of said children rose from the kitchen, one crying, the other laughing. Bogie emerged, still shirtless as a wild thing, and looked like he was ready to complain about his young sisters, but he closed his mouth when he saw the stranger. His posture took on that of his father, stiff-backed and stern, though on a ten-year-old it made her want to laugh. And then she wanted to cry, for no ten-year-old should have to pretend to be man of the house.

"Bogie, this is Mr. Kane. Our new boarder."

The boy nodded once and leaned against the doorframe between the kitchen and the sitting room, hands tucked behind his back, watching.

Ruth turned back to Kane herself, continuing her lecture. "My children know to leave you well enough alone, so I expect you do the same."

"Yes, ma'am."

She led him into the house and up the stairs. She opened the last door at the end of the short hall and stepped aside, averting her eyes. Kane walked past her and eyed the place. He smelled like fresh water and hard work, the kind of raw masculinity she hadn't had under her roof in months. She tried not to breathe.

"Wash tub's in the basement," she said quietly. "We've got hot water when the furnace is runnin', which is most days as long as I've got coal on hand. I appreciate you leaving that black dirt downstairs. There are clothing hooks by the basement door. Door's in the back of the house. Shower down there, too." She again eyed his neat attire. It was the only part of him that didn't seem to fit. Well, really, none of his clothes quite fit. They'd clearly been made for another man. Or he'd lost a lot of weight. Doubting herself, she asked, "I assume you *are* a miner, aren't you?"

"As of tomorrow, yes, ma'am."

Ah, that explained it. Fresh blood. "Don't suppose you have your rent money now, do you?" She rubbed the middle of her forehead, already suspecting what he'd say.

"No, ma'am. But they tell me they pay on Fridays."

She sighed. "They do." She shouldn't take in a stranger on his word. Heck, he hadn't even offered her his word yet. And yet, the spot had been open for months, and she desperately needed to fill it. The situation had changed, and her backup plan of going back to the factory was no longer an option, not with the baby on the way. "Fine." She dropped her hand to her side. "Pay as soon as you can. Do I have your word, Mr. Kane?"

"Yes, ma'am." He nodded and did a gentlemanly demi-bow.

She was about to wonder at his manners when the lace of one of the curtains fluttered in the breeze, sending a ping of loss to her gut. Unable to stand the room, she turned back down the hall before he could reply. If he didn't want to stay, he knew where the door was. If he did want to stay, well then, he had full range of the house, and it was a risk and an inconvenience she and the children would have to tolerate. Maybe she should have warned him that she owned and knew how to work a shotgun.

No, she admonished herself. *Stop trying to scare off every potential boarder. You need the money.*

She shut herself in the kitchen, which was now empty. Bogie had ushered his little sisters into the backyard, where they again seemed to be at peace. She didn't know what she'd do without him. He was young himself, and yet he'd stepped forward into so much responsibility. Ruth settled at the table and let her head fall into her hands. A sob ripped from her chest, only to be stifled. She straightened, wiped her eyes, then rubbed her belly. Then she began making dinner. The children and her miners needed to eat.

CHAPTER 3

Patrick sat on the wooden chair in the corner of the room, then pulled off his boots and wiggled his toes. It felt good to air his feet and stretch. He'd been traveling for days. A big toe poked through his threadbare sock, the last thing to replace, since it was the last thing people noticed. He looked around the room. It was plain, but neat. Creamy white paint and lace curtains showed care, though they seemed out of place for a men's boarding house. He didn't mind, though. They reminded him a bit of home. He hoped Ms. Ruth was as good a cook as his mother. There were two twin beds, one neatly made, likely his, the other tousled as if the occupant would be back any second. The other boarder wasn't tidy, as his pile of clothes in the corner belied, but at least he kept them in the corner. Or perhaps that was the extent of Ms. Ruth's housekeeping.

Patrick slouched back in the chair and rubbed his face, exhaling deeply. A job. A job at last. He'd been hop-scotching across the state looking for work, taking what he could get between cities, which was never anything more than temporary. Maybe here, in this little coal town, he'd be able to earn enough to build a life on. Anthracite though? Other than knowing it was a shiny black rock, he didn't know much about it. He didn't know how he'd like that deep, dark tunnel in the morning. But it was a job, and he hadn't lied when he said he learned fast. Surely, it couldn't be worse than sweating in the steel mill.

A small dresser next to his bed caught his eye, and he stood to walk to it. The top three drawers were full of men's clothes. The bottom three were empty. He assumed this was for his own meager possessions. He glanced at his rucksack, where it lay by the door. It only held a dirty outfit he'd been living in for weeks and a few more odds and ends. Thank goodness he'd kept one outfit clean. He knew from experience that no one wanted to hire a hobo. A clean—even if by creek water—neatly trimmed man in tidy clothes at least had potential. Something about first impressions and all that.

The putt-putt of an automobile sounded outside the window, and he pulled aside the curtain to watch as it pulled into the big house at the base of the hill. He'd noted the place on the way to the mine. A big two-story house, it stood alone with a wrap-around porch in its own copse of shade trees. It looked like a mansion compared to the rest of the miner housing in town. Really, it was the only house he'd seen in town that wasn't a double-family structure. It had to be the mine boss's house. His attention was drawn across the street, where a few men laughed loudly as they entered one of the bars. The place was just another two-family townhouse, only it had a sign out front and more cars parked around it. The patrons' English was laced with a hodgepodge of accents, some Irish, some Eastern European, some Germanic, and at least one from the good ol' Bronx. Patrick debated heading over for a drink. Wouldn't be bad to meet some of the other miners and town residents, get a feel for the place. For the job.

He stretched, then returned to the chair where he begrudgingly replaced his boots. As he headed out, he glanced at Ms. Ruth's wall clock, which warned he had only half an hour before dinner. That was plenty of time. He heard her in the kitchen, alternating between clinking dishes together and occasionally yelling out the back window. The children must be in the yard. He wondered how many she had. One was obviously on its way. Was she married? Widowed? He guessed widowed and remembered the lace curtains that had seemed to upset her. This must have been her and her husband's room, and then something happened that forced her to take in strangers like him. Risky business to be in, as a woman alone with small children. Even with a son who seemed to think glaring at people made him look older.

Patrick reached into his pocket, checking how much money he had left. There was one crumpled bill, enough for one drink. He didn't need the drink as much as he needed the information about the town and the mine. It would be a good investment. He stepped out of the house and walked across the street. The warm air of early summer was already cooling as the sun dropped lower across the tops of the forested hillsides. No green fields and pastures here. The woods crept right up to the edge of the black piles of coal tailings, and the tailings piles practically sat in the back yards of each house. The area was a cross between a forested wonderland and a barren wasteland. He'd spent the past week in coal country, and he still wasn't quite used to how the two coincided.

The bar was small, smoky with all forms of tobacco, and loud. Other than the round-figured bartender with her short-cropped hair and loud laugh, the place was dominated by men. They were mostly miners, judging from the black lines of dirt still etched into the creases of their knuckles and fingers. No one seemed to pay Patrick much attention, so he walked up to the bar and claimed an empty stool. He ran a hand over the smooth, polished wood in front of him, noting the rings left by many years of drinks. His heart pounded for a moment as he imagined *he* had drained all those glasses.

"What can I get you, sonny?" the bartender asked, flashing him a smile that revealed a broken front tooth.

His gaze snapped up. The woman raised her eyebrows at him, waiting. Then in a heartbeat it was as if she saw all his secrets laid bare. She nodded once, the corner of her lip twitching into a smile. "Gin and tonic, hold the gin?" she said that only he could hear.

Patrick nodded once and put his dollar on the table. "This cover it?"

She pocketed the dollar and stepped away to fill his glass.

The man next to him leaned over and pointed. "You should always ask for the Mount Carbon brew around here. They're one of few breweries that kept the alcohol in all through prohibition." The man's breath smelled of something much stronger than beer. "And the owner's a local."

"Maybe I'll have to try that next time." Patrick shrugged.

The man looked Patrick up and down as if seeing him for the first time. "Hey, you aren't from around here, are you?"

"Nope. Originally from Pittsburgh."

"Steel man?"

"How'd you guess?"

"Yer too clean." The man laughed loudly and stuck out his hand, the creases of which were lined in black dirt. "Name's Real Joe. Originally from Brockton."

Patrick shook the man's hand and offered his own name. "Where's Brockton?"

"About two miles down the road."

Patrick smiled. "And did I hear you right...you said your name is *Real* Joe?"

The big man nodded, his smile going wider. "Welcome to Maryd. You see, half the town is either Josephs or Johns, which gets a bit confusing, particularly as those names are even running with the same surnames within families. For instance, I'm actually Joseph John Coharchick the Fourth." He slapped his chest proudly. "But you see, my father is the only Joe in my family other than me still living, and he goes by the name of Stretch. And most of the rest of the town's Joes have already been divvied out names, so I'm left to be called by my real name, Real Joe." Real Joe took a long sip of his whiskey. The bartender deposited Patrick's drink in front of him then turned to help two more customers.

"That's an interesting scenario. So everyone has nicknames around here?"

"Pretty much. We got Brutus, Yapper, Red...behind me is Frankie, but his real name is Joe, too." He frowned in thought. "Not sure how he got his name."

Patrick took a sip of the tonic water, sorely wishing it was something stronger. He distracted himself by continuing the conversation. "So how did a town come to be called Maryd?" When he'd seen the job ad in the paper, it was part of what drew him. Not Maryville or Marystown. Maryd, lower case "d". Looked like a typo, but the residents were pronouncing the D, so it must not be.

Real Joe smiled a toothy grin. "Mine boss named it for his wife back when the town was founded, Mrs. Mary Dolores Dodson." He placed a hand on his heart and closed his eyes in mock devotion. "So romantic."

Patrick smirked. Women did funny things to a man, like having them come up with town names that didn't sound like town names. Even though he knew the answer, he prompted, "You a miner?"

"Of course."

"Any tips?"

Real Joe laughed. "You going down in the tunnel tomorrow for the first time, Steel Man?" When Patrick nodded, he let out one more chuckle, then shot the rest of his whiskey. He motioned to the bartender for more. "Well, you got quite the education coming to you. You look strong enough. We'll show you how to push cars, drill holes. Any man can move a shovel. Least you're not all soft like some of the city boys." He shifted in his seat and began his new drink. "What you best watch out for is the dark. Creeps into your head. I've seen it make men go mad, make them wonder if they'll ever see the light of day again. They get to the point where they can't go back down there."

"I'm not afraid of the dark."

"Maybe so, but have you ever truly been in the dark?"

"What do you mean?"

Real Joe leaned towards him, whiskey and tobacco strong on his breath. "Down there, when you lose your headlamp, it gets so dark you can't see your hand in front of your face." He held his hand directly in front of Patrick's nose, to the point that Patrick could smell the salty sweat of it. Then he withdrew. "When it's that black, not a ray of light, the mind starts to see things that aren't there. Shadows. Movement. You want to run, but what appears to be the tunnel is a solid wall of rock." He shuddered. "And that's when there's not the fresh blast of coal dirt in the air. After we blast, it's like you can chew the darkness."

Patrick turned back to his drink, wondering if Real Joe was trying to scare him on purpose or if he was just plain crazy. There had to be someone else, someone less drunk, in the bar. Someone else to become acquainted with, that wasn't going to just tell ghost stories to rookies like himself.

A rumble rose from the ground, and the bartender let out a curse, reaching out her hands to steady the glasses that rattled on the shelves around her. The bar went quiet, and then it was over. Patrick furrowed his brow, then looked back to Real Joe, who somberly finished his whiskey. Behind Real Joe, Patrick noted the glare of a tableful of hard-looking miners. He stiffened, sensing the tension now in the air could be explosive. Involuntarily, a fist clenched.

"Yo, Real Joe," a tall red-haired man shouted. The sound reverberated around the bar, where conversations were still muted. "How long they gonna keep blasting under our houses?"

Real Joe sighed and turned to the man. "Red, you know I don't call the shots down there. And they don't tell me what the plans are either. I'm just another gopher."

"Well, one of yous has gotta put a word in for the rest of us. It's gettin' ridiculous."

"I'll try again to speak with the boss. I know the foreman has been trying, too."

The men grumbled to each other but turned back to their drinks. Slowly, Patrick's fingers released until his hand was palm-flat on the table, albeit sweaty. He again turned his gaze towards Real Joe, hoping his new acquaintance would explain the shaking and the obvious tension.

"Mine's working its way under the town," Real Joe muttered. "Company claims they'll hit the richest vein of coal this town's ever seen. Only problem is, they're gonna keep digging until the town's down in the mine, too."

"Why would they dig below the town?" Patrick thought back to all the miles of forested hills he'd traveled over the last days. There was plenty of ground to mine around here.

Real Joe looked Patrick in the eye for the first time, studying him, judging him. Patrick met that gaze boldly, but not without a quickening of his pulse. He'd been invisible for a long time. How much did he want this new town to see? How much would they recognize him, remember him? Whatever Real Joe saw, he must have decided Patrick could be trusted.

"It's complicated, Steel Man. But the answer is always money."

Patrick smirked at that. "Isn't it always?"

Real Joe leaned towards him, as if they were conspiring. His voice dropped. "You responded to the job ad, I reckon, yes? I saw it in the paper, same as the rest of the county."

Patrick nodded and shrugged.

"Well, if you read the papers going back a few more weeks, the story starts to come together. The company mine just reopened, first time since the old land lease ran out at the beginning of the Depression. New ownership. New company. New plans for pulling coal out of the ground. New workers. Only thing is, the residents of this town are a lot of the same folks who were here when the mine company abandoned us back in '32. We remember when the mine company ruled the town, owned all our houses, paid in scripts that were only good in the company store." He straightened, rolling the base of his empty glass absently on the table. "Things ain't like that anymore."

Patrick waited for him to continue, but Real Joe seemed reluctant to elaborate. He placed his large hands flat on the bar and stared at his glass, then sighed. Patrick waited another moment, then drained his own glass and set it down with a final thunk. Real Joe's gaze again rose to meet Patrick's.

"So who are those men?" Patrick motioned to the table behind Real Joe with his chin. "They look like miners and yet they're talking like they aren't working with you down the company mine."

"Bootleggers." Before Patrick could question him further, Real Joe stood. "You'll learn soon enough. We'll get you down there digging tomorrow." Real Joe slid his hat off the counter and put it on. His expression softened as he gave Patrick a firm squeeze on the shoulder. "We'll find out tomorrow if you're afraid of the dark or not, Steel Man."

CHAPTER 4

Ruth set the pot down on the table with a little more force than necessary. Bogie looked up at her, face and hands now clean though his hair was as unruly as ever. His shirt was on, but untucked. His hand hovered over the table with a plate, midway through setting the table.

"Ma, you alright?"

She ran a hand through her wavy blond hair, which the humidity from the stove had loosened from its bandana. Then she laid a hand on his shoulder as she returned back to said stove to stir the evening's potatoes. "Just a lot going on, honey. Can you go fetch your sisters and get them cleaned up, please?"

Bogie placed the last two settings and slipped out the side door and down the steps. Ruth wiped her hands on her apron, then lifted the pot from the stove with two tea towels. The mashed potatoes steamed. Then she fetched the roast from the oven. Venison—she hoped the new boarder either couldn't tell or didn't mind. It took meat and potatoes to replenish the calories miners burned. But she wasn't running any fancy restaurant. At least the produce was starting to come in at the local farmers' market. And if she could summon the energy to get that garden in the back planted, that would help considerably. Energy was in short supply though, especially with the passenger in her belly.

Bogie returned via the side porch with the girls. Addy's pigtails bounced with her steps. At five, she fancied herself halfway to being a lady. She may play hard, but she kept her dresses neat—as neat as secondhand fabric and flour sack slips could be—and avoided the dirt. Dorothy though, she was a tomboy through and through. At three she was at the age where she had a ton of energy and no fear. Thankfully her two siblings kept her somewhat in check, otherwise Ruth would have gotten a stomach ulcer from worry months ago. Addy beelined for the sink to wash her hands, but Dorothy crawled onto a chair and started reaching her dirty hand right towards the steaming potatoes.

"Dot, go clean up." Ruth plucked her from the chair and set her back on her feet with a light swat at her bum. The little girl shuffled off. Addy helped her sister set a stool in front of the kitchen sink and together they washed their hands.

"Smells good, mama," Addy said.

"I agree with her completely," said Isaac, their first boarder, as he came up from the basement, freshly cleaned from the mine. He was an older gentleman with a grey beard flecked with black, as if he could never wash out the coal dirt. He'd only been staying with them a few months, but already he'd proven himself a kind boarder that was happy to keep to himself as long as he was fed. He tipped his head towards her. "Evening, Ms. Ruth."

"Evening, Isaac. All well at the mine today?"

"Blasting day, ma'am. Hard work begins tomorrow."

As if to prove his words, another boom—the second of the night—shook the dishes in the cupboards. Ruth instinctively reached to steady her glass, watching as the water within vibrated.

Isaac shook his head. "Sure don't seem right, this new tunnel we're pushing."

"How do you mean?"

"It's heading right under the town."

Ruth stilled. "I assumed they were just blasting bigger sections at a time, and that's why we can feel it."

"Well they are that, but it's also closer. The old veins have plenty of coal, it's just been a pain to access them. The flooding of the old works has pretty much ruined the old mine shafts. The new owners think if they follow this vein we'll hit onto the Mammoth vein like they did back in 1906."

"How far down are they?"

"Enough. I hope." He leaned forward and heaped food onto his plate. "I mean, you know the independent miners have been digging practically in their backyards for years now, to no ill effect. I just don't think the ground's been tested with a full on mine tunnel running under it."

Ruth turned to watch the girls slip onto their bench next to Bogie. He helped them. She knew all too well how the independent miners and bootleggers worked. She also knew the greed of the mining companies. She slipped into her seat and filled her plate, taking only a small portion of the meat. Her pregnancy-inspired food aversions were waning, but red meat was still hit or miss for now.

"Mishter Isaac..." Dorothy leaned forward on the bench, her elbows on the table, her little legs swinging.

"You think I could come down in the mine with you one day? I wanna see da tunnels."

Isaac chuckled. Before Ruth could scold the girl he answered, "The mine is no place for a child. Far too dangerous."

Addy cut in, "Bobby Cartwright said he went down with his dad once. He came back with his own bucket of coal and fossils."

Isaac swallowed, his lined face still bright with a smile. "Well, that's between Bobby and his father. But now fossils, that's something I can help you with. All we have to do is go for a walk down the back. I'll show you what to look for."

"Really?" Dot's eyes went wide. "Sh-well."

Ruth shot a glance at Bogie, who was silently picking at his food. Normally, he would jump into the conversation about fossils and rocks. He knew a lot about them, thanks to his father. But maybe that was why he was quiet. He missed him. And she could say nothing to console him.

They all looked up as the front screen door slapped shut. The new boarder had arrived. Late. Ruth had a sinking feeling in her gut. He'd been across the street, drinking. She hadn't even had time to tell him the house rules yet. No drunks. That was a firm one.

"Mr. Kane—"

He toed off his boots by the front door and walked to the kitchen in his socked feet. One big toe protruded onto the wooden floor. "My, that smells good."

"Mr. Kane, I don't allow—"

He held out a hand to Isaac. "Patrick."

Isaac shook it and introduced himself. Patrick settled down at the table next to Isaac, across from Ruth. The girls looked at him with curiosity. Bogie studied him with narrowed eyes. Ruth glowered.

"Mister Kane. I should have you know that I will not tolerate any drunkenness in this household. I know miners are accustomed to their drink, but I will not have any sign of it in my house."

Patrick straightened. "I'm sorry, miss—"

"Missus," she snapped.

He looked at her, stunned, as if he'd never had a woman speak sharply to him before. His posture softened, and he ducked his head. "Missus Flannigan. I'm sorry, I wasn't aware of your house rule. I do promise you, I'm as sober as I was this morning. Is there anything else I should know?" He glanced down the table. "Forgive me, here I am making myself at home among your family. I'll come back later, after you've finished." He stood and nodded to her and Isaac. "Missus Flannigan. Mister Flannigan."

Isaac chuckled. "Sit down, man. I'm not the master of the house. I'm your roommate. And Mrs. Flannigan here may run a tight ship, but she doesn't deny us a place at her table."

Patrick hesitated, but when Ruth gestured to a chair, he sat.

She was just overtired, that was all. Where were her manners? The man was going to pay her mortgage after all. All she had to do was give him a bed and feed him twice a day. If he wanted a drink or two, that was up to him. What more could be expected from a man? She steeled herself inwardly and forced a smile to her lips as an olive branch. "Please, Mr. Kane. Help yourself." She pushed the venison towards him.

With comedic tentativeness, he spooned food onto his plate. The group watched as he took his first bite, eager to see if he was revolted or enamored to the venison.

He closed his eyes with bliss. "Mrs. Flannigan, you should charge us more." He dug into his plate as if it was the first real meal he'd had in months. She again judged his ill-fitting clothes. Maybe it was.

As they ate, the girls barraged Patrick with a list of questions. He answered them all willingly, though some vaguely. It turned out he *was* a new miner, come from the steel mills in the western part of the state. Her judgement of him had been correct. Her first impression of him still stood, as that appraising eye of his continually flicked towards her, as if seeking her opinion, her approval. Well, she'd said her piece for the night. She pretended to be disinterested in the conversation around her. The wall worked, and Patrick didn't ask any questions about her family or her past. He wisely turned his interest to Isaac and began prying into his extensive knowledge of mining. Ruth rose to begin clearing the table, and the girls scampered off to play dolls in the living room. It wasn't until the dishes were almost done that she realized Bogie was still seated at the table, listening with rapt attention to the two men.

Not good.

"Bogie, can you pull the washing machine out of the basement for me? I'd like to do our laundry tomorrow."

Reluctantly, he nodded his head and headed off. He was so quiet, that boy. Always had been to a degree, but ever since—well, he was quieter now. She had to sit him down and talk to him. Maybe he had questions. She wouldn't be able to answer them, but at least he'd know he wasn't alone. He needed to know she was there for him. No matter how stressed she was, how thin her body and emotions were stretched, she *would* be there for him.

She finished her work in the kitchen and left the two boarders chatting about tunnels and dynamite and the best kinds of headlamps.

CHAPTER 5

Tuesday, May 31, 1938

The mouth of the mine yawned open, a hungry beast waiting to devour all the men of the town into the inky darkness beyond. Patrick stood at that opening in his new clothes—a set of blue coveralls and steel-toe boots—and wondered if he wasn't the greatest fool that ever asked for a job. He was already a week of work in debt to the general store in the center of town. If he added in what he owed Ruth for room and board, he was only going to see a few dollars to his name if he lasted the whole month. Would they keep him on a month? Did he want to stay a month? For a man who only worked a few months at any job, he was committing a lot to an occupation he knew nothing about.

He had to be a fool.

The whistle at the mine office called out the final warning to get on the mine train, and Patrick followed the last few stragglers into a car. The train was like none he'd ever seen before, a squashed, waist-high coal-fired engine with low cars just wide enough to sit one or two men on rough benches. The tracks were only about two feet wide. Today, there were three cars full of about forty miners, then another three box-like coal cars for hauling rock. Real Joe patted an empty seat next to him, so Patrick begrudgingly sat down. He knew Real Joe was looking forward to witnessing any sign of Patrick's fear.

As the train rattled forward and began to descend, the light of day faded to a speck, then was swallowed into black. They passed a set of thick wooden doors manned by a young man, and when the doors closed behind them, the darkness seemed to get even darker, despite their headlamps and the electric bulbs strung on a wire every twenty feet or so. It *tasted* damp. The temperature dropped, and Patrick wondered if he should have brought a jacket down into the mine. Then again, none of the other men had them. Maybe once they got working, he'd warm up. He suspected the gooseflesh that pebbled his arms was more from nerves than cold.

Wooden timbers supported the sides and roof of the mine at regular intervals. He distracted himself by watching the dark walls as they drifted deeper and deeper into the mountain. Chisel marks had carved the stone. Even in the dim light, he could see the sheen of moisture on every surface. Long hoses ran parallel to the tracks, and occasionally Patrick could see a pin-prick stream of water spraying out.

He pointed one out to Real Joe. "Why are they pumping water into the mine?"

Real Joe shook his head. He almost had to yell to be heard over the rumble of the mine car. "They aren't pumping it in, they're pumping it out. Water takes the path of least resistance. If we didn't pump, the mine would flood."

That made sense. They were going down.

"Takes a lot of pumping to keep it dry down here," Real Joe explained. "They're running twenty-four seven."

When the mine train slowed, they were in a rounded, low-ceilinged cavern where numerous tunnels intersected, their ceilings reinforced with thick timbers. The train stopped, and the engineer unhooked the passenger cars on one set of tracks as the men disembarked. Most of the miners headed off down the main tunnel, straight into the heart of the mountain, with long metal pry bars on their shoulders, as long as the men were tall. Their lights bobbed with their footsteps until they, too, were swallowed by darkness. There were no lights down that tunnel.

Patrick lingered near the cars as the train engineer repositioned the train and slowly backed down that main tunnel, following the path the miners had taken. It was still within sight when it stopped. Patrick turned to Real Joe, who lingered outside a wooden room built underground, flipping through papers on a clipboard.

Patrick approached as another burly middle-aged miner emerged from the room and looked over Real Joe's shoulder at the clipboard, then glanced at Patrick.

"Who's the new guy?" the miner asked.

"Patrick," Real Joe answered. "He's a newbie, filling in for Roger. Says he's eager to learn." Real Joe smiled, his face in shadow behind the glare of his headlamp. "Steel Man, meet our foreman, Hank Palvick. Most of the guys call him Pal."

Pal accepted Patrick's handshake with an iron grip. "Well, he ain't Roger, but anyone can work a shovel. Come along, Steel Man."

Real Joe chuckled as he hefted a pry bar over his shoulder and headed down the tunnel into the darkness, from where the sound of rock and metal colliding echoed. The foreman led Patrick down one of the lighted tunnels. Patrick gazed around in awe of the mine workings. The newly timbered beams made the air smell like pine. He ran his hand over one as he walked by, imagining the size of the tree the beam came from. The foreman noticed.

"You know why we use pine instead of oak, Steel Man?"

Patrick shook his head, then remembered how hard it was to see in the dark, and said, "No."

"If there's a push—when the rock inside the mountain here shifts or caves in—the pressure on a pine beam will begin to bow it. Pine's a softwood. Oak is a hardwood. Under that kind of pressure, oak would hold and hold until it suddenly snaps. By using pine, we can look for that bow, and it gives us an extra warning of when to get out."

The tunnel seemed to stretch on for ages. "All this has just been dug this year?" Patrick asked.

"Yup. Company is putting a ton of money into it, and we haven't pulled out much coal yet. But we will. We will." He glanced back at Patrick. "I don't think it's safe for you to work the newest part of the tunnel just yet, not right after a blast. That's where the rest of the men are. We'll get you down there to check things out tomorrow. Today, I want you down this branch of the mine. We started pulling coal out of this slope, but the winch broke. I hear you have mechanical skills."

"Sure, I'll take a look." The winch was in view, positioned over a darker hole that descended on a steep angle deeper into the earth.

"Well, here you go then. I'll be down the main drift if you need me." The foreman turned to go, then spun back to Patrick. "Hey, since you have electric lights down here, I'd turn off the headlamp and save the battery. They don't last long."

Patrick glanced at the bulky battery pack at his hip. "The store told me..."

"Just speaking from experience." Pal shrugged and went back down the tunnel.

Patrick sighed. The light was pretty decent down there, but it still would be tough to evaluate the winch without a headlamp. He went to the winch and eyed it over, then flipped on the switch. It hummed to life. He frowned. It seemed to be working just fine, though maybe it could use a little grease on the cables. He reached for a grease gun that sat nearby and started applying the black paste. He hesitated, then clicked off his headlamp. He could certainly grease blind. The electric lights had plenty of illumination for that job.

Then everything went black. Patrick froze, grease gun in hand, and stared into the nothingness. He thought he could see the winch in front of him, but when he reached a hand towards its shadow, he only touched air. A few inches below that, he came in contact with the cool metal. He let his hand rest there, letting that contact ground him to reality as he raised his other hand in front of his face. He could feel it, smell it, but he couldn't see it. He was blind.

The sounds of the mine became more noticeable. There was the drip of water, the distant rumble of the mine train. For a moment, he thought he heard something rustle down in the smaller tunnel at his feet. His ears strained, but the sound didn't come closer. Real Joe was right. A man could get spooked down here.

He reached a hand to his battery pack and flipped the switch back to on. Light flooded the tunnel and cut through the darkness. Patrick looked down into the dark, then shook his head. Someone must have bumped the light switch for the electric, not knowing the foreman had taken him down this way. He finished greasing the cable, made sure the winch was in fact working, and then worked his way back to the main tunnel, wiping grease onto his brand new pants all the way.

He was almost back to the main tunnel when the lights snapped back on and a cheer roared through the mine. The miners were gathered at the entrance to his side tunnel, and they all now hooted and slapped him on the back.

"I fixed the winch?" Patrick offered, his eyes wide with bewilderment.

Real Joe came up and put an arm around him. "Ain't about the winch, Steel Man. Wasn't broken. You passed the test. You finished your work even in the dark." He let him go to be passed around the other men.

One of the younger men laughed as he admitted, "You shoulda seen Willy when we hit the switch on him. He peed his pants!"

Patrick spotted the foreman, who sat on two stacked crates of dynamite, a smile on his face and his arms crossed. Patrick raised an eyebrow at his new boss, who only shrugged in apology.

"All right, back to work," Real Joe said, and the crowd dispersed. "Pretty dark, ain't it?" he asked Patrick.

"Pretty dark."

The foreman rose and handed Patrick a shovel. "Couldn't help ourselves, Steel Man. But maybe you'll make a miner yet." He motioned toward the darkness of the main tunnel, where electric had not yet been strung. "They got the loose stuff down. Go shovel the shale and let's get this place cleaned out."

Patrick found that there was a rhythm to the labor. Sledge, sledge, shovel, shovel, clang to load, start again. The experienced miners were working their way down the tunnel, testing the walls and ceiling with the pry bars for any loose rock. Every now and then, they'd find a loose section, yell, and a crash of rock would follow. They were followed by more men with shovels, including Patrick. He could taste the dust now, feel the grit of it between his teeth. Still grateful for work, he moved his shovel back and forth, scooping up the fallen rock. Around him, another team of men worked to place new timbers, ensuring the tunnel would safely hold. The men next to him alternated between working in silence, whistling, and chatting. Their headlamps bounced around the dark cavern, throwing shadows up the walls like the silhouettes of giants.

But he wasn't afraid of the dark. He'd proven that without even having to think about it. And as the day pulled on, he noted he wasn't intimidated by the enclosed space either. There were a lot of men in an area not much bigger than Ruth's hallway. Even when he realized the lack of space and thought about the tons of rock above his head, his pulse didn't quicken. He wasn't sure what that meant, that he could think about danger and feel nothing. Even mining couldn't cure his numbness.

When they sat in the mine train that evening, Patrick asked Real Joe how much rock he thought they moved. His muscles felt deliciously sore, the kind of sore that promised growth and reminded you you'd done something with your day. He hadn't had that feeling in a while.

Real Joe thought for a moment. "I reckon we moved about two ton per man today. That's about average."

When the mine train pulled toward the surface, Patrick had to squint against the harsh light of the sun that reached its fingers down the tunnel. Mimicking the men next to him, he turned off his headlamp. As they burst forth into the daylight, he blinked. All the men around him were black as the ground they worked, the whites of their eyes and teeth shining like headlights in their faces.

Real Joe caught his eye and smiled, his teeth like glistening ivory behind blackened lips. "You look like the rest of us, my friend."

Patrick looked down at his hands, which didn't even seem to belong to him. The backs of his hands were black with coal dust. His palms were just as dark, except for the spots where mild blisters had formed and ripped open. The sight of them brought on the sting, which he acknowledged by flexing his palms open and closed, amused at the pain. Here he'd thought himself a tough steel worker, and yet he'd shown how soft his hands had gotten after just one day. His coveralls were just as black as everything else. Well, more of a dark navy now instead of plain blue.

"Hope your landlady has a good wash tub, Steel Man." Real Joe slapped him on the back. "I've heard some boarders wash up with a garden hose every night. But think on the bright side...you made it through your first day. You proved you ain't afraid of the dark."

Patrick hoped he'd done more than that. He hoped he'd proven he was a hard worker, that he was worth keeping on. He hoped he could learn to be a miner.

"You coming for a drink?"

"Not tonight." Patrick shook his head, thinking of his pretty landlady and how furious she'd been that he'd even set foot in the bar.

It had been a long time since he'd been scolded by a woman, and coming from her tiny, yet fierce, frame, he had no inclination to get in trouble again. He needed a place to sleep, and if her cooking was like that every night, he had no desire to pass those meals up for oatmeal and biscuits at some soup kitchen in a city. Perhaps tonight, if he could manage not to anger her, she'd be more willing to talk, and he could get to know her better. Then again, it would be good to explore town a bit more while there was still daylight. It felt very good to be in the sun.

"There any place you recommend to go to take a good walk? I need to soak up this sunlight."

Real Joe laughed. "Oh, just you wait. In the winter, we go in in the dark, come out in the dark. You're right to enjoy every ray of light while it lasts." He pointed further down the road, away from town. "You go down that way a bit, and there's an old stripping hole. No fish in it, though there's plenty of frogs. Anyway, it's a peaceful spot. Gets you out of the house."

"Perfect. Thank you."

Real Joe gave a wave and headed home, and Patrick hiked up North Main to the boarding house, where he took a hot shower with a bar of soap that hardly seemed up to the task of removing coal dirt. He'd have to get some tips from Isaac. Did they sell special miner soap in the company store, too? When he reached for his clothes, which hung neatly on the hooks Ruth had described, he froze. He'd forgotten to bring clean clothes down to the basement. He eyed the filthy mine clothes, which, despite being protected from the worst of the mine dirt by the coveralls, still were sweaty and dusty. He hated to put them back on. Not only would Ruth be furious that he was tracking dirt through her house, but he'd have to shower again, wasting even more daylight.

With a grimace, Patrick cinched his towel tighter around his waist and padded up the basement stairs. He poked his head through the door to the kitchen, listening for Ruth or the children. All was quiet. He jogged barefoot across the living room, up the stairs, and had almost reached the sanctuary of his room when the door in the middle of the hall opened and he ran right into Ruth herself.

She shrieked.

He steadied her with one hand—he'd come close to knocking her over—and clutched the towel with the other. As soon as he realized what he'd done, his palm burned, and he released her, taking a step back.

"I'm so sorry," he mumbled. "Forgot my clothes..."

She stared at his bare chest with wide eyes. With one finger, she pointed behind her. "Go," she said in a small voice.

He cleared his throat and ducked his head as he stepped around her. Since she still stood frozen in the middle of the hall, he couldn't pass her without brushing her hip with his own. She still didn't move, but he darted the last few steps to the end of the hall and ducked into the room, locking the door behind himself. He leaned against it, face hot with embarrassment. For himself or her, he couldn't tell. A few seconds later, he heard her march off back downstairs.

So much for not angering his landlady a second day in a row.

Then again, she'd stared. Perhaps only at his chest, but he had the feeling she'd fought to keep her eyes that high. Odd reaction for a married woman. She smelled like mint and rosemary. Patrick shook his head. She was his landlady, and he wasn't a man to get involved in relationships—of any sort. They made things complicated. It was odd that he was even attracted to her.

Was he attracted to her?

She sure was pretty. He liked her brusque, matter-of-fact spirit. But she also had three and a half children and was *Missus* Flannigan. Though he'd yet to meet *Mr.* Flannigan.

He couldn't help but wonder what her story was. Time would tell. He'd have to stick around awhile, if only to pay off his rent and new clothes.

He dressed quickly, laced his boots on the back porch—thankfully avoiding Ruth on his quest back through the house—and then headed back down the steep hillside in the direction Real Joe had pointed. Definitely a day for the walk outside, not for prying deeper into Mrs. Flannigan's personal life.

It really was beautiful out. The air was still warm, but not hot. It was as if Mother Nature was caught between spring and summer, the time you really just ached to be outside. The farmers were probably out planting like crazy right now. It was also nice to be in the countryside in this kind of weather. Somehow, it seemed more noticeable that it was nice out. In the city, between the billowing soot of the factories and the dirty glass of the steel mill and even his apartment building, he never really seemed to notice the change in weather unless it was pouring, freezing, or baking hot. The steel mill had always been unbearable in those hot July heat spells. He was glad he didn't have that to deal with this year.

Before long, Patrick's feet had carried him out of town and down the dirt road past the mine. Hills of old coal tailings, the waste rock and pieces too small to sell, lined both sides of the road in massive piles, extensions of the hills they'd come from. The breaker was a way off, but still, all this dirt and rock had to be disposed of somewhere. The massive piles proved they used any convenient spot. What once had been forest was now barren piles of dirt. Funny, didn't coal itself come from forests long gone? It seemed to claim the forest twice.

Still, here and there, an occasional, hearty tree punched up through the ground. The leaves overhead trembled in a slight breeze, the light of the glorious sun reaching its fingers towards him. Patrick imagined this black coal path could be pretty if more trees could take root. He rounded a bend to see even more culm piles, some deep, full only with leaves, and some shallow. Then there was one full of water, as if a lake had appeared in the middle of the desert. Better yet, this small lake had a scattering of trees surrounding the edge, making it appear almost paradisical. It had to be the place Real Joe had mentioned.

Patrick walked down a bank to the edge, eyeing the murky water. It wasn't clear, but he'd seen worse fish ponds. The water sparkled in the bright sunlight. The silty coal dirt was firm enough to approach the edge, and thankfully not too mucky like quicksand. Patrick put his hands on his hips. The water stretched on for at least seventy-five feet. He could imagine himself swimming across the length of this little hole. Not today, not after he was clean. But maybe on a hot day, when he was black with coal dirt. Maybe he could even swim in his mining clothes, rinse the worst of the dirt off them, and thus save some laundry money.

He smiled to himself. He was starting to like Maryd. Who would have guessed this little town could have so much appeal? He set off around the perimeter of the water hole—stripping hole as Real Joe had called it—and continued to soak in the sun's rays until the very last minute.

He'd have to eventually go back to the boarding house and face Mrs. Flannigan.

CHAPTER 6

"Am I losing my mind?" Ruth asked her friend Edna. After running into Patrick while he was half naked, she'd escaped across the street. They were currently seated on Edna's back porch with glasses of mint tea. Their girls were playing together in Edna's backyard. "I should kick him out. I have to kick him out. I mean...what was he thinking walking around *my* house *naked?*"

"Sounds like he wasn't quite naked. He had a towel." Edna's blue eyes sparkled with amusement.

Ruth gave her a stern look. "A towel that barely covered anything."

Edna scooted to the edge of her chair, that old expression from their school days back with all its sparkle, just like when they'd talked about boys years ago. "I mean...is he handsome? Got any abs?"

"Edna!"

"Well, if you're gonna look, you should look."

"He's my boarder."

"He's a man. You're a woman. A woman currently without a husband. And you can't kick him out. You need the money."

Ruth gave her an exasperated look.

Edna held up her hands. "Look, I'm not saying anything has to happen. Just don't be hard on yourself for being human. In other words, you're allowed to look. And he's allowed to forget his clothes upstairs. Once. Now if he makes it a habit on a daily basis, then you need to call me and we'll both wait for him to come out of the basement—"

"Edna!" Ruth felt a blush rise to her cheeks, but she couldn't help but smile.

Edna giggled, then rubbed Ruth's shoulder. "So...how *were* the abs?"

"Pretty good." Ruth drowned her embarrassment in her cool tea.

"I knew it!" Edna cheered.

Ruth rolled her eyes. "You're married." Her smile faltered. "So am I." And very pregnant, which was a romance blocker if ever there was one.

"*Are* you married, though? I mean, how long does he have to be gone before you're allowed to stop waiting for him to come back in your life for however many weeks it lasts until next time?"

The mood plummeted. After a last swallow of tea, Ruth set the glass down on the side table with trembling hands. She leaned her head in her hands, tears threatening.

Edna put an arm around her. "Oh, honey." All trace of the mirth in her voice was gone. "I'm sorry. I should watch what I say."

"He doesn't even *know*." Ruth's voice shook. She clutched her arms around the subtle swell of her belly. "I can't help but think if he knew, he'd come back. Maybe he'd change." Not that the last three children had changed him. But he hadn't been this bad before the accident. Before—she gritted her teeth. Before.

Edna rubbed her shoulder. "Have you heard from him at all?"

"Not a word. I don't know where to send a telegram. I don't know if he's alive or dead. What if he *is* dead? What then? How am I supposed to go on in this little town alone indefinitely?"

"It's not right what he did. Not a person in town would disagree with that. My heart hurts for you. You deserve better. You at least deserve an explanation. No one would blame you if you moved on."

"But I *can't*. I don't know if he's *alive*."

"You could divorce him when he does show up."

Ruth looked at Edna sideways. Her friend was ever practical, and as such, often right. But she didn't understand the complexity of emotions Ruth held from her marriage. You couldn't be married to someone for ten years, build a life with them, have four children by them, and then just forget it all to move on. And yet the pain of Jack's leaving, the hardships he'd thrown upon the family without even a thought, had cut Ruth to the core. She was barely functioning, and the pregnancy certainly made things even harder. Having a man to help provide stability, at least financially, was a large help. This was the first time she'd have to do it with a baby, alone. How? By leaning on ten-year-old Bogie? How was that fair?

Her look must have told Edna everything. Edna knew her better than anyone. Old friends were like that. You couldn't go through grade school, puberty, and then the blissful beginnings of marriages side by side without a deep bond. Almost a sisterhood. Edna pulled Ruth into a strong hug again. Ruth considered crying, but decided she didn't have the energy. When the friends parted, Edna looked into Ruth's eyes.

"Look, it's all still so soon. Maybe he'll come back. Maybe he won't. In the meantime, it doesn't hurt to make new friends. You never know who you'll need to have your back."

"Friends." Ruth knew Edna could interpret that loosely.

"Bottom line, you take care of yourself. And I am always here for you, my dear."

Ruth nodded, then stood. "I should get back. Still need to finish cooking. Thank you for the tea."

"Don't kick him out. It sounds as innocent as he claimed. He's probably mortified." Edna smiled. "But if it happens again, don't forget to report back. I'm happy to come over if you need backup."

"Oh, you're so bad." Ruth rolled her eyes, but she couldn't help but smile.

They watched the girls play a few more minutes, then Ruth resolved that she really did have to get back to finishing dinner for her boarders. She and the girls were saying their goodbyes to Edna's family when Addy pointed down the road.

"Mama, what's that?" the little girl asked.

They all followed her finger to the rumble that came from the road at the base of the hill. A huge tractor-trailer pulled an even bigger machine. Its tracks hung off the sides of the trailer bed by a few inches, which didn't matter, since the tracks were so wide that there was still plenty securing it. The frame of the engine and cab towered so high it threatened to catch on the powerlines that hung over the road, thus why the truck driver was crawling along, leaning out the window of the cab to watch his clearance. The long arm of the machine lay folded and tucked next to it. And following all this was a second truck, with its entire trailer bed dedicated to a shovel big enough to drive a car into.

"Well then. Thus it begins," Edna grumbled. She crossed her arms in front of her chest and glared at the shovel.

Ruth rested a hand on Dot's head. The girls still stood staring in quiet awe. The children might not know the significance of the arrival of the strip-mining shovel, but the rest of the town did. Only a few weeks ago, the new Maryd Coal Company had announced its plan to strip mine all around the town. At first, the town had been enthusiastic about the mine reopening. But between the blasting heading under the town and the digging around their houses, the townspeople were holding their breath, hoping the company would agree to some limits before the projects commenced. Thus far, the company's position was they were doing everything legally, and thus they would do whatever they wanted. And those who had consulted attorneys had been told the company was in the right, and there was nothing that could be done from a legal standpoint. That wasn't sitting well with Ruth.

Ruth stared at the shovel as it finally passed under the electric lines and proceeded down the hill to the mine office. "We've got to be able to do something. Just because they're leasing the land around us doesn't mean they can dig right up to our back doors."

Edna's voice held a bitter edge. "Red's coal hole is right in their projected line of stripping. Of course, they want the easy coal. But then what are all the independent miners going to do? We don't have thousands of dollars to invest in the big deep mines. We *need* this shallow stuff."

It was Ruth's turn to reach a hand over to her friend and give her a reassuring squeeze on the shoulder. "We'll keep trying." She wished Jack were home. He wouldn't settle for doing nothing. Though, then again, his solution might be to take the law into his own hands and force the mine closed. Enough damage might get the company to listen. Ruth froze on that thought, then pushed it down again. No, there was still hope they could do things peacefully.

She said goodbye to Edna and headed across the street, her little girls' hands clasped in each of hers, swinging in rhythm to their small steps as if it was just another day in paradise. The girls' giggles reassured her. Surely, all that was wrong would one day be made right.

CHAPTER 7

Patrick couldn't wait for dinner to be over. It had nothing to do with the food. Truth be told, the food was what got him through it, and when Ruth offered him and Isaac seconds, he gladly refilled his plate. If he kept eating like this, he'd fill out his clothes again in no time. If Ruth thought he ate too much, she didn't comment. If she thought anything about him at all, it was impossible to tell, as she didn't talk to him at all through the meal, not even to berate him for the earlier incident. She couldn't even meet his eye.

That's not to say she was quiet. Dot was in rare form tonight. The little girl barraged her mother with a thousand questions on every subject that came to her mind. Ruth answered each with patience and a smile.

"Mama, where were the geese all winter?"

"They fly south, love."

"Mama, can I keep a baby goose?"

"No, dear."

"Mama, do I have to finish my tomatoes? They're mushy."

"That's what happens when we can them dear. They're all right. Eat up."

"What's that big shovel going to do?"

Patrick's ears perked at that. He'd seen the massive crane-operated shovel drive into town just like everyone else. He'd thought for sure it was going to catch those powerlines, but the driver was a talented man and managed to inch under them at precisely the right spot.

"They're going to dig coal," Ruth answered Dot.

Patrick wanted to cut into the conversation and ask his own questions, but he thought better of it. He was too new to town, too much an outsider to interrupt Ruth's family. He bit his tongue and resolved to ask Real Joe or Isaac more about the shovel later. As the conversation between Ruth and her children continued, he felt more and more like an intruder. An old ache stirred in his gut, a longing for a family of his own. He didn't linger on it. He excused himself to the porch as soon as he'd finished his second helping, topped off with a slice of strawberry-rhubarb pie.

The porch didn't offer much solace. He watched the patrons enter the bar across the street, longing for a drink himself. He couldn't afford one, he reminded himself. Maybe this was purgatory. If he had been out of money a few years ago, perhaps his life would still be on a different trajectory. He certainly wouldn't be scraping the bottom side of a black mountain, breathing in black dirt. Maybe when he paid his debts, he would allow himself one...to celebrate.

He leaned back and closed his eyes, listening to the sound of crickets. There was no breeze, just a little bit of humidity. They were weeks from the scorching heat of July, yet it certainly felt like summer was kicking into gear. He guessed that was one advantage of working down in the mine. It was going to be a consistent temperature down there all year. He could look forward to that escape from the heat. If he lasted more than a month at the job.

He startled as the screen door slapped shut.

"Oh. Sorry," Ruth said, frozen in place. She turned to head back into the house.

"No, join me. Or I can go in if you want me to. It's your porch." He stood to make his point.

She stared at him a moment, her hand on the door, then slowly released the handle and stepped around him to the other porch chair. The chair creaked as she gracefully sat down. "Nice night, isn't it?"

"Perfect night." Patrick reclaimed his seat and leaned back again.

They heard laughter come from across the street. Someone was having a good time over there tonight. He looked over to Ruth. She looked a bit tense, but she was settled back in her chair, her eyes closed as his had been moments ago. Patrick smiled slightly to himself. She really was a pretty woman. She had slightly olive-complexioned skin that already was soaking up a summer tan, shoulder-length hair pulled back haphazardly by a bandana, and striking hazel eyes. At least he thought he remembered them being hazel the first time he'd met her. He looked away. He would *not* make her uncomfortable with his gaze lingering on her figure, which, for a woman who'd already borne three children, had curves in all the right places. He couldn't help but ask, "How are you feeling? With the baby and all?"

She opened her eyes. Yup, hazel. The silence held a beat too long, and Patrick wondered if he'd overstepped. Maybe it was rude to ask about a pregnant woman's health. Of course, he was assuming she was even pregnant.

Good Lord, was she *not* pregnant and just that round? His pulse raced. He was sure digging a hole for himself. He quickly tried to dig himself back out.

"I just ask because my sister really struggled with her first. Our mother always seemed to handle it well, so Betty was very offended when her experience was nothing similar."

"It's as well as it should be, I suppose," Ruth said.

Patrick gritted his teeth. He was out of practice talking to women, and this one made it seem as if he was trying to lay siege to a castle. Yet he had a suspicion that once he could crack her walls, she was really a very lively and wonderful person. He saw that in her when she was with her children.

"How many siblings do you have?" she asked.

He looked over at her, surprised. Her knuckles were tense on the chair armrests, but she watched him expectantly, waiting. Her head inclined ever so slightly.

"There's nine of us actually."

"Wow, your mother had her hands full."

Patrick smiled. "Yeah, she's pretty amazing, even now that most of us are grown."

"Where's home?"

"Pittsburgh."

"You've come a long way. Maryd's a bit of a random place to stop."

"Needed a change." It was time to change the subject, too. He didn't want to talk about Pittsburgh. "What about you? Siblings? You from here?"

She nodded lightly. "Born and raised right in this little town. Had one older brother, but he died when the

Spanish Flu came through. Black lung took Dad a few years ago. Mama lives in Brockton now."

"I'm sorry for your loss."

Ruth stiffened. "Mama always says, 'The Lord giveth and the Lord taketh away'. Lost most of my family, but now I have my children. I wouldn't trade them for anything."

She didn't mention her husband. Patrick was about to ask when she abruptly stood. "Well, good night, Mr. Kane."

"Good night, Mrs. Flannigan." He nodded his head at her, and she disappeared into the house before he could wonder what he'd said wrong.

He wasn't usually a gossip, but anyone could see the woman had a lot going on in her life. Who could he ask? He'd asked Isaac when Mr. Flannigan would be home, and Isaac had only said he'd never met the man. Isaac was clear that he wasn't going to speculate on other people's secrets. How secret could an absent husband be in a small town, though? The neighbors knew. They had to. And yet, as the newcomer, Patrick still felt he should keep his head down and mind his own business until he got to know people better. You couldn't be a busybody if you wanted to avoid questions about your own life. Maybe he could get some old papers and page through them. If Mr. Flannigan was dead, there should be a write-up. No one could accuse him of prying into Ruth's private life if he was just reading newspapers.

CHAPTER 8

Wednesday, June 1, 1938

"Mornin', Steel Man," said the shopkeeper as he fed paper into a burn barrel alongside the store.

Patrick paused in the middle of the road. He'd only met the man once, had never told him his name, and yet here the man already knew him by his nickname. "Morning." Blast it, he didn't know the man's name.

"Fine weather today, ain't it?" the man continued.

"Sure is." Not that he'd get to enjoy it from underground. Patrick watched the man toss another large handful of paper scraps into the barrel, likely packaging materials. A large wooden crate sat at his feet, likely full of more. "Say, you don't happen to have any newspapers you wanna get rid of in there, do you? Old ones, of course. I'm a bit on a budget, as you know. Least until I get you paid back."

"Oh, I don't burn those. We save them to light the furnace."

Patrick lingered awkwardly. "Well, you think I could read them and return them?"

"I suppose so." The shopkeeper shrugged. "Won't need them for a while, and there's plenty. But waste not want not. When you're done, I'll take 'em back. No sense burning them without purpose, if you know what I mean."

"Sure thing, sir. Thank you."

The shopkeeper waved him off. "You're welcome. Stop by on your way home after work. Now aren't you late?"

The whistle blew down at the mine, and Patrick cursed under his breath. He waved and then took off running. He managed to leap into one of the mine cars just as the train began descending into the ground.

"Morning, Steel Man," said the man next to him, yet another he hadn't formally met. The kid looked to be about twenty, fresh-faced and clean-shaven.

"Morning," Patrick muttered. Then he sighed as they all clicked on their headlamps in the darkness. Dust swirled in front of the beam, and the lighting in the mine seemed dimmer today. He tapped his light, wondering if the foreman had been truthful when he'd said the batteries on the headlamps didn't last long.

"Not just you. The air's worse down here today." His seatmate frowned.

It was about time to introduce himself. "I'm Patrick."

"I know who you are, Steel Man. My name's Monkey."

"Monkey?"

The train slowed and stopped before the man could answer. The foreman hopped out of the front car and scanned the men.

"Where's Monkey?"

The man stood.

"Can you check this air shaft? If this one's clear, come back down the one at the back of the tunnel."

"Sure." The man hopped out of the car, and Patrick was surprised at his height—or lack thereof. He couldn't top much more than five feet. It didn't seem to matter, though, as Monkey jumped into the air and caught a beam that Patrick hadn't even noticed, then disappeared up a hole not much bigger than a man's body.

"Air shaft," Real Joe said from the seat behind him.

Patrick flinched. How was this new acquaintance always nearby?

The foreman had gotten back on the train again, and they continued to descend, though it seemed as if the trip went slower than it had the day before. Real Joe again leaned over his shoulder, this time with a lamp with a tiny flame flickering within. It looked like any other oil lamp, except the glass was different. Layered perhaps? Patrick took the lamp into his hands and watched the flame.

"This is a safety lamp," Real Joe explained. He held up a second one. "That one is yours now. Keep it on you at all times, or at least nearby."

"So the air *is* bad today? I'm not just imagining it's darker?"

"It's dusty. But it's not bad." Real Joe pointed to the light. "If that flame goes out, then you get out of this mine as fast as your legs will carry you. Better yet, if you can get to the equipment room down there—you saw that yesterday—you grab a gas mask and then sound the alarm."

"What kind of air puts out fire?" Patrick stared at that little flame. It held fast.

"Black damp, which is a lack of oxygen. If the ventilation gets bad, and the air is all carbon dioxide, you'll feel tired, then pass out and never wake up."

Another miner popped his head over Real Joe's shoulder. With a thick German accent, he said, "Und it has nothing to do vith the vet. Damp ist from our German dampf, for vapor."

Patrick nodded.

"But that's not all," Real Joe continued as the train pulled to a halt at the bottom of the tunnel. "See this flame? The blue of the flame is maybe a fingernail long. If that blue shoots higher, you better run. Firedamp makes the flame burn hotter. The mesh in the lamp keeps it from exploding. I assume you know what methane is?"

Patrick grimaced. "Methane and fire don't get along well."

"Real big boom," said the German.

"Thus the lamp." Real Joe tapped Patrick's lamp, then hopped out of the coal car. "Come on, Steel Man. You're on my crew today. We're drillin'."

The humid summer air hit the miners in the face like a punch as the coal train pulled into daylight. Between the dust of the mine and the thick moisture of the air, Patrick had to think about breathing for a moment. Some of the other men coughed it out, spitting out black globs of phlegm. Real Joe shoved a wad of tobacco into his lip, muttering that it helped with the dirt. Patrick drained the last of the water in his canteen and still he could taste the grit between his teeth.

"Later, Steel Man," Real Joe said, then headed up to town.

Patrick waved and followed after him, then noticed Isaac doubled over, still coughing so hard he was gasping for breath. The older man finally inhaled, relaxed, and straightened, but when he walked off his gait was slow. Patrick stopped. Isaac could have the first shower of the day. Though they'd both been in the dust all day, Isaac had been right up at the front of the mine tunnel with the most experienced miners. The old man was inspiring underground. He was confident and authoritative. He knew exactly what needed to be done and did it. The foreman even had a lot of respect for him, and Patrick knew the miners all had a great deal of respect for the foreman. You needed to trust the men you were with down there, and the experienced miners like Isaac, Real Joe, and the foreman all had proven over time that they deserved that trust. By default, Patrick found himself following the lead of the others.

But yes, Isaac deserved that first shower, which meant Patrick had some time to kill in dirty clothes that precluded him from walking through Ruth's tidy house. He headed for the stripping hole down the back.

From the edge, he eyed the murky water that pooled between the culm banks. The coal dirt made a beach around the hole, like dirty black sand. Trees shaded half the edge, further mimicking the beach, as if they were palms. If you could ignore the muck and murk, it didn't look too bad. If he came out covered in leeches, then he'd just pluck them off. Couldn't be worse than the Monongahela that wove through Pittsburgh. *That* he wouldn't swim in. He'd worked in industry long enough to know what the factories were pumping into it, and it wasn't fish.

No one was around, which was the advantage of a small town full of people with busy lives. With a final glance around, he pulled off his coveralls and clothes down to his underwear. He waded in, the cold water making him wince. The black mud sucked at his toes, but he only sank to his ankles. When he was up to his waist in the water, he pushed off the silty bottom, keeping his head high as the water engulfed his torso. He took a few strokes, then treaded water. He could no longer feel the bottom. He couldn't see what lay below, and he tried not to think about it. The water felt amazing. He ran a hand over his face, rinsing away the coal dirt from the mine. How could he worry about dirty water when he was even filthier than the water? He laid back and floated, imagining the coal dirt swirling out of his hair in dark rivulets. The clouds were blue in the sky. The sun warm. Maybe he should switch to bathing here every day.

"Hey! Mr. Kane! You'd better get out of there," a little girl's voice called.

Startled, he sat up and returned to treading water. Back on shore, next to his clothes, all three of Ruth's children stood watching him.

"Mama says the black water ain't safe," little Addy called.

Patrick frowned. He was in no mood to take orders from a little girl. "It's okay. I'm a good swimmer."

"So was Bob, and now he's dead," Bogie called out.

"Better come out...Mishter Kane," little Dorothy's voice warned, the sternest of them all.

Patrick figured he should at least humor the children, as they were so concerned. He took a few strokes back to shore and then waded out of the water. The black dirt of the mine still clung to his hands and forearms. He'd still need some soap. Maybe a bar of it as big as the bathtub. At least he'd gotten to cool off. He'd come back another day. "Don't you have someplace to swim around here?"

Bogie shrugged. "There's a lake a few miles away."

"A few miles? All these pools of water and no one ever uses them."

"Ain't safe," Addy said. Dorothy had taken to picking up pebbles and throwing them into the hole. Her brother kept a firm grip on her hand.

Patrick frowned. "I'm sure your mother just wants you to stay away until you're all good swimmers. She's a smart lady, your mother."

"We aren't telling tales, mister." Bogie released Dot's hand to cross his arms, taking up his manliest pose, made all the more humorous by his boyish voice. Patrick bit his tongue to keep from smiling. "Nobody knows where the bottoms of these holes go."

"They could go to the center of the earth," Addy said with all seriousness.

"Really now?" This story was getting more fantastical. Patrick reached for his clothes, shook out the worst of the mine dust, and started dressing.

"Dad used to say there was a great big serpent at the bottom, and when it opened its mouth, it sucked all the water, and whatever was in it, down to the bottom of the earth, never to be seen again." Bogie relayed this with great seriousness, so Patrick refrained from laughing. It was the first time the boy had spoken of his father.

"I don't 'member that stor-e," little Dorothy said from further down the black dirt beach. Addy jogged after her a few steps and caught her hand, just as she was about to get her feet wet.

Bogie gave Patrick the sternest look he could muster, then hurried after his sisters. They continued on a slow walk around the hole, Dorothy throwing rocks, Addy scratching a stick in the mud along their path, and Bogie playing the role of babysitter. Patrick shook his head, tied his boots, and hiked back to town. True to his word, the shopkeeper had a bundle of old newspapers set aside for him, tied with twine. He whistled as he swung his bundle and walked up the hill to Ruth's.

Isaac was finishing up in the bathroom when he got back, trimming his grey-white beard. He eyed Patrick's wet hair. "Where'd you shower?"

"I went for a swim in that hole down the back," Patrick explained. He still felt dirty, so he took a seat on the bench and started to pull off his boots.

"Brave of you. Bet it felt good though."

Brave? Since when was swimming brave? "The kids said much the same thing. It's a pool of water. I'm a good swimmer. There's no current. What am I missing? Or are you going to tell me there's a giant serpent that could suck me down to the very bottom of the earth, too?"

Isaac smiled. "I like that one. I'm going to have to remember that." He finished his trim and rinsed his hands in the sink, eyeing his handiwork in the mirror. "They aren't wrong. I guess you'd have no way of knowing, since you didn't grow up in coal country. But all these pretty little ponds, well, they ain't ponds. They're stripping holes."

"I know what they're called." Patrick gritted his teeth.

"Well, do you know *why* they're called that? It ain't because people strip off their clothes and go swimmin'." He turned to Patrick, who was now curious. "Stripping holes are formed a couple of different ways around here. One, they strip off the surface soil and rock to get at the coal, leaving a depression that fills with water. That's what that big shovel that drove in yesterday is for. Then there are ones that formed when water got trapped between the old culm banks. There's also the ones where the mines below the ground collapsed to create a sinkhole, which then fills with water. Same thing sometimes happens with old bootleg holes. Dirt covers the entrance over the years, or sometimes they even are blasted shut, and the depression holds water. So some of these strippings really *could* be bottomless pits. All it takes is that dirt 'plug' to let loose, and all that water disappears back underground."

A serpent—the mine—swallowing all the water and whoever was in it. Patrick cringed just thinking of how deep that network could take a person. They'd never be found again. "Is that what happened to Bob?"

"Who's Bob?"

Patrick shrugged. Maybe Bob was the tall tale, not the serpent. "So you're telling me, it could be a hundred degrees this summer, and no one is gonna go swimming in any of these little ponds anywhere near town?"

"Only if they're crazy. Or cocky about their swimming." Isaac lifted an eyebrow. "I guess no one's told you about acid mine drainage either?"

Patrick raised his eyebrows.

Isaac chuckled. "Just stay out of orange water, kid."

Patrick again sat on the porch that night, watching the patrons go into the bar. After a while, he realized the crowd was getting thick in there, and not many were leaving. Maryd wasn't a big town, and yet almost every household, man and woman alike, seemed to have sent in a patron. It was like a big town hall meeting. Curiosity piqued, he pushed up from his porch chair and crossed the street, hands in his pockets.

The little bar was packed inside, standing room only. Most of the crowd had their attention centered on a huge-framed miner in the front of the room. His head towered a good head over the rest of the men. He held a sheaf of pamphlets in one hand as he spoke.

"It is well past time that the companies stop trying to dictate what we can and can't do on the land we live on! We've been mining this land for generations. We know it better than them. It's a God-given natural resource that we should have full right to use without shame, guilt, or shipping regulations. We should be allowed to trade just as freely as the big companies! Enough of this selling better coal for a lower profit."

He got cheers throughout the crowd.

The man waved his hands, and the bar quieted again. "This is the same conversation we've been having since the mines closed, leaving you to fend for yourselves. But that conversation is changing here in Maryd. They want to strip mine all the coal from your backyards. They want to blast away the land from under your houses. Where will they stop? When the town is demolished? When your drinking water is poisoned with acid? No." He paused and shook his head, the crowd hanging on every word. "Maryd, the union will stand with you as you negotiate for what you need. For you do need something more than just fair trade now. Your livelihood and families depend on it. It is time we stood up to big coal and made them look at us. They needed our coal during that brutal winter in '34. They'll need it again in '38!"

Patrick flinched as cheers roared around him. The man speaking seemed finished and began handing out his pamphlets. Patrick took one as they came around. It appeared that the man was part of the Independent Miners Association. Patrick furrowed his brow.

"Hey, Steel Man!" Real Joe called from across the room. He waded through the crowd. "Didn't think you'd come tonight."

"Had to see what the crowd was about." He held up the pamphlet. "What is this?"

Real Joe took a sip of beer. "It's like I was telling you the other night. Company has one plan, and the bootleggers have another."

"I feel like I could get fired just for being here," Patrick admitted.

Real Joe pointed into a corner of the room, where the mine foreman was seated with a few other miners. None of them looked happy, but they weren't stopping the conversations or rebutting the speaker at all. "If they're here, we're okay to be here too. First amendment, free speech and all that."

"Fair enough." Still, it made Patrick nervous. He'd looked a long time for a job. He couldn't afford to lose this one now. He was about to bow out of the bar when he spotted Ruth. She was standing with a few other women, her arms folded across her chest while deep in conversation. A pamphlet stuck out of her hand.

Real Joe noticed his gaze. "Ah, you've met the lovely Mrs. Flannigan, then?"

"She's my landlady."

"Really now? Lucky you. I heard a rumor that she'd taken in a new boarder. Guess I should have put two and two together."

"She told me she doesn't like drinking, so I'm surprised to see her here."

"Ah, that would make sense." When Patrick shot him a raised-eyebrow look, Real Joe explained. "Her husband was a good friend of mine. And a dedicated drunk."

That explained a great deal. And Real Joe had used "was", which seemed to indicate the husband was no longer in the picture.

Real Joe's eyes lingered on Ruth in a watchful big-brother sort of way. Before Patrick could ask what had happened to Mr. Flannigan, Real Joe continued. "She's a fine woman. Pretty invested in this debate, too, since her father was one of the biggest independent miners in the area. He had a team of ten guys when he was working."

"She told me he passed."

"Yeah, the miner's lung got him in the end. It'll likely take all of us. He was a smart man, though. I learned a lot from him."

One thing Patrick was finding was that the miners all seemed to tutor under each other. It seemed mining was like any other trade or art; it needed apprentices to learn the tricks from the masters. He suddenly felt very immature, which was ridiculous since he was over thirty and had been making his own living for a long time. Yet in the coal industry, he really was just a baby. He'd seen children picking up coal from the roadsides, their little fingers and practiced eyes able to sort the shiny rock from the plain before they could even speak.

Real Joe pointed to the pamphlet. "Without the bootleggers keeping the next generation educated while the mines were closed, the industry would be dead. Maybe it already is. Strip mining is going to change everything."

Patrick couldn't help himself. He blurted, "Were you a bootlegger?"

Real Joe smiled. "Don't tell the company."

Patrick scratched his head. "I still don't understand this town. Everyone knows about the bootleggers, and yet they walk free. Isn't bootlegging by definition illegal?"

"Ah, and that's the crux of it, Steel Man. Is it illegal, or should it be legal?" He waved his glass of whiskey under Patrick's nose, and he caught a whiff that made him thirsty. "Are you ready for this lesson, my little miner?"

Patrick wanted the information more than the whiskey. He was getting the distinct feeling that his future depended on it. "I ain't little, but yes, explain it to me."

"Once upon a time—"

"Seriously?"

"You gonna listen or what? It's hard enough to talk over this crowd."

The bar was indeed loud, with a thousand conversations going on at once. Patrick sealed his lips and gestured for Real Joe to continue.

"Once upon a time, a town was built for miners. The miners worked and lived there. They moved their families there. They raised their babies, who had more babies, and they all worked in the mines. Then one day, Wall Street crashed, and boom!" Real Joe slapped his hands together, drawing the attention of a few nearby miners. "The mine owners lost their fortunes, and their very expensive mining operations closed."

"Tell him the whole truth, Real Joe," a man next to Patrick said. "They purposely bankrupted the mines to feed the railroads."

Real Joe held up a finger. "I'm getting there. This is advanced economics, which those of us without high school diplomas aren't supposed to understand."

A few miners laughed.

Real Joe pointed a finger at Patrick. The whisky in the glass in the same hand swirled dangerously. "Did you ever notice that most of the coal companies are tied to railroads?"

Patrick shrugged.

"You see, cities need coal to run their factories, power plants, and locomotives. Anthracite in particular makes the best steel, which makes the skyscrapers that form those city skylines."

"Certainly," Patrick agreed. That he knew firsthand.

"Coal is what has built this country and continues to build it. So the railroads, knowing this, knew that there was going to be a lot of business in shipping that coal. So they invested in the mines to dig the coal, then they cashed in when it came time to transport it."

"Brilliant investment."

"Exactly. But coal mining isn't cheap. It only takes one man to run a locomotive. It takes hundreds to run a mine. Not to mention, you can shut down a mine, but it's much harder, more impactful, to shut down a railroad."

"So they closed the mines after the crash?"

Another listener cut in. "One by one, starting in '29."

"Ours closed in '32. The lease with Lehigh Coal and Navigation was up. There was talk that someone was going to renew it. Heck, even General Electric from New

York City thought about it. But instead, they closed the mine, robbing the pillars as they went, sold all the equipment in the breaker and pump house, and left. Four hundred workers from this town were left to watch the mine flood into uselessness, wondering how they were going to feed their families. The town, then still owned by the company, was sold off in lots to the residents."

"But you all stayed? What did you do for work?" Patrick asked.

"We dug our own coal," said the tall, red-haired man Patrick had seen the other night. Red. He walked over to stand next to Real Joe. "You can't tell me it's illegal to continue selling what I can pull out of my backyard."

Patrick didn't dare argue.

One of his fellow company miners did. "But Red, you don't own the mineral rights on that land. That's what the Maryd Colliery is paying a fortune via lease for."

Red glared at the man. "I've been digging my coal hole for two years. They didn't have no lease then. You can't tell me to just forget about all those months of labor just to get it producing. I intend to work that vein until it's dry."

The company miner wouldn't be shaken. "There's independent miners who lease their own land. They're the ones the union is supposed to be representing. The legal ones."

"Digging in my backyard should not be illegal," Red insisted.

Real Joe waved the two men down. "Either way, it's not fair of the company to want to dig right up to our back doors and then blast under them. We own these houses now. We have mortgages on them. There has to be a limit."

Patrick cut in. "Go back a moment. Legal or not, you obviously are making a living selling your own coal, right?"

Red nodded and smiled. "We sell it all over. When the mines closed, the companies didn't account for the fact that demand for coal would stay relatively the same. Independent miners supply about five percent of the nation's coal...millions of tons a year."

"But how do you get it to market?"

Real Joe answered, "Funny you should ask. That's where those damn railroads come in. They won't let us ship bootlegged coal by rail."

"So we truck it," Red added.

"And no one gets arrested?" Patrick was still caught on that. How could something be illegal and yet the law was not enforced?

Red leaned toward Patrick, beer on his breath. "What jury is going to go against us? A jury of our peers from around here...all know someone doing exactly what we're doing. We're just trying to make a living, feed our families. By such, we're untouchable."

Patrick looked over at Ruth again, and their eyes met for the briefest moment. She quickly looked away, but not before one of her friends looked over, noticed him, and smiled. Patrick had a sinking suspicion he was being talked about. He could duck out or greet her and her friends. Would decorum dictate that he offer to buy her a drink? Did she drink? They probably had some soda on hand, too. Maybe the owner of the bar would let him buy on credit, just this once. He excused himself from Real Joe as the miners continued their debate and wove his way through the room. A miner passed him with a full pitcher of beer, and he had to look away to allow him to pass.

When he looked up, Ruth was gone.

CHAPTER 9

She felt guilty for leaving the children alone even for a few minutes, and yet she'd wanted to talk to Big Vic, the local leader of the Independent Miners Association. They'd met years ago through her father, and Jack had often had a liking for the man's business sense. Big Vic wasn't a miner himself anymore, but an independent bootleg breaker owner. He charged the miners to finish their coal and get it to market, or bought the raw coal from them, and in turn made his own, rather lucrative profit. It was an essential service, and without Big Vic, most bootleggers would be left selling coal to their fellow bootleggers. In other words, not selling it at all. With Big Vic, their coal got to markets as far away as New York City and Baltimore.

Most importantly, Big Vic knew almost every bootleg miner in the area.

"Hi, Vic, how are you?" Ruth smiled sweetly, wishing she'd put on a little bit of her lipstick. Gracious, had it been that long since she'd gotten out of the house for something other than church?

"Well, ma'am. How do you do?"

"Oh, I'm just fine. Do you remember me? Old Al's daughter?"

"Ah, yes! Ruth. Good to see you again."

"You as well. Glad you made it back into town." Someone else was already trying to get Big Vic's attention, so Ruth hurried it along. "You might remember my husband, Jack Flannigan? Have you by chance seen him lately?"

"Jack—" Vic's brow furrowed, then his face lit up. "Jack! Yeah, I remember him. Great guy. But no, I haven't seen him for a year or so." Again, someone jostled them for his attention. To Vic's credit, he fought to keep his attention on Ruth. "He still in the business?"

"Far as I know," Ruth said quietly, trying to hide her disappointment. "Well, thanks." She was gradually cut off by a group of men who were trying to show Vic a map of coal deposits in the area.

Big Vic craned his head over the crowd. "If I see him, what do you want me to tell him?"

Ruth paused. "Come home."

Bogie sat on the porch when Ruth got back across the street, his feet swinging in the chair as he'd done when he was little. Now his toes scuffed the boards. He was growing up all too fast. How could she pause, take a breath, and live in the moment again? So much time was dedicated to just surviving now.

"So has he seen him?"

Ruth settled into the chair next to Bogie, watching the bar patrons begin to disperse, their conversations lively with the theatrics of alcohol-dramatized gestures and laughter. Bogie knew she'd gone to talk to Big Vic. Bribing him with adult information was a trade for him taking on more responsibility, like helping with his sisters. Again, how was that fair to a child?

"No."

"If he doesn't know where Dad's at, no one will," Bogie said the statement with such matter-of-factness that it pained her. "Ma, you think he's alive? We'd know if he wasn't, right? Billy said the police come all formal like, with a telegram, when someone dies."

"I don't know, honey. I hope he's alive."

"And if he's alive, he's gonna come home, right? He wouldn't just leave us completely. Unless you kicked him out. Billy said you might have kicked Dad out, and that means he'll never come home."

She was going to have to have a talk with Billy's mother. "No, honey, I didn't kick him out." As if she could. The man was as stubborn-headed as a mule. If he wanted to stay, he'd have stayed. If he wanted to go, well, he was gone. "I'm hoping for an explanation when he comes home, just like you."

Bogie's legs stopped swinging, and he looked over at her. She braced herself for whatever hard question was coming next.

"Ma, I want to help the family and work. Billy said I could work with him and his dad. He makes almost ten dollars a week."

"Absolutely not."

"But..."

"End of discussion. You aren't going anywhere near a mine. Or a breaker. If you want to help out, you can help me cook and clean for the boarders. Or maybe feed

Mr. Petroko's mules every now and then. His back's been bothering him."

"Women's work..." Bogie mumbled.

"Excuse me?"

"Nothing, Ma." He promptly got up and went in the house.

"Good night," she called after him. She let her head drop back against the porch chair.

As if needing him to help with his sisters wasn't enough responsibility, now her son wanted to earn money, too. It was a noble thought. Yet Ruth knew well enough that Billy's father was a bootlegger, and that his operation was small enough, poor enough, to necessitate him putting his own son underground. Eleven-year-old Billy was a tough, wiry kid, and he was a good friend to Bogie. But Ruth knew well the risks of using a child to labor in a mine. That was why the government put an end to it years ago. Though rules didn't apply to bootleg holes. That was family business.

She closed her eyes and sighed, jaw tight as she thought of how stubborn miners were. Of course, that was when Mr. Kane decided to return.

"Evening," he said, stopping at the bottom porch step. "I would have bought you a drink, but you disappeared so quickly I lost you."

"I don't drink, Mr. Kane."

"Not even a good soda?"

That did sound refreshing, but she was loath to admit it, so she stayed quiet.

"Have I done something to offend you, ma'am?" Patrick asked. He took off his hat and twisted the brim in his hands. His hair stuck up at odd angles. His crestfallen expression almost made her pity him. Really, the man had done nothing wrong.

"No, Mr. Kane. Just a lot on my mind." She offered him a smile, but she could feel that it came out weak.

"Alright then, ma'am. See you in the morning. Have a good evening."

As the screen door slapped shut behind him, she wondered if she shouldn't try harder to make him feel welcome. As Edna had said, it really didn't hurt to have friends. She was going to need help when winter came. There would be no snow shoveling with the baby in hand. Would that, too, fall to Bogie? Who knew when or if Jack would show up, and even if he did, there was nothing wrong with having allies, fellow men who could help him see reason. He couldn't do this again to her. Maybe Jack would come home with a good excuse, and they'd be able to talk it out. But if he couldn't, well, then maybe Edna was right about that, too.

Ruth wasn't even sure which she hoped for.

CHAPTER 10

Thursday June 2, 1938

Buh-bu-bum. Buh-bu-bum. Buh-bu-bum.

Patrick stared at the ceiling, the night enveloping him like a dark blanket. The sound of Bogie throwing a ball reverberated over his head and in turn, through his head. Was he bouncing it off the wall? The ceiling? Certainly the floor of the attic, which happened to coincide with where Patrick lay. Apparently, the boy was as sleepless as he was. Patrick imagined Ruth sleeping in the room next to him, her hair tossed across a pillow, alone except for two little girls. Patrick groaned, rubbed his eyes, and sat up. Isaac still lay curled in his own bed, snoring.

Careful not to make too much noise, Patrick leaned over the bed and untied the string of the bundle of newspapers. He withdrew the top one without it rustling and spread it on the bed. It was dated a month ago. Too recent. Isaac said he'd been there four months, so Ruth's husband must have been gone longer than that. He returned it to the pile, then rifled through the stack until he found a few from about six months back. January 1938. He read the headlines, skimming pages, devouring in full every article about coal mining he could find, which there were plenty of. By the time the sun was up and Isaac woke, he was second-guessing his plan to keep his questions to himself. Maybe he should have just asked Real Joe last night. Or Ruth herself. There was no obituary, no arrests of a Mr. Flannigan. Heck, he didn't even know the man's first name.

How could a man leave a woman like Ruth? Surely, he must be dead. Then again, what kind of man was Patrick to have left his own fiancée in Pittsburgh? For a moment, he imagined her perfume on the air, the feel of her lips on his. It was that thought that kept him up almost until dawn, so that by the time the smell of breakfast and the noise of Isaac getting ready woke him, he felt as if he'd only slept ten minutes. He dragged himself through the new routine of dressing, eating, changing again to pull on his dirty mine clothes and coveralls in the basement, and then forced his weary body to the mine.

He crawled into the mine car and waited, yawning, while the other miners piled in. Real Joe again managed to find a seat next to him. Patrick ignored him, unwilling to talk today.

"You look like you were up all night. And you didn't even drink!" Real Joe said jubilantly. Patrick made a note to get a recipe for whatever kind of coffee Real Joe was drinking each morning. Later. When he was up for conversation.

The mine car lurched forward with a grind of wheels on tracks, and Real Joe mercifully grew quieter, so he didn't have to yell over the noise. They pulled into the dark tunnel and began their descent. Patrick let the rhythm of the mine car lull him to sleep. Maybe five minutes would be all he needed to refresh himself. Something changed in the rhythm though. Patrick opened his eyes and looked to Real Joe. Most of the miners had their headlamps on, and Real Joe's face was alight with the glow. The concern there was obvious. There was a squeal of metal on metal, and a shower of sparks lit the tunnel behind them. Was it his imagination or was the car picking up speed?

"We're speeding up!" Real Joe shouted to Patrick and shifted to his knees to better see down the low-ceilinged tunnel. Around them, the other miners also stirred with alarm, craning their heads to see what was wrong. Real Joe had to duck a particularly low beam, but soon turned back to the men. "I think the brakes are bad. Georgie's up there pulling the brake with all his might, and we ain't slowing!"

Patrick stiffened as they flew past the mine doors. The young man who worked the doors leapt out of the way, then stood on the tracks watching them as they continued down the slope, gaining speed all the way.

"You have an emergency brake on this thing?" Patrick asked. He was fully alert now, adrenaline surging through his system.

"Here!" Real Joe pulled a lever, and the car ground out a scream of steel. Sparks lit the tunnel. Several men covered their ears. But the car didn't slow down. The two other cars in front of them were attempting the same, and though one set of emergency brakes successfully engaged, they weren't strong enough to slow the other cars and engine that was still pulling them down the mine. Patrick peered down the tunnel to the engine, noting the driver was still wrestling with the machine, trying to throw the engine in reverse, or pull the jammed brake, anything. Patrick could also see they were running out of time. It wouldn't be long until the entire train crashed into the solid wall of rock at the bottom of the shaft.

"We've got to jam the wheels!" Patrick shouted. He looked around for anything he could stick under the car. They blew past a pile of wooden two-by-fours, and he snatched one, nearly smashing his head on the next support beam in the process.

"You'll lose your hand!" Real Joe shouted.

Patrick glanced from him to the runaway engine and then down into the darkness where the wheels of the mine car rolled. He took a breath, leaned over, and then shoved the wood in between the back two wheels. As soon as it was in place, it snapped out of his hands. Patrick flew back, uncertain if the wood would fly back up or if the car would derail. Maybe he'd killed them all.

The wood held, and the car began to slow. Another man took the handle of his sledgehammer and did the same, ducking out of the way as the wood threatened to smash him in the face. The car slowed more. The miners were still as the mine train glided to a stop, the nose of the train pressed against the wall of rock that marked the end of the mine shaft.

They were on tracks that had only been laid yesterday.

Patrick leaned against the side of the car, a cold sweat dripping down his back. There was a collective breath as all the miners processed what had happened. Patrick's heart pounded in his ears. Gradually, the rustle of fabric and creak of metal sounded as the miners pulled themselves out of the cars to check the damage.

"Brakes wore out," someone said.

"Melted clear through," said another miner.

"Bloody miracle we stopped."

Real Joe turned to Patrick. His eyes were still a bit wide. "You've got nerves of steel, not just a name."

Patrick smiled weakly. His knees felt like rubber, not metal. He pulled himself out of the car anyway and began inspecting the mine train. He observed much of the same as the other men. He also noted that the cars were so coated with dust and rusted from the constant moisture of the mine that it was no wonder certain parts failed to engage. He turned to the foreman, who'd been along for the ride and was a bit white in the face.

"This train has got to be serviced. It needs grease, cleaning, new gears that aren't rusted solid—"

"Can you do it?" the foreman asked.

"I—yes." Patrick nodded once.

"Then do it. We need to get out of this hole tonight. Can't mine without blasting, and I ain't staying down here when we blast. And I ain't walking up that drift. Get it done." The foreman gestured for the engineer to back the train to its normal parking spot at the tunnel intersection. Patrick hopped in the car behind the engineer for the short ride as the other men got out their drills and started preparing to lay dynamite.

That cold prickle fingered its way up Patrick's spine again. Did he really want to be down there while they were playing with explosives? Too late now.

A few of the men gave him an appreciative wave as the train backed away from the worksite.

The train stopped. "Get us topside," the engineer said, then drove the engine down another tunnel to hook up to another string of coal cars.

Suddenly alone in the big central tunnel intersection, Patrick closed his eyes and sank onto the damp metal of the tracks. He forced himself to breathe once, twice. It was just another day on the job. So what if they'd all almost died? He'd signed on because he wanted a dangerous job. He wanted to feel alive. Well, he sure did that. And he knew with certainty he didn't want to be dead. That was reassuring. He slapped his knees then pushed to his feet. He went over the cars a second time, now with the benefit of the electric lights in addition to his headlamp, and then headed into the storage room to get what he needed.

Perhaps his career change wasn't going to be very dramatic after all.

Patrick was just finishing his lunch when Real Joe showed up.

"I'll tell you, if anything else goes wrong today, we're all pulling out of here early. Even if we do have to walk." Real Joe headed for the storage room.

Patrick brushed crumbs off his hands and stood. "What's happening?"

"They were clearing out the last of the coal in the chute down tunnel two, and the trap got stuck. About a ton of coal overflowed onto the tracks before we could get it shut again. All that had to be shoveled by hand. I don't know if men are just spooked from this morning and not thinking, or if all this is an omen that we need to get out of this dang mine for the day." He frowned at Patrick's lunch pail. "Did you just eat lunch?"

Patrick also frowned at his lunch pail, as if the tin had done something wrong. "Well, yes. My belly's been growling, and I don't have a watch. The cars are done, and I swear I didn't take longer than a ten-minute break."

"You don't know what time it is?"

"Hard to gauge by the sun down here."

"It's ten A.M. You've got a long day to go yet."

Patrick cursed under his breath. He had thought it was closer to at least two. His internal clock was way off today.

Real Joe read his face and smiled. "You're not the first one that's been alone down here and done that. A little advice...always leave a little water in your canteen. Drain it when you can see daylight again. Only thing worse than running out of food early and working on a hungry belly is being out of water, thirsty, and unable to rinse the coal dirt out of your mouth." He found what he needed in the storage room and threw the box over his broad shoulder. "You think you have this train set that we won't die getting out of here tonight?"

"Yeah, she'll work now. Kinda in rough shape. I thought this was a new mine."

"The bosses are using as much old equipment as they can. Catch up with Georgie and go over that engine, too. We're counting on you, Steel Man." He headed off into the dark, the light from his headlamp bouncing along the corridor. "Whisper to that metal...make love to it...make it purr..."

Mercifully, Real Joe faded into the distance.

True to his word, by the end of the day, Patrick had the train operating better than it probably had in years. He and Georgie even took it for a ride partway up the drift and back, just to make sure all was well. The train engineer seemed pleased and took a few loads of coal up with the engine, just to be sure. Thankfully, the engine had never been the problem, just the brakes connecting to the cars. Still, more than a few miners looked at the train warily as they climbed in. The foreman did a walk-around, which Patrick felt was just for show. If the foreman knew what to look for in regard to the mechanics of the mine cars, he never would have let the train leave that morning. He couldn't hold it against the man, though. He was a miner, not a mechanic. He cared about his men. Patrick joined him to point out all the things he'd tweaked, so the foreman would know what to watch for in the future.

The signal was given for the train to ascend, and even Patrick couldn't help but hold his breath. He watched for daylight. What was he doing, risking his life for black rocks? He hadn't even gotten a paycheck yet. He liked working with his hands. He even liked being underground—it felt like an adventure. But he wasn't keen on dying or worse—getting hurt. If he was going to end up as a mechanic again, he might as well stay above ground.

There was nothing for him here.

He saw the daylight cut into the gloom and not long after, he felt the mist of rain on his skin. Overcast, and still it felt bright to be back on earth. He took a deep breath. He could smell diesel fuel and taste the grit of the coal dirt, but he could also smell the pines from across the tailings field. The miners began to cheer. Then their cheers turned to be directed at him.

"And the Steel Man gets us home!" Real Joe boomed out.

With wide eyes, Patrick took congratulations and thanks from all sides. He tried to be humble and tell them, "It wasn't just me..." but they weren't listening. The men were all smiles, despite the brutal day, as they piled out of the train car into the misty air.

"Come to the bar tonight," Real Joe invited. "My treat."

"I dunno..."

"Seriously, you need to live. We almost died today. We owe you a drink. Now come join us and live while we can, and we'll all listen to the blasts of our hard work. I'll make sure you're in bed plenty early to be rested tomorrow."

Patrick was too tired to think. "What's tomorrow?"

"Payday, my friend. Payday!"

CHAPTER 11

Ruth shook out one of Dot's dresses, the fabric making a sharp snap in the breeze. It had started as a good day for wash, or more importantly, drying wash. This morning, the sun had been out, the breeze blew and still, she'd managed to time everything wrong. She'd hoped the clouds that had rolled in that afternoon would part, but instead they'd unleashed a mist of rain, which now led to bringing in damp clothes. They'd have to finish drying on the clothing line that hung in the upstairs hallway. She sighed. That was even more work, as now she'd have to hang everything twice. Why was she even bothering to fold things? Absently, she snapped one of Bogie's shirts and squinted at the horizon. The sun was down. Twilight was upon them. The ground was done shaking for the day from all the blasts down in the mine. The boarders were fed. And there was still a list of things she had to get done. It started with getting this wash in, soon followed by getting three overtired children to bed.

"Girls, how about you help me?" They were seated on the damp grass at her feet, dolls in hand, glassy, tired eyes watching her.

"You said not to help last time," Addy pointed out, but begrudgingly pulled herself to her feet.

"I did, didn't I?" The girls had spent more time running around with sheets over their shoulders like superhero capes—an idea inspired by Bogie and his friend Billy's brand new comic—dragging the washed clothes through the grass, than transferring wash from line to basket. "Well, let's be quick about it this time." She snatched one of her dresses off the line with a sharp tug that sent clothespins flying through the air. The girls giggled. Dot was the first to reach out a tentative hand and jerk one of her dresses down. The dress came down and covered her head. Ruth couldn't help but smile at the expression Dot made as she tried to extricate herself. When the little girl emerged, she let out a giggle that warmed Ruth to the core. That smile could light a room of strangers.

The baby within her kicked. Her hand went to the place. If only Jack could see this.

The girls had half the wash in the basket by the time she'd blinked tears from her eyes. She finished unpinning the rest, rolled the damp clothes into balls, and tossed them into the overflowing basket. Addy picked up the escaped clothespins, and Dot stood on tiptoe to reach the very last dress. It hung at the highest point of the wash line, and her fingertips could just touch the hem. She jumped. Her hand clenched the fabric. This time, instead of clothespins flying, they held, and a rip cut through the backyard. The entire hem of the dress was now in Dot's hand. She stared at it, blinked a few times, and then looked up to Ruth with tears in her eyes.

"I sorry, ma-ma," she gasped out, and then squinted her eyes shut into a wail.

Ruth didn't have the heart to scold her. She squatted down next to her and pulled her into her arms. "It's alright, love. That was my game. I underestimated those clothespins."

"But it was my fa—" she sniffled— "favorite."

"I know." Ruth couldn't help but smile to herself. She'd fought Dot tooth and nail to put that exact dress on last week. Dot had insisted it was too girly because there was tiny little flowers on it. "I can sew it. You'll see." She stood, scooping Dot up with her. Her back felt the strain, but it was worth it to have her little girl nestled into her shoulder. "Now, everything seems worse because you're tired, so let's get to bed. Addy, come on dear. Bring Dot's doll, please."

So with one child in her arms and one close behind, she climbed the stairs into the house and to the upstairs bathroom, where she hastily cleaned up both girls and got them into nightgowns. She got them down to bed and mercifully, they fell asleep as soon as they said their prayers. Then it was on to Bogie, who, after hours of playing ball with his friends, had gotten home and was emerging from the bathroom now.

Ruth ruffled the damp hair that was starting to grow over his ears. He was due for a trim. He had a towel around his waist, his lanky frame drawn up as tall as he could in imitation of his father. Gangly as he was now, Ruth had no doubt he would fill into his body and be as handsome as his father, too.

"Did you have fun?" she asked him.

"I hit a home run, but then Billy and Sammy both got home runs when I pitched. I've got to work on my curve."

Ruth smiled at the determination in his eyes and traced his cheek with her thumb. "We'll work on that this weekend."

There was a flicker of something in his eye then, as if he was going to spit out some retort but thought better of it. Then there was the echo of sadness she knew came from missing Jack. She kissed him on his forehead and stepped aside so he could climb the stairs into the attic.

"Love you, sweetheart. You can open the windows up all the way up there. Weather is supposed to improve tonight."

"Already did, Ma."

He disappeared up the stairs, leaving Ruth alone in the hallway. She could hear Isaac snoring down in the main bedroom. Every now and then he coughed, and she recognized the start of miners' lung. The man had toiled underground as long as her father had, if not longer. She wondered if he knew what he had. Even if he did, there was nothing she nor he could do, at least not if he wasn't willing to quit working and stay above ground. The practical side of her wondered what she would do if he couldn't pay rent. Then she felt guilty for even considering putting such a kind man on the street. She wiped her forehead with the back of her hand, suddenly tired. What else was there to do tonight? Tidy the kitchen for the morning, do her weekly ledger, get herself washed up for bed, and actually sleep. That wasn't too bad. She stretched and rubbed her aching lower back.

She was sitting at the freshly cleaned kitchen table with her grocery receipts, planning the boarders' meals for the next week, when the screen door to the kitchen slapped shut. She looked up into Patrick's brown eyes. At night, they looked like deep pools of chocolate. Or mine tunnels into darkness. Yes, maybe that later.

He shifted his weight, and her gaze settled on the wash basket on his hip. She frowned at it, for a moment confused as to why his basket looked so much like her own.

"I figured you didn't intend to leave this out."

She snapped back to reality and leapt to her feet. She'd forgotten the wash again. Now it would be covered in dew and even wetter. She moved to take it from him. "Jeez, I'm sorry. Thank you."

He still held the basket on his hip. "I can take it upstairs for you if that's where you want it."

"Oh, you don't have to..."

"Ruth..." He cleared his throat. "Mrs. Flannigan, I really don't mind. I'm going up anyway. Just tell me where you want it."

"Hallway," she said quietly. Now that was a novelty if there ever was one. Never had Jack offered to carry a basket of clothes. Nor had her father for her mother, for that matter. And here was a man she was supposed to be serving, being...helpful?

Ruth followed Patrick up the stairs, noting how he made the basket look light, even though it was heavy with wet clothes. She again rubbed her lower back. He raised his eyebrows at her when they reached the landing, and she pointed near the bathroom door at the end of the hall. He set it down quietly, as if he was aware the girls were sleeping on the other side of the wall.

"Thank you."

"Anytime, ma'am. You need help hanging them?"

"I'll just do it in the morning."

He hesitated, then looked down at the basket. "Things generally dry faster if you hang them. Don't get as musty either."

She sighed and reached for the clothespin bag. He was right. When she reached into the wash basket, her knuckles brushed his.

"You don't have to help, Mr. Kane."

"Not ready to sleep yet anyway," he said as he took two clothespins from the bag and pinned up one of the girls' dresses with practiced precision. Then he hesitated. "Unless you want me to go."

She pinned up her dress, smoothing the wrinkles in the fabric. Edna's voice echoed in her head. It was alright to accept help. "You're fine."

They pinned a labyrinth of wet clothes in the narrow hallway, elbows and fingers brushing occasionally. The house suddenly felt very small and stuffy. She felt a blush climb into her cheeks and desperately wanted to distract them both.

"So what do you think of mining?"

She watched Patrick withdraw a pair of Bogie's trousers from under her smallclothes. The heat in her cheeks grew hotter. She hastily gathered her things and tossed them onto the nightstand in her room. They could dry in there. Later. She glanced over at the girls, who were fast asleep. She pulled the door shut behind her.

Patrick continued as if he hadn't noticed. "It's been an interesting week. I don't mind the dark or the small space much. It's hard work, but that's what I signed on for. Today we had a bit of a runaway train incident, though. Dangerous work those men do."

"Well, you're one of them now," Ruth pointed out.

"I guess I am."

"Did they let you play with the dynamite yet?"

"Naw. Maybe next week." He smiled, and she couldn't help but stare. She had the feeling he hadn't smiled much lately, at least not real smiles. His whole expression changed. His eyes grew softer, brighter. His shoulders relaxed, which somehow made him seem taller.

His gaze met hers, and she held it a moment, a smile playing at her own lips, then forced herself to look away. The clothes were hung. The hallway was barely big enough to fit them all, and the line that ran from doorframe to doorframe the length of the hallway strained under the weight.

"Thank you," she whispered.

"Anytime, Ruth." He tipped his head and ducked into his room with Isaac.

She didn't bother to correct him.

CHAPTER 12

Friday June 3, 1938

Patrick thought of that paycheck the whole time he worked, clearing rock from the blast the night before. Every shovel stroke seemed to be another dollar. By the end of the day, his back ached, his hands were raw, and yet he felt more alive than ever. The other men had a similar pep in their step, despite the collective exhaustion. Pay meant money, money meant drinks, drinks meant an escape from the drudgery of labor. They all could afford to forget the day before.

After they unloaded from the mine train that evening, Patrick followed the rest of the men to the mine office just off Main Street, where a rough line formed. Men were handed their pay and then headed back up to town. Patrick shifted back and forth on his feet. He knew he owed the store for his clothes and headlamp, plus room and board at Ruth's. He knew the math wasn't going to be in his favor this first paycheck, but hopefully this week he'd be well on his way to paying off his debts. And maybe he could keep just a dollar for himself.

The clerk handed him his slip, and as he left the mine office, he ripped the envelope open with his thumb. A few feet outside the door, he stopped. There was a paper statement scrawled in barely legible handwriting detailing his income, subtracting taxes. It wasn't enough to cover what he owed the general store for his mining clothes, let alone his board with Ruth.

Patrick stared. All that work over the week, and he still hadn't made money at his new job. He owed money. He crumbled the paper in his hand.

Isaac appeared at his side and laid a hand on his shoulder. "It gets better after the first few weeks, now that you have appropriate supplies." He steered Patrick up toward town. "No, it'll get better. Once you take on more responsibilities down there, you'll see the pay raise."

"I forgot they take taxes," Patrick said in a daze.

"Government wants their share of our sweat. Been a while since you worked above the table?"

Patrick nodded. His visions of a cold drink at the bar faded. He was going to have to escape down to the stripping hole again. The weather was decent, but not hot enough that he wanted to plunge into the cold mud pit. One day, when he did get paid, he was going to hitch a ride out of this town and find out what more there was to do around here. He excused himself from Issac and headed down the hill to the stripping hole. He nodded greetings to more than one of his fellow miners along the way—he was now one of them after his "heroic" efforts the day before. Maybe he'd sit for a while. Maybe he'd take out his frustrations by throwing rocks into the inky black depths. Either way, he needed time to be alone.

Ruth was there, stretched out on her back, soaking up the summer sun. Patrick hadn't prepared himself for such a vision. He stopped about twenty yards away and stared. Her blonde hair was her pillow, the strands shining like gold in the light. Her bare legs, strong and muscled from hard work, stretched long into the grass, pointing towards the water's edge. Her stockings and shoes were discarded next to her. She had dainty feet, slender and graceful. She was still, with both hands cradling the slight bulge of her belly. She looked so peaceful, so beautiful.

Patrick swallowed.

He turned to return back to the house. To hell with her rules, he would go to the bar and drink a few drinks tonight. He'd pay his debts next week. After surviving this week, he deserved it. His boot sent a slight cascade of shale down the embankment, which made Ruth look up. On noting him, she sat up and straightened her hair, a slight frown on her lips.

It would be rude to ignore her now. He turned. "Sorry to disturb you."

"No worries. I should be starting dinner soon anyway." As if to explain her idleness, she quickly added, "The girls are with their friends tonight, and Bogie is playing baseball with the boys, so I thought I had time for just a moment—"

He held up a hand. "You don't have to explain yourself to me. You deserve time for yourself, too." He took a few steps down toward the water. "Or at least you should. For what it's worth, you're raising a great bunch of kids."

She smiled slightly. "Thank you for that. I try." She pulled her skirt a bit lower down over her knees and turned back to the water, which sparkled as if it were made of silver. The greens of the trees around the hole reflected back, making the waste pit look as if it were a peaceful pond.

The silence grew awkward, and Patrick debated whether he should excuse himself. Maybe if he walked a bit further, he could find his own little pond to sit next to.

"How's the mine?"

He took her question as an invitation to join her. He approached the last few strides and sat on one of the larger rocks next to her. "Moved a lot of rock today. Everyone survived."

Out of the corner of his eye, he caught her sideways glance. "Something else happen?"

"No, thankfully. Just a long week."

"It's a dangerous business." She picked up a piece of shale and let it flake apart in her hand. It didn't take much, just the pressure of her thumb. "Rumor has it you worked steel before this. What made you change to mining?"

He thought about giving her the same excuse he gave everyone else. Yet somehow he thought she deserved more.

"You don't have to tell me." She shook her golden hair and turned back to the water. She let the rock sail out over the water with a casual throw that had enough power to raise Patrick's eyebrows in appreciation. It settled with a plunk.

Suddenly, Patrick didn't want the conversation to end. He wanted to talk to someone. "I got fired."

"Lots of people out of work right now."

"They got laid off. I got fired." He took a deep breath. "I made a mistake in the steel mill. I was a mechanic, and instead of fixing the piece of equipment like I should have, I put a patch on it. Wanted to be done for the day. When it broke, it was spectacular." He savaged a handful of grass, picturing the molten metal flying. The screams still echoed in his head as if he'd heard them yesterday, not years ago. Then the smells rushed back to him, that metallic tang of iron and blood. The guilt was what crushed him.

Ruth didn't need to know all that.

He crossed his arms to hide the tremor in his hands. "I hopped a train to Bethlehem. Tried to work steel there again. But my mind wasn't in it. I'm not comfortable with the noise or the heat anymore."

She was polite enough not to pry into the details. She sat, her forehead furrowed. So at peace with his vague description was she that Patrick wondered what horrors she herself had witnessed. Surely the mine car incident was not the first in this town, nor the worst. Her next words solidified his suspicion. "How can a man move past that guilt? I understand acknowledging that remorse, but why let it destroy your life?"

"I wouldn't say my life is destroyed. Just different." He looked at her quizzically and realized she wasn't talking about him anymore, but someone else. Who?

Before he could ask, she turned the conversation again. "But why mining? Why not farming in the fresh air? Or driving a truck? Or even the railroad. There are so many fields for a man with mechanical skills. Why something so dangerous, so deep underground, you practically become a monster?"

He laughed at that, startling them both. "Miners are monsters now? My dear, now I must ask how you ended up in a mining town with that kind of sentiment."

Her lips pressed into a thin line. "I fell in love with a miner, the son of immigrants. Got pregnant." She suddenly looked angry and wiped off her skirts, then started pulling her shoes back on, not even bothering with the stockings. "Doesn't matter, he's gone now."

"I'm sorry, I didn't mean to upset you." Patrick was taken aback at the rapid mood change. He beat her to her feet and reached down a hand to help her up. She looked at it, hesitated, and then accepted. Her touch felt like fire, and Patrick didn't immediately release her. There was a piece of grass in her hair, and with his free hand, he picked it out.

He hadn't thought about the action, but when he looked back at her eyes, they were wide with shock, like a doe caught in the headlights of a car. Her hand tightened on his, and suddenly there was a rush of new emotion on her face, as if she wanted to kiss him.

Even though every thought in his head warned him that it was a bad idea—she was his landlady—the look she gave him held not just desire but desperation in it. She promised a passion he'd long denied himself. His thumb traced the back of her hand. His heart pounded in his chest, and for the second time since he'd arrived in the little patch town of Maryd, he felt life rush through his veins and all the joys and pains that came with it. It was the first he'd felt that rush in a circumstance that wasn't near-death in a long time.

"Ruth..." he breathed, her name a question and yet sweet on his lips.

It broke the spell, and her expression changed again. She withdrew her hand from his, broke eye contact. She took a step back, dusted the grass off her skirt. With a brusque nod, she headed back up the hill towards the house.

Patrick sank onto a rock. Ruth's departure took the breath from his lungs. How...how could he feel so much so quickly for someone who was still grieving and thus wasn't even ready to feel herself? No relationships, he'd told himself. He didn't plan to stick around for long. He never did, not since Pittsburgh. Now, he could picture himself staying here in Maryd, settling down. The mine was an adventure. The physical work gave him purpose and vitality. He'd feel even more alive when he finally got a real paycheck and felt like a man again. Maybe he *could* settle down. Moving from city to city was exhausting. Looking for new work, a new meal, was its own kind of exhausting.

Could he picture himself with a family?

Patrick picked up a piece of shale, flaking it apart as Ruth had done. He noted a shimmer in the rock and looked closer. There was a perfect fossil of an ancient vine, each delicate leaf etched into the stone. He sighed. The small treasures of this place just kept appearing. He needed to give himself time. And maybe that was what Ruth needed, too. Who knew what her full story was? The simplest question—what happened to Mr. Flannigan—was the one she seemed the most adept at avoiding.

Luckily, time was something he had plenty of.

CHAPTER 13

Jack was going to come back. He had to. She was a fool to think he wouldn't. She couldn't go around thinking things like she just had. For goodness' sake, she wasn't some love-drunk teenage girl who could make googly eyes at any man who talked to her. She was a landlady. She was a mother. She was a *wife*.

Ruth lectured herself in circles all the way back to town and then beelined it right to Edna's house. Edna was sitting on her back porch watching the girls play. Her expression lightened when she saw Ruth, then faded to concern.

"Honey, you still have time. The girls are fine. Go relax—"

Ruth felt the tears fall, her eyes blurry. No words were really necessary, but Ruth managed to whisper, "He's coming back, right? Edna, he has to come back." Her voice shook as she blinked the tears away, all while Edna rose to her feet and put her arms around her.

"Oh, honey." Edna held her tighter.

The women stood like that a long moment, until the girls ceased their playing and took notice.

"Mama?" Dot questioned.

Ruth pulled away and wiped her tears. She forced a smile. "I'm fine, love. You go play. I'll come and get you girls before bed, alright?"

"How about you let them have a sleepover tonight?"

Edna's daughters, Maisey and Elaine, danced on their toes with excitement, big smiles on their faces as they clutched their friends' hands.

Edna looked at Ruth earnestly. "Please?" Quietly, she added, "You haven't had a break in ages."

Ruth hesitated, but her resolve was weak. "Okay, if you girls want to."

Dot and Addy smiled as their friends cheered, but they were reserved as they went back to their game. They may be young, but they knew something was going on. They knew their father was missing, though they may not voice it as clearly as Bogie did. Ruth turned to Edna with wide eyes. Her arms circled her belly.

"I don't know how I'm going to do it. How?"

Edna took a deep breath. "You take one day at a time. And I'm here for you. Ruth, this whole dang town's here for you. You know that."

Ruth nodded.

Edna hesitated. "After all he's done, all he's put you through, you still love him, don't you?"

Ruth turned slightly and looked off into the distance, over the piles of old mine dirt, out over the valleys where, somewhere, Jack was probably crawling around in some coal hole. She took a deep breath. "You know how deep a mine goes?"

Edna furrowed her brow in confusion. "Well, yes."

"That's how much I love him."

If she was going to have a night off, she was going to take it. Ruth put dinner out for her boarders, made sure Bogie was fed before he set off down the road to Billy's, and then pinned her hat into her hair as she ducked out the door with a polite smile at Isaac. Thankfully, Patrick was nowhere to be seen. She strode out of town with long strides, heading south towards the gas station where the bus ran on its route between Tamaqua and Pottsville. She didn't make it off Main Street before a Model-T pick-up pulled next to her and slowed. She instinctively took a step away, her eyes flicking to the driver with a wary glance, but it was only Real Joe.

"Heya, Ruth. You going to Gig's with the gang?"

"Yeah, Real Joe. You gonna give me a lift?"

He stopped and reached across the seat to pop open the passenger door. "For you, always, darlin.'"

Ruth rolled her eyes but slipped in and shut the door.

Real Joe pulled out, the Model T's engine roaring.

"Can't believe you're still running this thing," she said to herself.

Real Joe glanced at her. "Hey, she's still fit as a fiddle. And besides, you know she works double-time."

Ruth smiled. As the daughter of an independent miner, she knew some of the bootleggers used the engines of their Model T's to run the winches for their coal holes. They also used the trucks to haul the coal to the breaker or to the buyers in the cities. She glanced in the back, which was empty. "Where's your haul?"

"I've been down the company mine all week." He leaned forward over his steering wheel. "Party tonight, then work double-time all weekend. Hole's about to start producing."

She leaned back in her seat. "Good for you."

"What about you? You get a night off from the kids?"

"Yeah, Edna insisted."

"Swell. It'll be like old times."

It was the wrong thing to say, and they both knew it. Ruth looked out her window and sighed. Their group of friends was not the same without their ringleader, Jack.

"You heard anything from him?" Real Joe asked quietly.

"Nope." She let the silence linger, then turned abruptly to Real Joe. "Don't you think I should have? Or you should have? No one—no one—knows nothin'. He could be dead down in some hole until all that's left is his bones."

"He ain't dead."

"How do you know?" she asked with a bit more force than necessary.

"Cause Jack—drunk and dumb or not—ain't stupid." He frowned as he pulled into the busy parking lot of the dance hall in Middleport, just a few miles outside of Maryd. "What I mean is, when it comes to mines at least, safety is his chief concern. If he *is* dead—and he ain't—then it ain't in a hole. And he ain't dead, because if he's above ground, they'd've found his body."

There was some rationale to that. But that made the truth of his absence by choice worse. Real Joe got out of the truck, and Ruth followed, not waiting for him to come around to open her door. They looked towards the dance hall as the sounds of music and laughter filled the air. Bright lights flashed within, where their friends waited. The scene was so counter to Ruth's mood, she suddenly had no desire to go in.

Real Joe gently took her elbow. "C'mon. The gals will be here. My sister has been itching to see you for months. She always asks about you."

Ruth sighed. "I've been thinking of her, too. It's been too long." Maybe she could invite Trudy over for pie one of these days. Or invite her for tea. Or—just go inside the freakin' dance hall and say hello now.

Real Joe smiled, but he released her elbow. He folded his arms and leaned against the hood of the truck. They stood there a while, watching the locals wander into the hall. She felt Real Joe's eyes studying her, but her mind was too emotionally exhausted to make her feet move towards that much happiness.

"How's your new boarder?" he asked quietly.

"Fine." She felt the heat rise into her cheeks again. Thank goodness it was dark.

"He's a good guy. Been working with him all week."

"Yeah?" She tried to keep her voice indifferent.

"Yeah. Not bad looking either, not that I'm much of a judge. That's what my sister says."

Ruth clenched her jaw.

"Level with me, Ruth. I won't judge. Is there more there?"

Her eyes flashed up to his. "Where is this coming from?"

"Honestly...Mrs. Vilchick said Mrs. Fisher saw him bring in your laundry basket. Scandalous."

Ruth wanted to laugh, and for a moment the smile quivered on her lips, until she remembered how Patrick's fingers had brushed hers as they hung that wash. Her silence made her seem guilty. She met Real Joe's eyes. "I am loyal to my husband."

He studied her a long moment. "Of course." Then he dusted his hands on his clean trousers and offered one to her. "Well then, my lady. Am I assisting you to the dance floor or would you like me to take you back home?"

"Would you?"

Without having to clarify which she was referring to, Real Joe smiled. He opened the door of the truck for her, and wordlessly they returned to Maryd, where he dropped her off at home before returning to the festivities himself. Ruth stared up at the house, the window in the front bedroom shining with the light of a bedside lamp. The curtain moved ever so slightly, as if a person had just peered out. She felt in her gut that Patrick had been watching. She heard a newspaper rustle through the open window, yet another reminder that the men in that room were not Jack. He never had the time—or desire—to read the paper. She imagined Patrick up there, feet propped, paper in hand, and her heart ached with loneliness, then guilt.

Even when he wasn't there, even if he wasn't dead, she couldn't escape Jack's ghost.

CHAPTER 14

Saturday, June 4, 1938

Saturday morning dawned with a muggy heat that only grew more intense as the day wore on. Patrick managed to avoid Ruth for most of the morning by sleeping in and thus eating a cold breakfast, and now this afternoon, the heat gave him a good excuse to escape back to the stripping hole.

He stood at the edge of the water, eyeing the black depths. The water called, cool and welcoming. He'd told himself he would just put his feet in, but walking barefoot in the muddy shallows was squishy, and the rocks were sharp. The warnings from the children and Isaac echoed in the back of his mind, but the heat was winning.

"Ah, the heck with it," he said to himself and stripped.

He splashed into the dark coolness, letting it envelope him. He dove down, then reemerged to shake the water out of his hair like a golden retriever. He wanted to whoop, but refrained for fear the children would again show up to ruin this moment. He paddled out further, feeling the water soothe his sore muscles. Then he lay back and floated, closing his eyes to the bright sun overhead. At least there *was* sun, glorious light. He swore to himself he'd never complain about heat again, as long as heat was a side effect of sunlight. He could feel it burning through his eyelids in the most pleasant way.

With his eyes closed, his senses heightened. He heard the gentle splash of the water as he moved. He smelled the pond-like decay of the murky water. He tasted the sweat that still hung to his upper lip and washed it away. He felt the water cool his skin, the power of his muscles as they obeyed his command to swim.

He was alive.

His imagination roared back. He thought of the serpent that drained the holes. Then, on a more practical level, he wondered what was really underneath him. The hole could be seven feet deep, the bottom just out of his reach, or it could be thirty or a hundred feet. There was no way to know. He reached out a hand, felt the water pull at it. He could see only an arm's length down into the water. When he treaded water, he couldn't see his feet. He pulled himself upright, treading to test his theory, which was correct—he could not feel the bottom. He held his breath and let himself slide down in the water, searching for the bottom with his toes. Again he felt the pull of the water around his legs, gentle as a caress of a tiny stream, but no bottom.

Still underwater, he stilled, his focus shifting to that caress. He could still feel it, even when he held his breath and didn't move. If he was in a stagnant pond, with no in or outflow, why was there a current?

Patrick kicked once hard and burst back through the surface of the water. He shook the water out of his hair and looked around for a stream, a pipe, any kind of inflow. There was none. The water around him was calm, only disturbed by his own movement.

The stories from the children and Isaac echoed in his mind. His heart thudded. Now, unable to relax, he gave up the swim and headed back to shore. He stood there looking out over the surface of the stripping hole, waiting for it to yield its secret, as if the water serpent would show itself. He shook his head. He was letting the tall tales of this town get to him. He scraped the water off his body as best as he could with his hands, then dressed. With one last look at the stripping hole, he turned towards the house.

He hadn't gone more than ten steps when he turned back, plucked a stick from a nearby tree, and walked to the water's edge. He sank the stick into the mud, an obvious marker of the water line. He'd come back tomorrow and check to see if the serpent had swallowed any water.

When Patrick got back to the house, Ruth was struggling to unload two armfuls of groceries while her girls literally ran circles around her. The girls were laughing their heads off, obviously deep in the depths of some game. Ruth kicked the car door closed with a foot.

"Thanks, Edna!" she called, and Edna drove across the street to her own townhouse.

Ruth shifted the groceries in her arms. One of the paper bags started to rip, and she yelped. Patrick sprinted the last few steps to her side and caught the bag just as its contents started to spill out. Ruth breathed a sigh of relief and blew a stray piece of hair out of her eyes. Patrick was caught off guard by how pretty she was, with a light coat of pink lipstick and rouge on her cheeks. He froze, feeling heat rise into his cheeks. So much for avoiding her. He should look away, but he couldn't.

"Thank you," she breathed.

The spell broke. "Anytime. You want me to take that one, too?"

"No, I've got it." She turned to her daughters. "Girls, let's go."

The girls ran ahead of them up the porch stairs. Patrick caught the screen door and held it for Ruth, and she gave him a slight smile as she walked past.

That was an improvement.

He followed her to the kitchen and set the torn bag on the counter, catching a few cans as they spilled out. Groceries secure, he looked at the can in his hand. "Tuna? Been a while since I've had that."

She blushed. "I've been craving it. Makes no sense. My last pregnancy, I couldn't stand the smell of fish. Now I'd have Bogie fishing down in the creek every day if it weren't dead. He made a grand effort for a while until the boredom got him."

Patrick pulled items out of the bag and set them on the counter for her. "He seems like a great kid. What's wrong with the stream?"

Her eyes flicked to his. "You haven't gotten to look in our creeks yet, have you?"

He shook his head.

"Orange, all of them. They say it's because of the mines. They pump the water out, as you know. It flows into the creeks. Only problem is, mine water isn't just mine water. It soaks up all the weird chemicals that occur underground. Turns our streams orange with poison." She sighed. "We get our drinking water from a dam that was put in years back. So far, the water is clean. But now with the company digging anywhere they please, who knows what will happen."

Patrick watched as she clenched her jaw, frustration evident in how she plopped the bag of flour into the cupboard.

Ruth glanced up. "You shower already?"

Suddenly, Patrick was aware of his wet hair and the wet spot on his backside where his wet underwear soaked through his pants. He swore, then clapped a hand over his mouth and apologized.

Ruth smiled.

"I, uh, have some cleaning up to finish," he said. He looked around the kitchen, noting the faint trail of coal grit he'd tracked on the otherwise pristine floors. "And then I'll get the rest of this mess."

She waved a hand at him. "It's fine, Patrick. I've got this in exchange for you rescuing my bag of groceries. Go get yourself cleaned up." Her eyes sparkled, and Patrick was almost breathless. "Don't forget to take clothes down with you."

He swallowed down the heat that threatened to rise into his cheeks. "Yes, ma'am."

It was only on his way down the basement steps that he realized she'd called him by his first name.

When he climbed in the shower, he turned the water on cold.

CHAPTER 15

Sunday, June 5, 1938

The temperature eased overnight, and by the time Ruth and the children got back from church, the humidity was starting to lift, and a decent breeze was blowing. Good laundry weather, not that her pile was large enough to be worth doing. Edna, however, was at it in full force. So just for something to do, Ruth and the girls went across the street. Bogie opted to stay home and read his latest comic.

"It looked like you had quite the hero yesterday." Edna nudged Ruth's side. Ruth nudged back. "He seems like such a gentleman."

Ruth had to admit that yes, both of her boarders were gentlemen.

"Only one of your boarders is close to your age though. And looking at you like he's starting to fall in love."

"Oh my. That's far too strong a word."

"Okay. He likes you." Edna shrugged. She snapped out one of her husband's wet shirts and hung it on the clothesline.

"Stop trying to dramatize it. You told me to make friends. I'm making friends."

Edna smiled, a clothespin between her teeth. She hung another shirt. "And he doesn't seem to frequent the bar. At all."

Ruth snorted. "I think that's only because he's too broke."

Edna laughed. The sound was overridden by a screech of delight as all four of their girls raced into the backyard. Their bare feet pounded the grass as if they were elephants, not tiny girls. Dot stumbled, and Ruth flinched, bracing for the tears, but the little girl picked herself up and charged after her big sister, not one to be left behind.

"What are you girls playing?" Ruth called out.

"We're in the Olympics!"

"The Olympics! Well, then we must have an official race. Shall we start at the wash line?"

The girls sprinted back to their mothers and lined up with their backs to the wash line, damp sheets enveloping them when the breeze blew. Little lungs heaved, and their faces were flushed.

"Two laps around the house. On your mark, get set, go!"

The girls took off, and for a few steps, Dot even managed to keep up, her little arms pumping. She fell behind before they made it around the side of the house, but Ruth was sure she wouldn't give up. Her face, mud smeared as usual, was etched with determination.

"Olympics?" Edna asked. "Where'd they get that one from. They were too young for the last Olympics."

"Probably Bogie. He's been reading a lot lately. First, he was sweeping the floors of the shop to earn a few cents for comics. Now, Mr. Moore has been giving him old magazine issues from the store. Most are pretty old, but Bogie doesn't care, especially if they mention sports. Last week, he had the girls running around in capes like

'Superman'. He must have read that comic cover to cover three times by now."

"Superman? What's it about?"

"From what I can tell, a man born on another planet with superpowers. Strength, speed. The power to save the world. You know, the usual attributes that most men long to possess."

Edna laughed as she hung the last of the clothes. "Pity we don't have real-life supermen. I wouldn't mind one that could blast the laundry clean and dry with just his eyes."

Ruth would take a man who simply was around, but before she could say such, the girls barreled back into the sheets. Maisey won, pumping her fists in mid-air. Her sister and Addy were close seconds. Addy leaned over, breathless with her hands on her knees. And Dot continued to run and run until finally she crossed the finish line, her face beet red with exertion.

"Well done, ladies," Edna praised. "I think you should take a break from the Olympics for a while now, though. Want some mint tea?"

They nodded, too exhausted to speak.

"Can you pick some mint?" Edna pointed to a patch of wild mint that grew down the back of the yard. The girls hurried off.

"You think I should get a job in the factory instead of hosting boarders?" Ruth blurted out, watching the girls. She'd been thinking ever since Real Joe had reminded her of her friends from the mill, some of whom were still there. She'd worked the garment floor like the rest of them until she was married. She was good at it, and her old boss would take her back. But it was long hours, crap pay, and hard work.

Edna furrowed her brow, a clothespin between her teeth. "What about the children?"

"School will start again in fall. Maybe I could convince my mom to come in the evenings until I get home."

"Dot won't be ready for school for a few years yet. And more importantly, you're expecting, Ruth. No one will hire you when they know you won't be able to work soon. How would you feed that baby if you're at work?"

Ruth's mouth pressed into a firm line. A tear threatened at the corner of her eye.

"Good God, Ruth. You aren't thinking..."

She clutched an arm around her belly, suddenly overwhelmed by a fierce sense of protection. "No, I'm not thinking. You're right. It's impossible. Maybe in another year. We just have to make it until then."

"Oh, honey." Edna pulled her into a hug. "Look, you're gonna get through this, Jack or no. We'll make sure you don't starve."

The girls approached again, their hands full of bunches of sweet-scented mint. Ruth and Edna pulled away from each other. Addy's smile faltered, unsure of what she should feel. Ruth pressed a smile back on her own face to reassure her daughter. Addy's smile returned. Lying a hand on Dot's head as the little girl tried to shake the dirt off the roots of the mint plant, she said, "I think we need some sugar cookies to go with that tea. Who wants to help me?"

The girls skipped ahead of her around the house just as a pickup pulled in front. Red hopped out, his flaming hair sticking out a thousand ways with sweat. His freckles were concealed by a layer of coal dirt, as was the rest of him. His girls rushed into his arms anyway.

"Daddy!"

He kissed them both on the heads and scooped them up, a daughter on each hip, with ease. "How are my fine ladies today?"

"Good," the girls echoed.

Edna came from around the back, a smile on her face. "Good run today, Red?" She kissed him on his dirty cheek.

"Full load, delivered and paid for. Not bad for summer."

"Wonderful."

"Hiya, Ruth." He nodded to Ruth.

"Hi, Red." Ruth smiled at Edna. She noted the twinkle in her friend's eye. The woman was still as lovestruck as the day she met Red. Ruth put her hands on Addy's shoulders. "How about I take the girls over to make those cookies at my house, and we'll bring you a fresh batch over in about...two hours or so?"

The girls didn't wait for Edna's reply but instead squealed and wiggled to get down from their father's arms. Addy and Dot led the way across the street, all of them holding hands.

Edna waved as Red placed a kiss on her cheek. "Thank you," she mouthed.

Ruth waved and followed the girls. She owed Edna. It was good to have your best friend across the street.

Patrick heard the shrieks of laughter before they even burst into the house. He watched from the window as the neighbors shared a long kiss and then disappeared into their house hand in hand. In the Flannigan household, it sounded like a herd of elephants had invaded. He'd been working to get through his stack of newspapers, which at this point had just turned into something to do, since he'd given up on finding anything about Mr. Flannigan. As the elephants continued to stampede and trumpet downstairs, he quit. No one could read with that noise. Not even Bogie, who he heard clomping down the attic stairs to join the party below.

Patrick rubbed a hand over his eyes. He could nap—out of the question with that noise. He could go across the street and have a drink, which he didn't have money for. He could go down to the stripping hole and walk around with wet pants again. Or, he could go downstairs and see what Ruth and five rambunctious children were up to.

To the kitchen it was.

When he walked into the kitchen, he was greeted by the sweet scent of mint and six faces.

Ruth looked up from the kitchen sink, where she ran handfuls of mint plants under the water. "Oh, sorry. Didn't know you were home. We'll be more quiet."

"No need." He took in the flour and sugar bags that sat open on the table. Dot already had a smudge of flour across her forehead. She stood on a stool that looked all too precarious, reaching deep into the sack. "You, uh, want some help?"

The stool slipped from under Dot, and Ruth caught her before her chin could clonk on the table. In the process, the mint fell on the floor and the flour bag tipped, spilling white powder onto the kitchen table in a puff that blew up in the other girls' faces. They made faces, then burst out laughing. Ruth tried to scoop up the flour, but her hands were still wet and thus created a sticky paste. She looked up at Patrick in exasperation. He couldn't help but smile.

"Okay, sure." She pointed at the flour. "You measure."

A few minutes later and the cookies were in the oven, the tea was steeping in a big pot on the stove, and Patrick was seated on the bench with Bogie on his right and Dot on his left, and he was more tired than he had been from his week working the mine.

Ruth was still moving, cleaning up the mess, including the flour-covered children.

As she smiled at him, dishrag in hand, he was suddenly struck by how domestic the scene was. This could have been his life. A room full of children. A wife barefoot in the kitchen. Food in the oven. A bed upstairs. That hollow feeling returned to his gut, and he felt himself grow distant. He didn't belong here. He needed to move on. His fingers clenched the edge of the table until he finally pushed himself away and stood.

"Mr. Kane?" Bogie looked up at him with curious eyes.

Patrick couldn't answer. "I have to...go."

"The cookies will be out in a minute." Ruth's smile faltered.

"Enjoy." He nodded to them all once and then walked out the kitchen door. He breathed in the summer air as if there could never be enough of it on the planet. And then he walked the railroad tracks until dark, when he finally resigned that he had to stay in Maryd at least long enough to pay Mrs. Flannigan for his room and board.

CHAPTER 16

Monday, June 6, 1938

The mine wasn't bad on Monday. The work kept Patrick's hands busy, so he couldn't think. At least not about anything but what they were doing. The blasting last week had left a lot of rock to clear. The tunnel would be longer still. The old timers said they were close to hitting the coal vein in Tunnel One, but they weren't quite there yet.

Now that he was back above ground, he could list a dozen reasons he needed to go for a swim. Chief among them was that he needed to keep his mind off of Ruth, and that included staying out of that house until it was time to eat and sleep. It also gave him a good excuse to spend time in the sunshine away from his fellow miners' requests to get drinks from the bar. Maybe he could make this his routine. Maybe he could even take his meals to go and eat them down here. That would give him even more space.

He reached the bottom of the hill and looked up, expecting to be greeted by the sparkling water. There was none.

He looked around. Had he taken a wrong turn? Maybe it was on the other side of the culm bank. He'd just been too lost in his thoughts. It had been a long day after all. He walked up the bank, his boots sending showers of tailings down to the muddy pit below. There was no water on the other side either. Patrick narrowed his eyes, confused. Then, as he scanned the mud hole, he noted his stick from the day before, not far from the edge of the dry bank. It jutted from the mud proudly.

The entire stripping hole was empty.

Patrick's eyes widened. It was downright spooky to look at. The depression went down a good twenty feet. Perhaps the children's father was right, and there was a serpent at the bottom. He could even make out the swirl of mud, like a serpent's tail that marked where the water had run. And the worst part was that he couldn't tell where it had gone. There was no hole in the center of the once-pond. There was no stream leading out. It was just that waving line of mud leading to smoother mud, as if the earth had sealed itself once all the water was gone.

Patrick sat on the culm bank and stared. It had drained in less than twenty-four hours, as if the entire pond was merely God's bathtub. What if he *had* been swimming? How strong had that faint current turned? He made a note to have a chat with Ruth's children that night, to thank them for the warning. He wouldn't have known such a thing was possible. And they should know that their father was a smart man, whoever he'd been, because the serpent at the bottom of the hole could swallow everything.

There wasn't even a leaf left in the black mud.

"Then the serpent leaped high, opened his mouth…" Patrick raised his hands to show how the serpent had risen out of the water, his hand the giant mouth. "Then he dove back down." His hands plunged back to the table, almost taking a water glass with them. "And then with a swish of his tail, all the water was gone." He did knock a water glass as he demonstrated the swish, but Ruth caught it with a warning look. He finished the story by smoothing his hands across the table, his eyes wide.

Dot stared at him, wide-eyed. He got a chuckle out of Isaac.

Addy looked at him suspiciously. "Mr. Kane, you're kidding."

"It's true! Go see for yourself." Patrick straightened and shrugged.

Bogie said, "See, Ma, I told you Dad's stories weren't all crazy."

Ruth had to blink away tears, and Patrick was immediately overcome with guilt. That hadn't been his story to tell.

Thankfully, Isaac changed the subject. "Bogie, did you hear about how the team did this weekend?"

"Billy said they won again!"

"Scored back-to-back runs. The whole league is talking."

The conversation turned to baseball, and Patrick ate his food in silence, his moment of theatrics passed. Every now and then, he glanced at Ruth. Her mood had lifted, and she smiled at Isaac and Bogie's conversation, but she did not meet his eye. Patrick lingered in the kitchen with her after everyone else had filtered out. He cleared plates, and she finally looked up at him with surprise.

"Thank you."

"Of course," he said gently. They worked in silence for a while. She washed while he dried. He didn't know where everything went, so he just started a dish pile on the table.

"The children miss their father, don't they?"

She scoffed. "If only he knew."

"He been gone long?"

"Four months or so." She motioned to her belly. "Just recently enough to leave me with this."

"I'm sorry." As soon as the words left his mouth, he regretted them. He meant he was sorry for her loss, sorry she had to raise a baby by herself. He hoped she didn't think he meant he was sorry she was pregnant. What if she wanted that baby? Then again, what if she didn't, and maybe he *should* be sorry she was pregnant? He opened his mouth to try and clarify, but she had already turned away.

And changed the subject. "So what really happened down the back?"

He followed her lead and let the conversation move on. It was soon. She'd need more time to mourn of course. "Just like I said. The water got all swallowed up."

"The whole strippin' is dry?"

"Completely. Not a leaf left. As if it's just been a mud hole forever. That happen a lot around here?"

"We hear about it every now and then. I wouldn't say its common, but it does happen. This is mine country. You can't dig holes in the ground and expect everything to remain stable on the surface."

"The kids said something about Bob?"

Ruth frowned for a moment, then her eyes widened. "Oh yes. That was over the mountain in Tuscarora. He went swimming in one of those pools. He'd been warned, but he really was a good swimmer. Very strong, too. He did it every single day, unless the water was iced over. I think he would have gone then, too, if his wife would've let him. But one day he went and didn't come home. His wife checked the pool, found his clothes neatly folded to the side like they always were. But no Bob. She called the police, thinking that he'd drowned. They came out with a team and dredged the whole stripping hole. It wasn't even that big, maybe the size of the one down the back. But they never found his body. And they never found the bottom of that hole either."

"They couldn't find the bottom? Doesn't everything have a bottom?"

She inclined her head towards the muddy puddle Patrick had swum in just days before. "If that had a bottom, then where did all the water go?" She smiled wryly as Patrick relented. "In Bob's hole, the water didn't even drain. The theory is that the mine underneath opened, sucked him down in a whirlpool, and then closed itself back up as it pulled in debris. That was maybe five years ago, and they still never found him."

"His poor widow."

"She was devastated. Took her years to get over it. If you can even call it that. She's remarried now. Actually just saw her last week at the farmer's market."

"So she was able to move on?" Patrick asked quietly. He asked as much for curiosity in Ruth's reaction as for hope for his own past.

Ruth looked at him pointedly. "It was very painful." She grew quiet. "For as long as there have been stripping holes, there have been drownings. Had one here in Maryd just a few years ago. I don't like to think about it." She rinsed the last plate and watched it drip over the sink. "It was a little boy. Bogie knew him. His friend dropped a ball, and when the boy went to reach for it, he slipped into the stripping. The bank was too steep, too loose, for him to grab hold and pull himself out. He couldn't swim yet. All his friends could do was scream. Adults were there within minutes, and still they couldn't find him. They dove and dove." She finally handed the plate to Patrick.

He dried it slowly, listening.

Ruth turned back to the sink. "I never saw a mother with such grief. I never saw a town gather together like this one. We all stood by the banks of that hole and took turns holding that family up as a Navy diver came in to look for the body. We surrounded it. We mourned with them. We then went to the funeral. The whole town. Hundreds of us." She dried her hands. "You know how deep they found his body?"

Patrick waited.

"Eighty-seven feet." She met Patrick's eyes. "That's why I don't need to warn my children to be careful around those holes. They know. Bogie knows. He lost a friend. He stood there with me as we watched the diver."

"Was this in the hole that just drained?"

Ruth shook her head. "Different one. Other side of town." She met his eye. "Do *not* try and swim in there."

Patrick had no choice but to nod. Though he knew he now would have to scout out this other hole for curiosity's sake. He picked up the dried stack of plates. "Where do these go?"

Ruth wiped her hands on her apron and then shooed him out of the kitchen. "I've got it from here. Thank you."

Patrick nodded. As he got to the door, she called after him. "Just so you know, Steel Man, all the little depressions you see between the culm banks out there…stay out of those, too. Bootlegging isn't a new concept around here. Been going on for almost a hundred years. You never know which one of those little valleys between piles is just a valley and what's a lightly covered mine that could send you straight down a hundred feet. Water or no, we tread with caution around here."

"Good to know. Thank you, ma'am." He tipped an imaginary hat and left her, emotions rolling for reasons that had nothing to do with losing his swimming hole.

CHAPTER 17

Tuesday, June 7, 1938

The whole town. If Ruth had had her bed to herself that night, she would have tossed and turned. Instead, with the girls pressed next to her side, she lay perfectly still and stared at the ceiling. *The whole town.* They had done it before in solidarity with that family. What if they could do it again, this time before disaster struck? What if they could gather another two hundred souls and—do what? March on the mine? Demand that they not strip mine, protect their coal holes, and protect their houses? What could they possibly do to convince the mining company to listen to them, when the law itself was on the company's side?

She must have fallen asleep for at least a few hours, for when she woke up, she had a new resolve. She would have to talk to Edna, but the makings of a plan whirled in her head. She missed Jack more than ever, but instead of sadness, now she brimmed with anger. How dare he leave? And to think that she still valued his opinion and had to acknowledge that he was smart enough to know the solution to the problems the town was facing, and yet he wasn't there to do anything about them...it made her furious. She let her hand drift to the baby she carried, wondering what Jack would think of that, too.

What did Patrick think? Why did she care what Patrick thought?

To keep her hands busy after her boarders went to work, she started the wash. She had two wash tubs, a garden hose, and an old wooden wringer that had been her grandmother's. The thing was about ready to fall apart. Submerging the clothes in the tubs wasn't hard. The agitator in the electric wash tub helped with the scrubbing. It didn't take more than that when the clothes were free of coal dirt, one plus of Jack being away. But the rinsing and wringing…lordy, how she hated wringing. She always felt like her arm was about ready to fall off after she was done cranking each piece of fabric through. The alternative, hand wringing, was even worse. Back before Grandma had given her the wooden wringer, she'd worked her hands so hard she hadn't been able to lift her baby the next day.

Ruth made it through half the pile, changed the dirty water twice, then looked at the soaked clothes that lay in the basket, ready to wring. Then she looked at the clothesline. There was a nice breeze rolling today. Surely, they'd dry by nighttime. She called Bogie over, and together they hung the dripping wet clothes on the line. The line sagged so badly that the hems of the shirts touched the grass. Bogie looked to her with eyebrows raised. She nodded once.

"All done for now." She wiped her hands on her apron, which was now soaked with wash water. The girls played in the grass nearby, picking violets for their dolls. "How about we go for a walk?" She was more than a bit curious to see the stripping hole for herself.

Patrick hadn't exaggerated. She stood on the bank with the girls' hands in hers, Bogie nearby, and stared. It was gone. Her peaceful getaway was now just a pit of black mud. When the shock wore off, they went down the bank closer, careful not to go where the mud still sucked at their shoes.

"You all remember why I tell you to stay out of these places, right?"

The girls nodded.

Bogie whispered, "My friend."

Ruth nodded. "Just don't forget. Don't let your friends convince you otherwise. This is as close as we get." She picked up a rock and let it sail out of her hand. It landed far out in the mud pit with a satisfying thuck as it struck the mud. The children copied her, and soon they were laughing as they tried to throw their rocks the furthest.

Ruth sat down at the same spot she'd been a few days back, when Patrick had come down. The view was very different. She let another rock sail. He'd looked like he wanted to kiss her. Her, a married woman. What kind of man was he? One that carried groceries, washed dishes, and held doors for women. Did he know about Jack? Surely, one of the gossips in town would have told him. Had she wanted him to kiss her? Didn't matter. She hadn't. She wouldn't. And she needed to stop thinking about him.

Her throws were more playful than forceful until she noted how hard Bogie was working on his own throw. It was baseball season after all. She rose back to her feet. She laid a hand on his shoulder to get his attention, then let a rock sail clear across the muddy flat, a distance almost as wide as the entire baseball field. The girls cheered; Bogie frowned.

"Step and follow through," Ruth explained.

Bogie chucked one with force and anger. It didn't go far. He stared after it, his shoulders slumped. Then he turned to her, his eyes narrowed with a glare that caught her off guard. "What would you know anyway? This is why dads are supposed to teach kids to throw."

Her mouth dropped open, but she quickly shut it. *He was grieving.* "Who do you think taught me how to throw?"

Bogie glared a moment longer, then picked up another rock, flicking off mud with his thumb. The girls moved off just a little bit, their own throws exuberant and comical. But Ruth wasn't in the mood to laugh.

"When your father and I were dating, we'd come down here. He taught me how to skip stones. And we threw rocks just for the fun of it, like we are today. We'd have competitions between ourselves, the prize a kiss." She smiled faintly at the memory. There were happy times with Jack back then. "I'm not sure if he regretted or was glad that he taught me to throw so well. I didn't let him win much."

"Why'd he leave, Ma?" Bogie let a rock sail with a perfect throw. "Doesn't he love us?"

Ruth turned him toward her and pulled him into a hug. She kissed the top of his head. "I love you. So, so much."

The weather changed and became overcast well before the laundry was dry. The breeze slowed. The wet clothes hung heavy on the line. Ruth frowned out the kitchen window, debating if she should take them down again, but the sky wasn't ominous. Maybe they'd be okay to hang until tomorrow, which surely would be a sunny day. She certainly didn't want a repeat of hanging them upstairs with Patrick's help again.

Thankfully, she was better at cooking than laundry. She loved to mix ingredients, experiment with adding a little more or less of something. Just like her grandmothers had taught her, she cooked by feel and taste and consistency, not by measure. If the dough for the biscuits was runny, she knew to add a little more flour. If the tomato juice in the vegetable soup was too bland, it could be remedied with a hot pepper—though likely not an entire one. That depended on the size of the pepper, of course. Thus, she was lost in her cooking, the familiar smells of her kitchen enveloping her like a warm blanket, when she heard the front door open and shut. She glanced at the wall clock. It was early for the miners to be done. She gave the pot a few more stirs, then turned around.

Ruth stared at her husband as if he were a ghost. Surely, he would disappear again. Perhaps he'd been a ghost all along. That life before was a dream. When had they ever been happy, in love? Surely it couldn't be this same lifetime.

No, her children wouldn't exist if he were a true phantom.

He didn't even have the decency to show up sober. She could smell it on him from across the room. And the smile that played on his lips was only further proof. At least he was a happy drunk, not a mean one. Most of the time. But that didn't negate the fact that he was a drunk, and he was standing in her kitchen, hat in hand, beaming at her as if he'd come back as the mine boss himself with a million dollars.

She doubted he had a dollar to his name.

Slowly, she set her wooden spoon down on a saucer and turned down the stove. Her hand trembled. Food was costly enough; no sense burning the boarders' dinner. And if the tremor in her bones was any indication, she needed a moment to think. She wiped her hands on her apron, then turned to face him.

His face was as handsome as ever. Ruddy-complexioned, his short-bristled beard lined his jaw. Her mother had always hated such a rough appearance, but Ruth found it hard to resist. It made him a man. Then again, what kind of man left his wife and children to follow the drink? She folded her arms across her chest, looking him in the face but avoiding his ice-blue eyes. She knew from years of experience that they weakened her. He knew it, too.

"Ruthie, I missed you." He took a step towards her but she had the wherewithal to hold up a hand. He stopped, looked down, twisted his hat.

"You've been gone four months, Jack. Four months with no word. I didn't know if you were alive or dead."

"Been hard to get word to ya."

"Didn't have two cents for a telegram? Spend it all on booze?" She hated the sarcasm in her voice, but she didn't bother to mask it. Part of her wanted to run sobbing into his arms, let those strong arms hold her, tell him about the child that grew in her belly, while the other part of her wanted him to walk out the door and not come back.

Just like he had four months ago. How could two such drastically different emotions co-exist?

"Weren't no place to send one."

"Really now?" That was even harder to believe. Every town had a telegraph office these days. Or at least a *post office*.

He shook his head, took a deep breath. "I was up north, wilder country."

Ruth folded her arms. "And you couldn't discuss such a change with your family? Or take us with you? Just abandon us in this tiny mining town." Her voice was rising now. She closed the distance between them, her eyes narrowed. "You know what I think you are, Jack Flannigan? You're a coward. You didn't have the courage to quit the drink. So you abandoned us!"

His eyes sparkled now that she was within arm's reach of him. "You've always been beautiful when you're riled, Ruthie." He reached for her, his strong hands closing on her upper arms and pulling her firmly but gently the last step towards him. Then his lips were on hers with all the passion of their youth. Only she could taste the whiskey. Which reminded her he hadn't changed. She pulled herself away and slapped him.

He didn't pursue her as she retreated across the kitchen. She turned on the stove and was hastily wiping tears away when she heard Patrick ask from the doorway, "Everything okay in here, ma'am?"

She shot a glance over her shoulder. Patrick, though not tall, was still stocky enough to fill the doorway. He and Jack were evenly matched. He was eyeing Jack, fingers flexing. He must have heard them and come straight up from the basement, as he was still black from head to boot with coal dirt.

Jack's face changed then. The happy drunk was gone; the hard miner who longed to drown in a barrel of beer returned. Without taking his eyes off Patrick, he asked her, "So ya been cuckolding me while I'm gone?" His voice was like icy steel. Anger seldom rose in him, but when it did, it had a tendency to explode like the dynamite he wielded.

Ruth slammed the spoon into the pot, and the sauce splattered. "He's my boarder, Jack. There's two of them. I had to do something to pay the mortgage when you disappeared."

The two men didn't soften to each other.

Ruth gritted her teeth, took a towel, and wiped up the sauce. "Mr. Kane, *this* is my husband Jack."

Patrick didn't extend his hand. His eyes still on Jack, he asked, "Ma'am, I'll ask you again. Everything okay in here?"

"Fine. Dinner will be ready in about another twenty minutes."

He nodded once. "I'll be back in a few then."

She heard his footsteps retreat to the front porch, the screen door slapping closed behind him. He was staying in earshot.

"Boarders?" Jack growled.

"What else was I supposed to do?" She threw up her hands, slapping the towel against her thigh.

"Take in laundry, be a secretary. Something that didn't involve men living in this house with you."

"I've got three small children to raise. How am I supposed to be away all day? As if finding work was that easy—"

"Where are these men sleeping? The basement?"

"Our room," she said quietly. "I've been sleeping with the girls."

He stared at her. "They're sleeping in my bed?"

"No, I sold our bed so I could buy groceries for a week. Two used twin beds are much cheaper."

She turned back to the sauce, which was starting to stick to the bottom of the pot, and wiped her eyes. It was better when he wasn't here. Then he didn't make her cry.

"I made you that bed. As a wedding present. With my own two hands." His voice was laced with shock and hurt, and yet it seemed to growl.

"Then I suppose it was mine to sell," she snapped. Then she took a deep breath and closed her eyes. It would do no good to keep fighting him. Really, no one was more hurt that the bed was gone than she was. It was an exquisite piece of craftsmanship, a fact she'd pointed out to him many times when she'd tried to get him to quit mining. And yes, it was their marriage bed, in all the meanings that term held. "I had to do something, Jack. The girls are too young for me to go back to the mill." Not to mention, she was in no physical condition to work like that. She wasn't going to tell him why just yet. It said a lot that he was too drunk to notice.

Jack walked to the kitchen table. He pulled a thick envelope from his pocket. He slowly set it at her place at the table. "My earnings from the last few months." The hurt in his voice was back. He pulled his cap onto his head, then ducked out the kitchen door.

"Jack…" He didn't turn back. "Jack!" He kept walking.

Ruth swallowed back tears, turned off the stove, and retrieved the envelope. It was full. A good couple of hundred dollars, almost a full year's salary. She sank onto the bench, numb. He hadn't done it the right way, but he *had* done it. He'd provided as he promised. Now the question was, was he going to come back? Or was he gone this time for good?

CHAPTER 18

Patrick gripped the armrests of his porch chair with white knuckles. *Jack* Flannigan. This man was quite alive, judging by the steady stride of his walk, even while drunk, the solid shoulders, and the voice that had brought Mrs. Ruth Flannigan to tears. Patrick could still hear Ruth banging pots and dishes around in the kitchen, muttering under her breath, even as Jack ducked into the bar across the street.

She'd never said anything about her husband being alive. He'd never asked, though he'd wanted to a thousand times. If he'd known, would it have changed anything? Maybe. Definitely. This was why he didn't have relationships. What had been his first thought? Don't make it complicated? Well, now it sure was complicated. The first woman he'd been interested in for years was a married one. And in a strained marriage to boot, if his five-second appraisal was worth anything. He certainly didn't mess with married women. Why hadn't she said anything? Had he imagined the look of longing she'd given him?

Maybe he had. It was always her, after all, that had thrown up that barrier between them when he'd gotten close. At least now he knew why.

Jack hadn't even given him a second glance when he'd walked across the street. He'd exited the house through the kitchen door, which had taken him out of Patrick's direct path, and yet there was a firm set to his head that showed he was consciously avoiding Patrick's gaze. Beyond that, it was hard to tell just what the man was feeling. Angry? Suspicious? Then why not meet Patrick head-on? Maybe he was disappointed in Ruth's homecoming. That lady had some spice to her after all—she'd told it to him like it was, no doubts there.

Patrick debated checking on Ruth versus going over to the bar to find out more about this mysterious Jack, the husband risen from the dead. He was still kicking himself for missing the signs. Should he apologize to Ruth? No. Nothing had happened. He was not going to apologize to a woman for being kind, nor for looking at her like she could be loved.

Loved. He really was losing his marbles.

He slapped the handles of the chair and stood, striking off down the road. Dinner or not, he couldn't be in that house yet. And he certainly wouldn't be caught in the house without Isaac and the children, not while her husband sat across the street, ready to come over and clock him good at any moment. The weather was cool and dreary, the clouds foretelling rain in the night to come. He started off down the hill, back towards the mine. Soon, Isaac and Real Joe would be coming up from the mine. They were setting dynamite to blast again, and all men not necessary to the task had been sent up early, like him. He had quite a few questions for Real Joe, like why he hadn't mentioned that Jack was alive.

The mine cars still hadn't returned to the surface, so he stepped into the mine office as fat raindrops began to fall. The mine boss and the clerk were deep in a heated discussion in a back office. He closed the door with a little more force than necessary to announce his presence. He awkwardly waited, hoping they would soon finish or at least come out to acknowledge him. Maybe he could talk them into a raise. He could work weekends, service the water pump and fan above ground. Anything to keep him out of Ruth's house.

"I'm telling you, the miners are getting more and more reluctant to keep digging. They don't want to keep heading under the town," the clerk said.

"They aren't running this mine. I am!" said the boss.

"You won't have a mine if they go on strike."

"They don't get paid if they go on strike. They don't get paid, they can't pay their rent or feed their families. They need to dig. And this is where we're going to dig. I have a lot of money invested here. I need a fast return."

The clerk was quiet for a moment. "And what if they're right? What if we are too close to the surface, and we jeopardize the town?"

"We are hundreds of feet down. They've been bootlegging from their basements for years with much shallower mines and nothing happened."

"They don't use dynamite under their houses."

"You mean didn't."

"I mean don't."

The mine boss exhaled. "Out of their *basements*. Well, if they can scratch enough coal out of the floors of their basements to make a living, just imagine what else is down there. And I own the rights! Their concerns are only because they don't want us to break into their precious, illegal holes. I'm telling you, the stability of the town is just fine."

"We can feel the ground shake with every blast."

"You think I don't feel it, too? I live here, just like you."

Patrick caught a glimpse of the clerk throwing up his hands through the cracked door. "Look, you're the boss. I did my job and told you what I know. I'm just saying, if you don't want trouble, then you'd better post a watchman." There was the sound of papers rustling. "I'm going home."

The clerk paused just inside the office doorway.

"Watchman, you say," the mine boss mused.

"Roger Clemens is out of work with an injury. Bum knee. He could use the work. I hear he's a good shot, too."

"Hire him."

The clerk opened the door and walked out, only to startle at Patrick's presence.

"Afternoon." Patrick tipped his hat.

The clerk frowned at him, then looked past him to the gathering clouds outside. The wind was picking up now, the rain still holding itself to splatters but threatening more. He shoved his hat on his head and, without a word to Patrick, ducked out of the office.

The mine boss crossed his arms over his chest and looked Patrick up and down. "Can I help you?"

"Just looking for more work, sir."

"We aren't hiring."

Patrick scratched his temple, then straightened his hat. "Well, that's fine. Because technically, I already work for you." He was still filthy from his day in the mine. He straightened. "I'm a mechanic, sir. I've got most of the equipment down below working up to speed. But I'm short on cash and have plenty more time this coming weekend. I'd like to work on the pump and the fan and whatever else you have topside."

"We have a mechanic topside."

The rain played accompaniment to the silence between them.

The mine boss sighed. "I'm not the monster the men make me out to be. I'm just trying to run a business."

Patrick nodded. "Of course."

"You think the town will be compromised if we keep digging? Or are the men really just trying to protect their bootleg holes?"

Patrick shrugged. "Honestly, I don't know enough about mining yet to say. But things sure do shake up there when we blast."

"That's what my wife says, too. She's worried about her china." The mine boss leaned against the doorframe between the back office and the pay desk. "You the guy they call the Steel Man?"

"Yes, sir."

"What brought you to mining?"

"Needed something different," Patrick answered vaguely. Eventually, he'd need to come up with a better story. People in this town were too nosy. As if no one had ever changed careers before. Then again, most of these men were multi-generational miners.

"Well, you'll certainly find something different in mining. Never a dull day." The boss ran his eyes over his filthy clothes. "Well, Steel Man, I'll let you know if we need more help. Good night."

Patrick nodded and exited into the storm, just as the clouds let loose. He lifted his face to the sky, letting the rain wash the coal dirt away. The ground beneath his feet rumbled with a boom that was unrelated to the thunder. The rumble above and below seemed to resound in his soul, as if the world echoed the struggles around and within him. He steeled himself as he stepped into Ruth's front yard, uncertain of what he'd find in the house. He ducked past her wet laundry, each article now so soaked it hung to the ground like a line of failed dreams.

CHAPTER 19

Ruth made it through dinner without crying, despite the fact that one of her favorite vases had fallen off the windowsill with the latest blast down in the mine, and the power was out from the storm. They ate by candlelight, and yet the mood was so tense it wasn't the least bit romantic. The children were as quiet as she was, except for occasional bickering between the girls and Bogie. They did clean their plates, though, so the spaghetti and sauce must have been good. She couldn't taste anything. Her food went down like lumps of cardboard. But the baby needed food, so she ate. It wasn't about her anymore. If it were about her, she'd have left town long ago, and Jack would have gotten a rude wake-up call when he came home to an empty house.

He did not show up for dinner.

The boarders knew she was struggling. Patrick, of course, had witnessed her and Jack's altercation. He must have said something to Isaac, for Isaac was exceptionally gentle and polite, but withdrew as soon as the meal was over. Patrick looked like he wanted to say more—surely he had questions—but he, too, seemed distracted. She owed him an explanation. Or did she? She'd always insisted she was Mrs. Flannigan. What more could he have thought?

She hadn't acted like a Missus.

She'd have to talk to him. Apologize for whatever flirtation she'd participated in. It never would have gone anywhere. Right? No, that gut-aching longing to be noticed, appreciated, and loved would never have been fully realized. She was married to Jack.

The thought made her want to sob with loneliness. *She was married to Jack.*

He came back that night still drunk, a few hours after the power had clicked back on. Ruth was up, cup of tea in hand, seated on the couch, waiting. He staggered over and flopped on the couch beside her. She winced as the tea threatened to slosh over the lip of the cup.

"Can I still sleep in my own house?" he mumbled.

She nodded to a blanket and pillow, folded neatly on the end of the couch. "You best stay down here until you're sober." She rose, annoyed by him just being in the room. "However long that takes." She moved for the stairs, then turned over her shoulder to look at him. "Jack, I always loved you when you were sober. Tell me now, is that man gone for good? Or is he still in there somewhere?"

He merely stared at her. She turned on her heel and quietly padded up the stairs toward her tiny bed in the tiny room she shared with her tiny daughters.

"Ruthie..."

She paused, hand on the banister.

"Is the baby mine?"

Her heart thudded. "They're all yours."

Ruth forced herself to turn away. If he wanted her reassurances, she didn't have the energy to give them. If he wanted to celebrate the coming baby, she didn't have the courage to hope he'd feel enough to change his ways and act like a father. And if he *didn't* want to celebrate—that reaction she couldn't handle at all. So, numb and ignorant to his response to her pregnancy, she crept into the girls' room and curled into bed next to Dot. The little girl's hair was in need of washing, but she still held some of her baby scent.

"Mama?" Addy whispered from Dot's other side.

"Hmm?"

"Is Daddy gonna stay for a while?"

"I don't know, love."

"He didn't tuck us in."

"He doesn't feel well."

Ruth's eyes closed, and she was just about asleep when Addy whispered again, "Mama?"

"Addy, you need to sleep, love."

"Mama, is Mishter Isaac and Mishter Patrick gonna leave?"

"I don't know." She hesitated. That depended a lot on Jack and whether he stuck around or not. She thought of the envelope of money he'd given her. She didn't need the boarders, at least for now. But that money wouldn't last forever if he left again.

"I'd like it if they stayed." Addy yawned. "Mishter Isaac tells good stories. And Mishter Patrick makes you smile."

Ruth held her breath as Addy nestled closer and reached her arm over her sister to grab Ruth's hand. Before long, the little girl's breathing evened out into the soft sighs of sleep. Ruth exhaled slowly and squeezed her eyes shut, feeling the moisture of her tears pour down her cheeks. She hugged Addy and Dot close, all while wishing the man downstairs was the one holding her. Was it too much to wish for someone else to play the role of protector?

CHAPTER 20

Wednesday, June 8, 1938

Breakfast the next morning was oatmeal, which Patrick wasn't surprised at and yet couldn't help but be disappointed in. It was hard to go into a day of tough labor on oatmeal, while eggs and fried potatoes, and better yet, a side of bacon, would have given him the energy boost to push through the day. But oatmeal it was, and Ruth wasn't around. Bogie was helping Addy pour her breakfast, and Patrick could only assume that little Dorothy was still fast asleep. He and Isaac ate their oatmeal without complaint, though Patrick wished for a spoon of sugar. But Ruth had coffee perking on the stove, and that was done to perfection. He drank it black, as coffee was intended to be drunk.

After throwing on his mining clothes, he followed the steady stream of men down toward the mine. Just as he passed the mine office, Ruth emerged, her face red with anger. She didn't see him at first, but when she did, she looked conflicted on whether to ignore him or not. Patrick shoved his hands in his pockets and walked towards her. Thankfully, she stopped when their paths met.

She glared at him, her lips in a thin line. Patrick wasn't quite convinced the anger was directed at him, though, so he stood his ground, cocking his head to the side. "All okay?"

She pushed a wisp of hair behind her ear with abrupt force. "My best vase broke last night because of the blasts, and all the company says is 'put your glassware in a more secure place'. I'm about ready to go down in that mine myself and shut it all down."

Patrick met her eyes, waiting. There was a lot more than that going on.

She dropped her gaze. "Jack's gone again. And he ain't down in the mine." Her coal cracker accent got stronger when she was mad.

"I'm sorry—"

"Ain't your problem," she snapped. Then she lifted a shaking hand to her forehead and closed her eyes. "Patrick, I'm sorry. I didn't mean to—"

He held out his hands. "It's fine. I understand."

"No, you don't. How could you? I should have told you about Jack, about why I was taking in boarders. If I misled you—"

He shrugged, more cavalier than he'd felt the night before. "It's not like anything happened. I'm just surprised you didn't mention him."

"I just…" She bit her lip, which sent a jolt of attraction through his body. Her voice dropped to a whisper. "He left without a word a couple of months ago. Abandoned us. It's complicated. But when you showed up, all kind and gentlemanly…I forgot my place. It won't happen again."

Patrick scuffed the ground with the toe of his boot. "You deserve better, you know."

She kept her gaze averted. "I know." Then she straightened and smoothed her dress. "But it is what it is. And you'd best be going before you miss the train down into the mine."

Patrick tipped his hard hat at her and moved towards the mine.

"And Patrick—" she called. "Be safe down there."

"Yes, ma'am."

Ruth went straight to Edna's, her stride long and quick with anger. It was hard to believe that yesterday morning all she'd woken to was ideas—about Jack, about the company mine—and overnight the world had turned upside down, demanding action. Jack was back, no sense worrying about him anymore. The company's blasts were getting more intense, as her vase proved, so her worrying was no longer worrying but an actual, actionable concern. She'd put on her brave face and walked down to speak with the mine supervisor about her concerns, as a mother first and foremost, only to be given the run around of excuses that she *knew* would lead to no action. And then there was Patrick. At least that confrontation and awkward conversation were off her list of things to do.

She didn't bother knocking on Edna's door. She let the screen door snap shut behind her and looked down the house, with its open doorways, straight into the kitchen. Edna and Red looked up from their places at their kitchen table, eyebrows high and eyes wide with concern.

"Oh good," Ruth said, striding through their house. "I'm glad you're both here. We need to talk. Tell me if I'm crazy."

Red rose to pull out a chair for her and then listened with rapt attention as she put her ideas before him.

"You're crazy," he said when she was finished.

Ruth looked down, pulling at the fringe of a cloth napkin. Then she stood, the anger bubbling within her again. She didn't want to unleash it at her friends. They were right. She'd counted on them for their honesty.

"Wait—" Red caught her arm. "I didn't say it wasn't a good idea. Let me talk to a few others. Quietly."

Ruth's eyes flicked to Edna, whose lips were pressed in a flat line, her eyes sparking with anger Ruth knew was directed not at her, but the elephant that had been circling the town for months.

"You better talk fast, Red." Edna turned to her husband. "Your career is on the line. And she's right, we need the whole town on board. Independent miners, bootleggers, and company miners alike."

Red released Ruth's arm and stood. She had to look up to keep eye contact.

Edna continued next to him. "I'll talk to the other women."

Red nodded once, resolve in his gaze. "I'll convince them. Though it would be easier if the ringleader were home. He can talk a man into anything."

"He's back," Ruth blurted. Her gaze dropped back to Edna, who leapt to her feet. "Last night. He's still drunk. And he's gone this morning. But I think he's back."

"Ruth—" Edna pulled her into a hug, no words necessary to understand the flood of emotion this revelation brought.

"Don't tell him," Ruth said to Red. "Not yet. He's not ready."

Red pursed his lips. "I agree. But this is too pressing to wait. I'll do what I can." He turned to the kitchen door and pulled his cap over his flaming red hair. Edna followed him, then stood on tiptoe in her bare feet to kiss him goodbye.

Before Edna could turn her focus back to Ruth, Ruth excused herself. "I have to get back to the kids." And thus she dodged a dozen questions and managed to keep the tears at bay a little longer.

A day of action, a day of action, she reminded herself. There was no need to keep waiting.

It wasn't a safe kind of day. It was the kind of day where everything seemed to go wrong, which put all the miners on edge. The rock in the main tunnel was unsteady after the blast the night before, which one crew was working on. Patrick had joined up as a shovel man with the crew in Tunnel Three, which was supposed to be the safe, established tunnel, but today was anything but.

"Slam it shut, I tell you! Slam it shut!"

Coal roared down the wooden chute from the cavity above, filling the narrow tunnel and covering the train tracks. Isaac threw his weight into the slide that cut off the flow from the chute above, but it was jammed solid.

"Use the sledge!"

One of the younger miners smashed the slide with a sledgehammer. The board moved, but the impact broke the support. Expletives were uttered, but the miner had no choice but to hit it again, which finally sent the board home. The flow of coal stopped.

The miners stood and wiped their brows for a moment, disaster averted.

"That's the second time in a week," Isaac said with disgust.

Patrick traded places with the man with the sledge, peering into and up the chute. "This bottom board has a gouge in it. That's why it's catching. How do we get this chute empty so I can work on it?"

"We fill the cars. Only problem is, we need a working slide so we don't have to keep picking coal off the ground."

"What if we just install a second slide as a backup?"

"Great idea, but how you going to do that when the coal's jammed in there all the way to the top of the chute?"

Patrick shone his headlamp up the chute, wary of any loose pieces of coal that could come flying down on his head. Most of them were the size of footballs or even larger. It certainly was full.

"I'll have to add on an extension. If I reinforce it enough, it should at least get us through until this chute is empty. Then I can fix the whole thing properly." He laid a hand on the broken chute support, feeling the wood wiggle with the lightest touch. The coal shifted.

"Do it," Isaac nodded. "The rest of us, let's get this cleaned up so the man can work."

They wheeled an empty coal car closer and began the laborious task of clearing the rails. Patrick and one of the other men walked back to the supply room for the wood and tools he'd need to make the chute extension.

"Heard ol' Jack Flannigan's back," the man said and spit a stream of tobacco juice on the ground.

"Appears so." Patrick glanced at the man, his headlamp illuminating the man's sharp features. They hadn't yet met. There was something about the man's tone that put him on edge, like he was ready to pick a fight.

"Guess you'll have to give his wife back to him now, eh?"

Patrick stopped walking, letting his headlamp illuminate the man's face. "Excuse me?"

The man shrugged. "Pretty woman like that. Lonely. Deadbeat husband. No one'd blame ya for offering her a little comfort." He smirked.

"It's not like that. It never was like that."

"Somebody saw you two down by the stripping hole. Before it drained. Said you were getting mighty close to each other."

Nothing went unnoticed in this town. "Well, nothing happened." Patrick walked on ahead, eager to get the supplies and get back to work.

The miner grew quiet, yet Patrick still felt a prickle under his skin. He hadn't even been here two weeks yet. Poor Ruth. She didn't deserve to have her name drug through the mud. Maybe for his next job, he'd find a monastery where they took vows of silence, since apparently talking to other people got him in trouble. They reached the supply room, and Patrick quickly loaded the miner's arms up with wood. Then he grabbed the tools he needed.

The miner fell into step beside him as they returned to Tunnel Three. "Better watch out for Jack. Just friendly advice." The miner smirked, then lengthened his stride to reach the others.

Patrick tried to push the whole conversation from his mind as they worked to build a solid extension on the chute. He added extra two-by-fours underneath to ensure it would hold and not rip the whole thing off and cause a bigger problem. By the time he was done, the men had the fallen coal cleaned up, and an empty car was wheeled into place. Then it was the moment of truth. The slides were pulled, the coal rushed down to fill the car, and then the slides were shoved back into place. The top, old one was still an issue, but the bottom one did its job. They filled four more cars that way until the chute was empty and ready for the next blasting. Patrick got a good look at the problem slider. He'd have a project ahead of him in the morning, but he knew he could replace the boards and get things greased to run smoothly again.

He was anxious to get out of the mine and into the sunlight by the time his crew walked back to the main tunnel and the mine car. But once there, the foreman was in a heated argument with another miner. The miner pointed to the ceiling. "Our town's up there."

Pal threw his hands in the air. "What would you have me do? I live here, too. I've had the conversation with the mine owners a dozen times, but they insist we do it this way."

"It's too much for the ceiling."

"And their engineers say it isn't. So who's right? You got a college degree?"

The miner's glare was visible even in the dim light. "Just a few generations of education down here."

The foreman took off his helmet and rubbed his forehead, his eyes closed. "Look, I'm in the same boat as all of you. But if we want to keep our jobs, we've gotta do the work the bosses ask us to. They ask us to mine, to pull coal out of here. I do my darndest to keep you all safe. I advocate for you. But until someone comes up with proof that our houses are threatened, we don't have a legal foot to stand on. They own the damn mineral rights to this ground. And we work for *them*."

The miner turned and spit. No one in the mine had further words to argue. The foreman slapped his helmet back on his head and went ahead of Patrick to the lead mine car.

After the incident with the car brakes, Patrick had taken it upon himself to check the cars before they went up and down the slope each day. The other men appreciated it, often assisting by pointing their headlamps where he needed light in order to expedite the process. When his circuit of the short mine train was complete, he sat in the car with the others and breathed.

"I still can't figure out what happened to those brakes," one of the men said, almost to himself, as he leaned over the edge of the car, looking at the offending brakes while they waited for the last of the miners to load.

"The perfect storm of rust and dirt. Made one of the pins break, which prevented the brakes from engaging," Patrick said. And from what he could tell, that's all that had happened. Though most of the company's equipment, like the mine cars, had been sold back in 1932, he had noticed the company was trying to source its new equipment as conveniently as possible, which meant some of it was used. The mines were hard on metal and wood.

"But those pins are in there solid. Double-wired and then soldered."

Patrick furrowed his brow. He had noticed the same, thus his daily checks. But all the other pins were holding firm. Perhaps this one had just worn the wrong way until it snapped.

Another miner chimed in, his legs crossed as he leaned back against the side of the car. "I just hope them bootleggers aren't trying to sabotage *us* now. First the cars, then the chute. We're really down on production this week while we fix everything."

The miners looked at the man. The silence of the mine surrounded them. Only the distant drip of water could be heard.

"I certainly hope that isn't the case," Patrick said. "Because that would be attempted murder."

The engine of the mine train fired up like a dragon in the darkness. Deafened, the men rode in silence into daylight.

CHAPTER 21

The heat of the sun washed over Patrick like a salve. The humidity of a Pennsylvania summer clung to his skin and filled his lungs. He closed his eyes, relishing it. He breathed deep, his first real breath of the day. When he blinked his eyes open, the sun was gone. A pit settled into his stomach. Was even the light of day being sucked into the mine? Had he imagined it? He turned his face skyward, frowning at a cloud. The wind streamed around the miners as they exited the mine car. Another storm was rolling in, complete with black clouds and thunder. Patrick felt as if he'd missed a day of his life.

"You're getting sun fever," Real Joe said from next to him. He lounged back against the side of the mine car. He let out a snort. "Just wait until the days are short, and it's dark when we go down and dark when we come out. Makes you wonder if it wouldn't be better to work at night."

Patrick thought for a moment. "I've never been one to sleep in the daylight. But I guess we have to sleep sometime."

"Eyes closed during the day or down in the mine during the day. Either way, we're doomed to never see the light."

"We didn't see much sun in the steel mill either," he admitted to Real Joe. "Might not be underground, but we worked in a big metal building, no windows. Well, a few dirty ones up high, I suppose. They didn't let in much light. The electric lights and glow of the molten iron lit things."

Real Joe pushed off the mine car and stared past Patrick. "Well, would you look at that." He motioned towards the mine office, where a police car sat. The officer was taking a man by the shoulder and shoving him—rather roughly—towards the car. Wind blew dried leaves past them, accentuating the tumult of the weather.

"Miner?" Patrick asked.

"Yes and no," Real Joe said quietly. "He's a miner all right, but he doesn't work for the Maryd Colliery."

Patrick looked closer, then recognized the man. "Jack Flannigan?"

Real Joe nodded. "Wonder what he's gotten into now." He stuffed a wad of tobacco in his mouth. Rumor had it that it helped with the grit of the coal dirt, but Patrick hadn't tried it yet. A corner of Real Joe's lip turned up as he looked back to Patrick. "How's Ruth taking it?"

Patrick avoided his eye. "Haven't asked her." It wasn't his business to share about the fight he'd walked in on yesterday, or how Jack had skipped out of the house before Ruth had woken up.

Real Joe waved at the officer, who tipped his hat to Real Joe as he slipped into his car. As he drove past them, he rolled the window down and stopped. "Hiya, Real Joe."

"Fred." Real Joe leaned past the officer to greet the drunk in the backseat. "Jack. Welcome home. What'd you do this time, bud?"

"Gave the mine boss a piece of my mind. They won't hire me." His voice lisped with a hint of drink.

The officer looked up at Real Joe. "I'm gonna let him sober up a bit before I give him back to his wife. He's talking all kinds of nonsense that the colliery is gonna make the town fall into Hell."

Jack started to mumble from the back seat, then promptly threw up on the seat.

The other three men cringed.

"You sure his wife'll want him back?" Real Joe chuckled, then slapped the top of the cop car as the officer pulled away, cursing.

Patrick watched the altercation silently.

What was it that Ruth had seen in the man? Maybe he'd been different back when they'd met. Maybe she'd gotten with child young, and they'd had a shotgun wedding. Bogie had to be what, ten? Whatever their story, he pitied her now. The man was a trainwreck. Thankfully, he in no way felt threatened as the other miner had indicated he should be.

"Hey, you wanna get a drink?" Real Joe asked.

Patrick considered it for a moment. "Still waiting for that first real paycheck. Gotta get the debts cleared."

Real Joe laughed. "You likely won't, the way you're running through clothes." He glanced at the new tear in Patrick's coveralls. "Hope you can sew. They've got needles for sale down the general store, too."

Real Joe was still laughing as they parted ways, and Patrick hiked up the hill to the boarding house—Ruth's house. Jack's house. Isaac was already in the basement, washing up.

"So how do I get these clothes clean?" Patrick asked as he stripped out of his blackened shirt. It stank of sweat and felt crusty.

"I don't even bother. Just wear them until they have more dust than the mine. Then send them across the street to Mrs. Krajnak. She soaks them for a whole day before she starts scrubbing and rinsing."

"What does she charge?"

"Less than the cost of new ones."

Isaac ran a towel through his hair and turned his attention to trimming his beard in the small mirror above the sink. Patrick slipped into the shower. The hot steam of the water felt even better than the humidity outside. The mine might be damp, but it was a different kind of damp than the humidity topside.

"How long you been mining?" he asked Isaac. The man was old, which didn't mean he'd mined his whole life, but he was respected enough down below that Patrick suspected he was a lifelong mining veteran.

Patrick heard a ting as Isaac set his scissors on the sink. The water in the sink turned on. "Long time. Started in the breakers as a boy. They didn't limit ages back then like they do now. Then I was a mule man. Then moved down with the men. Spent some time as a car pusher back before they mechanized things. Now I'm just a blaster. They think after forty years that I know a thing or two about structural integrity and how to prevent cave-ins." He coughed, and Patrick heard him spit into the sink. "Damn dust," Isaac mumbled. It was the first time Patrick had heard him swear.

Patrick turned the shower off and reached a hand through the curtain to grab his towel. He'd heard talk throughout the mining towns during his travels about local football teams attracting some of the miners. Their muscles were honed from a lifetime of labor. Of course, the sport of the hour in Maryd was baseball, not football, but Isaac, age aside, was a burly man.

"You ever play football?"

"Nothing formal. Though once I played with Tony LaTone himself. He left the mines to play for the Pottsville Maroons. They won the 1925 World Championship. Funny story that."

Patrick stepped out of the shower. "Oh?"

Isaac had a wistful look on his face as he stared at the lines of his own face in the mirror. "They won that championship, but the NFL bosses took it away. Said it was a technicality in the paperwork. The team is still fighting to get it reinstated. In the minds of the Pottsville residents, they won, fair and square." He turned to Patrick, a twinkle in his eye. "Those were fun years. Tony was a car pusher, too."

"I played a little back in grade school. Not much time for it after you start working, though."

"Tell me about it. What position did you play?"

"Quarterback, actually." He smiled. "I liked calling the shots back then."

"You don't now?"

"Higher stakes now." Patrick frowned as he dressed, his mind going back to the steel mill. Unfortunately, he seemed to be taking on more and more responsibility in the mine, too. He had a gift for seeing what needed to be done and then opening his mouth to point it out. The men were starting to respect him. Most would consider that a good thing, but that was the opposite goal of this job. He had wanted a job where he could just put his head down and work. He didn't need responsibility.

They were interrupted when Bogie walked in. His clothes and face were nearly as black as their own had been. Patrick didn't think too much of it, but Isaac froze in place. The boy turned tail and tried to go back outside, but Isaac caught his shirttail.

"Not so fast. I thought your mom said you weren't to work in the mines."

"I'm not working in the mine," Bogie mumbled.

"Sure does look like it." Isaac released the boy and stood looking him up and down, frowning.

Bogie slouched beneath his gaze.

"Well, out with it, man. Your secret's safe with us. You bootleggin' or working a breaker?"

"Bootlegger's breaker," Bogie mumbled.

Patrick's eyebrows rose. The news was not pleasing to Isaac, whose gentle countenance furrowed into a frown. Patrick wondered if he was remembering his own days as a breaker boy.

Bogie looked up, a spark in his eyes. "You aren't gonna tell my mom, are ya? I know she said not to work, but she needs the money, and Dad's back, but he still ain't workin'. I wanna help."

The two men glanced at each other, then back to Bogie. Patrick wiped his hands on a towel, then carefully hung it to dry. Isaac looked conflicted.

When he turned back to Bogie, hands on his hips, Patrick offered, "How about this? I won't bring it up, but if your mother asks me, I ain't gonna lie. This is between you and her. But I'll tell you, the little I've gotten to know your mother, she's far more hurt by lies than she is by someone making a mistake. If I were you, I would talk to her about this. Today. Not when she finds out some other way."

"He has a point," Isaac added.

Bogie shook his head firmly. "Not yet. Not until I get my paycheck and can give it to her."

The men exchanged another glance, then Isaac held out a hand and motioned Bogie over to the sink. "Let's see how bad your hands are then."

Uncertain what Isaac meant, he peered over the boy's shoulder as Isaac cranked on the sink. As the water ran over the boy's palms, he winced, and it didn't take much to see why. His fingertips were raw, red, and cracked from hours of picking through rock in the breaker.

"They'll toughen up," Isaac encouraged, gently washing the boy's hands with soap and water. Bogie's face screwed into a grimace, and his eyes blinked rapidly as he fought off tears. "When you're done cleaning up, put this on." He handed the boy a jar of salve.

Not wishing the boy to be more embarrassed over his tears than he already was, the men left him to the basement bathroom alone. As they climbed the stairs, Patrick couldn't help but think that the boy's intentions were noble and that he had a point. It was summer, no school. He was old enough to work, much like Patrick himself and Isaac had done as boys. Why wouldn't his mother let him? He asked Isaac such.

"You ever been in a breaker?" Isaac replied. When Patrick admitted he hadn't, the miner went on. "Back in the day, the boys' job was to sort the coal. Little hands are the perfect size for the work. We sat on benches, the conveyor roaring underneath us. As if the noise wasn't bad enough, there's the dust, and the rocks themselves are hard on your hands." He showed Patrick his palm when they reached the top of the stairs. His fingertips were thick, with calluses thick enough to stick a needle into without feeling. Patrick himself had some thick callouses, which he was grateful for with all the work he was doing down in the mine, but his fingertips were still fingertips. "Took me years to build up the natural protection I needed. And even then, sometimes the callouses catch and just rip off. But that's not the real issue. Sometimes things got stuck, or a boy fell. My best friend in the breaker sat two rows down from me. He was telling some joke when he reached for a piece of shale and slipped. Before anyone could do anything, he got caught in the conveyor and crushed. He was nine years old."

Patrick followed Isaac into the kitchen, where Ruth was finishing dinner. The smell of beans and fresh bread wafted around the room.

Isaac quietly added, "You implemented the labor laws in the steel mills, didn't you? Back in '24?"

Patrick nodded.

"Well, it may be illegal for boys Bogie's age to work now, but it doesn't mean they don't. The bootleggers are a secretive bunch to start with, and when they need workers, well, they use who they can get. He's probably working for his friend's daddy." Isaac threw a furtive look towards Ruth, who still worked at the stove. "You know that young man who opens the doors in the mine? Look at his leg. Or lack thereof. He was a breaker boy back before the law kicked in. Mine boss took pity on him and let him man the doors to keep working. He'll never earn a full miner's wage, though."

Patrick shook his head, then slipped into his chair.

"If you two are whispering about the horrors of that mine, you better keep whispering," Ruth said as she set the pot down a bit forcefully in front of them. She turned back to the window and yelled, "Bogie! Girls!"

The men heard a scurry of footsteps from the porch stairs and, within a few seconds, the girls appeared. They sat down at the table, their dolls next to them. Ruth again yelled out the window for Bogie. The storm was now here, with fat raindrops pelting the yard. Reluctantly, she sat down.

Just as they all had stacked their plates with food, Bogie came up from the basement. He stood at the end of the table, hands behind his back.

"Where've you been, child? Come eat," his mother called.

"I'm not a child anymore," Bogie answered quietly, but firmly.

Every person at the table froze.

Bogie took a deep breath and plunged ahead. "I'm a man now. With a job. Today was my first day. I'm gonna contribute to the family."

Ruth's eyebrows raised. "Oh? Doing what?"

Bogie lifted his chin. "I'm working at Billy's dad's breaker, Ma." Then he slowly took his red, bandaged hands from behind his back and slipped onto the bench next to his sisters.

Patrick tried to keep his eyes averted. This was clearly a family matter he didn't need to be privy to, and yet he was loath to leave his delicious dinner. Isaac saved the day.

"You know, Patrick, sometimes it's nice to watch a storm. What do you say we go finish our meal on the front porch?" Without needing further encouragement, they stood and left Bogie to his mother. They could hear her yell from the front porch even then. Though the porch kept the worst of the downpour off of them, they still were misted with precipitation as the thunder rolled overhead.

"She really is passionate about keeping him away from mining, isn't she?" Patrick asked.

"Wish all mothers were."

A cop car turned at the bottom of the hill and made its way up North Main. Patrick had a feeling that Officer Frank's timing in dropping off Jack couldn't be worse. "Shame the boy feels he needs to be a man."

"We all have to grow up some time," Isaac said dully. "At least most of us," he added as they watched Jack stagger from the back seat of the car, Officer Fred's hand under his elbow to steady him. The rain grew heavier, pelting the men.

"Gentlemen," Fred acknowledged, then left Jack swaying on the bottom step of the porch. He quickly drove away.

The miners watched Jack, who glared at them. Then he pulled himself up the porch railing, more with arms than staggering feet, and disappeared into the house without a word.

Isaac leaned back and sighed. "We should go across the street for a while."

Patrick couldn't agree more. Even if he didn't order anything, he needed distance from the Flannigan family. When the rain slowed, he and Isaac pulled the brims of their hats low over their eyes and jogged across the street.

The bar was quiet, likely due to the storm. They slipped onto barstools. Isaac ordered a Yuengling. Patrick, empty-pocketed and claiming dehydration from the long workday, ordered water.

"What do you know about Jack?" he asked Isaac.

Isaac pursed his lips. "About as much as you. He was gone before I started boarding with Mrs. Flannigan. I knew she was married, but I still don't know what the story is. I'm new to town, out of a Mahanoy City mine, so I don't know Jack." He caught the bartender's eye, and she took advantage of the slow business night to come talk to them. "Mary, you know Jack Flannigan's story?"

"Aye, whole town knows it. He killed a man. Couldn't handle the guilt, so he drowned himself here. Then one day, he was just gone." She smiled her missing-toothed grin. "Always good for business when he's back in town."

"He murdered someone?" Patrick asked in shock.

"Naw." She smacked a towel on the bar in front of him. "That ain't what I said. He *killed* someone." When Patrick still wasn't comprehending the difference, she leaned towards him. "Down the mine."

Isaac looked from her to Patrick as if he were a translator. "Mine accident."

Mary smiled mischievously. "No one witnessed what happened that day, but his mining partner came out dead, and Jack ain't been back underground since."

This didn't make sense to Patrick either. "But he was down at the mine office. Asking for a job."

"Maybe so," Mary nodded. "But there's lots of jobs that don't take a man underground."

CHAPTER 22

Ruth was shaking. How dare Bogie disobey her and go down to that breaker! How dare he! The defiance in Bogie's eyes was what bothered her the most. He had his father's eyes after all. That fire, passion for what he believed in, was what had made her fall in love with Jack. Until it backfired. Now Jack's son, the son she cherished, wanted to follow in his father's same reckless footprints, all the way down into the mine. The rational side of her brain reminded her that he technically hadn't gone into the mine, but everyone knew a miner's life started as a breaker boy.

"Bogie, why on earth would you disobey me?"

"We need the money. I want to help."

"That isn't your place. It's mine."

"Well, you can't do enough."

Ruth felt as if she'd been slapped. She straightened. She heard her tone grow icy. "Do you not see the food in front of you on the table? Do you not have a roof over your head, to keep out of the howling storm outside?" The thunder clapped to punctuate her words.

Bogie glared at his plate, unwilling to meet her eye.

She pushed her plate away, leaned towards him, and folded her hands neatly on the table. Her appetite was gone anyway. "Do you understand why I don't want you anywhere near the breaker or mine?"

"You say it's dangerous," he mumbled. Then he brazenly met her eye. "But Billy and the other boys are all working. They're just fine. And then they have pocket money for whatever they want."

"So you would risk life and limb for some candy and comic books?"

Bogie held her gaze a moment longer, then had to look away.

"You know Sam Bartasavage, who lives down the street?"

"He works for the mine, too," Bogie mumbled.

"You know why he only has one leg?"

Bogie's face turned red. He continued to stare at his plate.

"John Bogden Flannigan—" Her use of his full name got his attention, and he raised his blond eyelashes to her. "I do not want you to end up like Sam. You have a thousand opportunities for work that do not involve putting your life at risk for a mine owner's profit."

"But my friends—"

"Your friends are not my sons."

He folded his arms. "I'm sick of girls' work. I'm sick of babysitting and washing dishes and helping clean. Besides, you know what they say about you, Ma? They say you're running around on Dad, and that's why he left."

Ruth straightened. She shot a glance at the girls, who had been watching the whole exchange with fascination, their mouths gaping open. It didn't matter what the other townsfolk said; her own son was not going to repeat it in front of his sisters.

"Go to your room until you learn to think before you speak," she ordered.

"I don't have a room," he snapped back. "I sleep in that hot oven of an attic, remember? Since we need the money you get from boarders just to survive."

He must have recognized the danger in her eyes. She had never used a belt on her children, but she had always made it clear she wasn't opposed to it. Talking back was on the list of things she absolutely didn't tolerate. He ducked his head and left, obediently making his way up the stairs.

The girls sat wide-eyed in silence. Addy looked ready to cry.

"Finish your dinner, girls."

"I don't like beans," Dot whispered.

Ruth dropped her head into her hands.

She didn't look up as the screen door to the front porch opened and closed. The boarders were back. She sighed, then raised her head, ready to put on a brave face. Her composure again fled when she saw Jack, swaying with his inebriation.

The girls lit up at the sight of him, the first glimpse they'd gotten since he had arrived. He'd spent more time in the bar than he had with them. Nevertheless, the girls didn't know that, and they rushed into his arms. His face softened with something akin to surprise.

"Addy. Dot," he slurred, swaying slightly. "You grew."

Ruth just stared as the girls babbled on about how tall they were, what their dolls' names were, and how excited they were to see him.

"Good, good," Jack said. He pulled himself from their grasp and walked to the table. He had to catch himself with a hand on the last step. His chair creaked as he flopped down in it. Without acknowledging Ruth and ignoring the girls, he pulled the beans toward himself, then looked around for a plate, since there was no setting for him. His eyes finally lifted to Ruth.

She sighed and rose to get another plate out of the cupboard. When she placed it before him, he caught her wrist.

"I'm sorry, Ruthie. I tried to get a job today, but they still won't have me."

"I wonder why," she replied with sarcasm lacing her tone. She pulled her hand away. The storm was letting up outside. The girls had forgotten about their dinner. Dot still hadn't eaten her beans, and she likely wouldn't. "Girls, let's go wash up for bed."

"Already?" Addy whined.

"Now." Her tone left no room for argument. If one more person in this family questioned her, she was going to quit. Go on strike like the rest of the unions. Let the lot of them cook and clean and take care of themselves for a change.

The girls obeyed, giving their father one last hug, which he barely reciprocated as he shoveled food into his mouth like a starving man.

A few minutes later, while Ruth knelt by the tub shampooing the girls' hair, Addy asked, "Where's Daddy gonna sleep?"

"The couch. Same as he did last night."

"Are you gonna get your old bed back now that Daddy's home?"

"No, honey. I had to sell the big bed."

Ruth was exhausted by the time she put the girls to bed, and since it was still somewhat early for them, they continued to babble even when she turned the light out.

She gently closed the door and laid a hand on the wall. She took a deep breath, then slowly exhaled, trying to build her reserves. She could hear Bogie throwing a ball against the wall up in the attic, which he wasn't supposed to do in the house, but she didn't have the energy to start a new fight. The child inside her didn't help the exhaustion radiating through her bones, but she had to deal with Jack first.

He was still in the kitchen, slouched back in his chair, eyes closed, plate empty. Without a word, she cleared the table and started washing dishes. When he spoke, she startled and nearly dropped a plate.

"They look just like you."

She kept her back to him, continued washing. Did he know how Dot had his sense of adventure? How Abby's smile was the mirror image of his own? Did he know how much Bogie missed him?

"Your son took it upon himself to start working today," she said quietly.

"Really? Good for him."

"In a bootlegger's breaker."

Jack stayed silent, and Ruth turned around, wondering if he had fallen asleep again. He was frowning into his water glass.

"He sees us struggle and is willing to risk his life to support this family. As if he's the man of the house." She leaned against the sink and crossed her arms.

He avoided her gaze. "Mine company wouldn't take me."

"Do you blame them, you drunk? You're a liability."

He shook his head. "I'm gonna get sober."

"When?"

"Tonight." His eyes flicked up to hers, then away again.

"God, Jack. I so badly want to believe you. You're a better man than this."

"I gave you the money."

"I'd rather *you* than the money. I haven't seen *you* in a long time." She turned back to the sink and rinsed the last of the forks, then pulled the drain. As the water whirlpooled away, she leaned against the counter. "You can't do it halfway, Jack. You have to give it up altogether. You know it."

"I know."

"Then why can't you? I don't understand. You chose drinking over us."

Still, he avoided her eye.

"It's like you aren't even here, even when you are here. Ever since—" She shook her head.

"You want to know what happened that day?"

"Only if it will help you," she said quietly. She turned back to face him, but didn't move to sit with him. His face was skewed in pain.

"Got anything to drink?" he asked. She glared at him, then slowly, purposefully, filled his water glass from the tap and set it down gently in front of him. If he wanted to prove to her he was going to quit, he'd have to start by drinking plain water. He downed half of it as if it were whiskey, then took a deep breath. "I was supposed to be the one down in that branch of the coal hole that day. We'd been at it hard for weeks, and she was producing nicely. Hamy was out delivering, so Rhys took over the winch. I knew the second branch was about ready to start producing, and I wanted to be ready to roll with it when Hamy got back. So I left my mining partner alone."

He took another sip of water. "The day before, Ed had joked about how his half needed more dynamite, so we could break into the old West Mammoth vein. Well, we each went down our separate tunnels, prying loose rock from the ceiling like we always do. I could hear him work as I started setting the new charges on my half of the mine. After a while, I realized it was awfully quiet."

Ruth closed her eyes.

"I yelled, heard nothing. So I walked down the tunnel to check on him. When I got to where the coal vein had been, there was a new void in the wall. He actually *had* cracked into one of the old Kaska mine tunnels."

"And he didn't come get you before he went in?"

Jack shook his head. "He was in a mood. A whole network of new tunnels that we didn't have to dig was the perfect temptation. Not sure what was going on at home, but he didn't have his usual respect for the mountain that day."

"And it claimed him." She knew he'd been crushed by a rockfall. Jack had carried his bloody, broken body out of the mine and never been the same since. She'd gone to the closed-casket funeral along with most of the town. She'd taken up the collection for his widow herself. She cocked her head to one side. "You don't blame yourself do you?"

Jack shrugged.

Ruth quickly moved to sit next to him and took his hand in her own. "He knew the risks, same as you. You both had the same job. The mountain just claimed him that day. This was not your fault."

"*His kids...*"

"What about *your* kids? You have a family, too. What would we do if it *had* been you?" She hastily wiped a tear from her cheek. What would they have done? Perhaps life wouldn't be so much different from what it was now, as his disappearance had jerked her into a whole other kind of grief. "Jack..." She squeezed his hand. "Don't leave us now."

"I'm not dead," he snorted.

"Right. You aren't. But you aren't *here* either."

CHAPTER 23

Thursday, June 9, 1938

Ruth woke up the next morning to the smell of bacon and eggs. At first, she thought she was dreaming, then she panicked that she'd overslept. The clock indicated it was still early, not quite five thirty, her normal morning start time. She again wondered if she was dreaming, but now she could smell coffee, too. If she held her breath, she could even hear the sizzle of the bacon. Were one of the boarders cooking? Now that, *that* would make her angry. This was still her house, her food. Begrudgingly, she pulled herself out of bed and put on her robe, careful not to wake the girls. The door to the boarders' room was still shut.

She padded down the stairs, smoothing her hair into some form of presentability. The couch was vacant, the blanket and pillow she'd given Jack neatly folded and set aside. Maybe he was gone again. He didn't even sleep here last night. She gritted her teeth and faced the kitchen. At the doorway, she froze. There, a shirtless man stood cooking the delicious-smelling breakfast, singing to himself under his breath. He hesitated to take a drink of coffee from his mug, and she watched the muscles in his back ripple. Her heart pounded.

"Jack?"

He spun, spatula in hand, and his face lit up. His smile faltered slightly as he took in her shocked expression.

"I, uh, hope you don't mind. Hope this is what you were thinking for breakfast."

She shook her head and then nodded, stunned. He was not only cooking, but he was sober. "Yeah, sure." Uncertain if she could trust her legs, she pulled up a chair at the table and sat.

He poured her a cup of coffee and set it down in front of her. "You still like it black?"

"Yes. Thank you."

He turned back to the stove and started mumbling Jimmy Rodgers' "Kisses Sweeter than Wine" under his breath. His voice was a rich baritone, evident now even when he wasn't singing full force. She remembered him singing in church. He should have been with the choir.

The hot coffee was perfection. She could make a pot well enough, but something about how he made it was an art form. She closed her eyes for a second, reminding herself that he'd left her. He was sober now, but there was no guarantee he'd stay that way. She cleared her throat.

"You're up early."

He shot her a look over his bare shoulder. "I guess I'm getting back in the rhythm of things again."

She again eyed the sharp contours of the muscles across his back and chest, the smattering of hair that accentuated pectorals grown hard from a lifetime of hard labor. She was almost embarrassed, and then she remembered she was married to this man. She was allowed to look. He caught her eye, his own sparkling. She knew then he'd set this up on purpose. He wanted her to look.

She looked away, going back to her coffee. "The boarders will be up soon."

He winked. "Don't worry, I'll be decent by the time they stir."

She set the cup down as he flipped a helping of bacon, eggs, and home fries onto a plate. "Jack—what is this about? Don't do this to me. Don't pretend everything is the same if you're going to just leave again."

He set the plate down in front of her. "I'm not playing."

Tears brimmed at the corners of her eyes. "But this is like the old days. And since then...since then you *hurt* me."

He knelt in front of her and took her hands in his own. "I meant what I said last night. I'm gonna stay sober, Ruthie. I'm going to provide for you. You have the money in your hand *now*. We won't need boarders. Bogie doesn't have to work." She trembled, and he squeezed her hands tighter, craning his head to force her to meet his eyes. Then he took his hand and gently laid it on her belly. "You've made me realize what I need to do to take care of my family."

She covered his hand with her own. Oh, how she'd longed for his touch, his recognition of the life he put inside her, just like he had recognized the rest of their children with unbridled joy. Still, it was hard to trust after he'd hurt them so badly. He'd left. She'd had to scrape out an income so they didn't end up homeless. He'd chosen alcohol over them. And yes, he'd come back with a stash of money, but where had that come from? She was still afraid to ask.

And now he was saying that was all in the past.

"It's going to take me some time, Jack. I can't just forget."

He pushed to his feet and kissed her on the forehead. "Fair enough."

He returned to the stove and removed the rest of the food from the heat. He covered each pan and dish so they would stay warm until the boarders came down. On cue, they heard someone stir in the upstairs bathroom. Jack went to one of the hooks by the back kitchen door and donned a shirt, watching Ruth's eyes as if he performed some kind of seductive reverse striptease. In a way, it worked, and she felt that old flutter in her core. He walked back over to her and kissed her lightly on the lips. She didn't protest. Couldn't. Though a tear did slip down her cheek.

"Ruth Flannigan, I am so sorry," he whispered. "I promise you, I really am going to try."

They heard footsteps on the stairs and Ruth hastily nodded. She wiped away the tear.

"Morning," Jack greeted the newcomer.

"Morning, yourself. Isn't this a nice treat?" Isaac said.

"How do you like your eggs?"

Ruth knew Isaac preferred sunny side up, but he told Jack he had no preference. He took what was offered and sat at the table across from Ruth, a twinkle in his eye when he looked at her. She offered a slight smile back and dug into her own food. A few minutes later, Patrick joined them. He offered less surprise at the chef—perhaps he assumed she'd done it all—and yet Ruth couldn't help but notice he seemed quiet. Distracted. Perhaps he was still mad at her for not being transparent about her husband's existence. Though that didn't quite seem right either. Neither Jack nor Patrick said anything other than short cordial greetings to each other. She could feel the tension between them.

The miners headed to the basement to change into their mine clothes, then headed out. Bogie appeared in a rush, pulling on his socks as he hopped across the kitchen on one foot. Soon, he added a piece of toast to his wrestling.

"Whoa, son, what's the rush?" Jack asked him.

"I'm late for work!" Bogie rushed. He avoided his mother's eye. He ignored his father completely.

She felt herself tense, the anger rising. They'd *talked* about this. She'd said *no*. She debated how best to stop the bull-headed ten-year-old. Scream at him? Lock him in the attic? Saddle him with extra chores? That would only make him hate her more.

Jack looked at her, then turned back to the spectacle of Bogie trying to dress, eat, and run out the door all at once. He stayed silent. Ruth's temper rose.

"John Bogden—" she began, but then Jack held up a single finger and shook his head.

Bogie seized the opportunity to duck out the kitchen door and take off running down the street.

Ruth turned to Jack and her wrath snapped out like a whip. "How *dare* you undermine me? I told him no. Now you go—"

He again held up a single finger. "Hear me out."

Ruth poured herself a second cup of coffee, her hands shaking with rage.

Jack pulled out a chair next to her.

"You know, I was his age when I started in the breaker, too."

She frowned into the steam that rose from her coffee.

"I'm going to team up with Rhys and Hamy again. They're mining on the opposite side of town. Winch shaft."

"You're changing the subject."

"We'll go back to Bogie in a moment. Look at me. Please, Ruth."

Her eyes flicked up to his. The blue pierced her own with an earnestness she hadn't seen in years. He really was ready to try. He was going to stay in town, work. She knew the men he spoke of. They were good, hardworking, independent miners whom he had worked with before. They'd been going underground since they were teenagers, and they were also some of the most safety oriented men she knew. They'd lived through Ed's accident along with Jack. They were good men. Still, she had to ask, "You think bootleggin' is better than trying again to work for the company? If they start strip mining and you can work above ground—"

Jack took her hands. "I need to have control again. Ruth, for the sake of my head, I need that. I don't want to be in a position where a life has to be gambled for someone else to get rich. I'll leave that to card-playing." His gaze wavered from her eyes for a moment, and her heart pounded, wondering if he'd gone back to another of his old vices to bring home that stack of cash. He focused back on her, that determination returning to his eyes. "I trust Rhys and Hamy."

She inhaled slowly, then exhaled, her eyes never leaving his. "Fine then." She reached out to touch his hand. He immediately clasped hers, their pulses pounding as if their hearts were trying to sync.

"Now, do you mind if I get our son fired?" he asked with a sparkle in his eye. "I'll go down and talk to Billy's dad now. Unless you think we should give him the chance."

"I don't care how we do it, but we'll make ends meet so that he doesn't have to work in mining." She nodded. "Get him out of there."

"I'll let him work today yet. Give the boy some pride in himself. But I'll tell William to pull the plug tonight."

Ruth nodded in agreement. Maybe another day of sore fingers would make Bogie feel better about not having to return as well.

Jack turned to face her, a lusty look in those blue eyes. "Now, wife, the boarders are out of the house. The girls are still asleep. Can I prove to you how much I love you?" He brushed a lock of her hair behind her ear, his rough, calloused fingers caressing every piece of skin they made contact with.

She closed her eyes, as much to block those seductive blue eyes as she did to hide the longing she knew rose in her own. "Jack—not yet. You need to give me time." She opened her eyes and fixed him with a firm look, not unlike what she used on the children.

He pulled away, and instantly she missed the connection. Was he mad? No. Just reserved. Maybe he really did understand what his absence had done to them.

"I'm going to head down and talk to William about Bogie." Jack stacked plates next to the sink. "And then I'm going to meet with Rhys and Hamy. I'll probably be back late."

She nodded. "Supper's at six."

CHAPTER 24

It was a long day underground.

When Patrick came out of the mine that evening, he was exhausted, frustrated, and even a little mad. The conditions were getting to him, as grateful as he was to be working. Was he really working though? He was still as broke—no, more broke—than he was when he'd first come to town. The men kept promising him that this next paycheck he'd have money in his pocket. It wasn't like he didn't have a roof over his head and meals in his belly. He didn't like owing Ruth.

The mine was making great progress. The new tunnel was moving ahead. The veterans said they'd hit coal any day. Saleable coal that is, not just the minimum needed to run the water pump and the ventilation fan on the surface. They told Patrick that when they did start working a solid vein, boy oh boy would the cars be moving then. Patrick couldn't help but wonder if the bootleggers didn't have the right idea, the more lucrative one. If they pulled coal out and sold it, they pocketed all the money, not just a flat wage. Where did they sell it? To the homeowners looking to fire their furnaces and hot water heaters? To industry? To the steel mills, which ran better on anthracite than any other fuel in the world? He just needed access to that world.

Bogie's voice carried across the coal yard. "What'd'ya mean I'm fired? I just got hired! And I've done everything you told me to for the last two days!"

Patrick's head snapped around to watch. The boy was standing at the main intersection of town, a decent distance from the mine entrance, and still, his voice carried.

"Bogie, it wasn't my doing," a man was saying. His voice only carried on the wind. "You did great work. Proved yourself well. But your father said on no condition are we to keep you hired on."

"My father got me fired?" Bogie's voice still carried. A few of his friends flanked him. "He's the whole reason I have to work!"

Gently, the man said, "You'd better talk to him about it."

Bogie put his hands on his hips, smoke practically coming out of his ears. "Well, do I get paid for my two days?"

"Sure thing." The man presented an envelope. Bogie shoved it down in his pocket.

"I'm gonna talk to my father, Mr. Kolpack. I'll be back tomorrow, just you see."

"If he gives his blessing, Bogie, we're glad to have you back."

Bogie stormed up the hill, his friends in tow.

Real Joe appeared at Patrick's side. "Gotta give it to the kid. He's got spunk."

Patrick couldn't help but feel bad for Bogie. He was just trying to help his family. He hoped for the Flannigan family's sake that Jack didn't run out on them again.

He chewed the inside of his cheek, even considered asking Real Joe for some of his chew. "Gotta ask your advice, Real Joe. I think I want to start bootlegging. I need more money than I'm making in the mine. You think anyone would take a rookie miner like me?"

Real Joe pushed a wad of chew into his lip as they walked into town. He shrugged. "The men like you. You might be able to join up with a crew. You don't know mining, though."

"I can learn."

"Maybe."

"You know anybody looking for another miner?"

Real Joe gave him a hard look, working the tobacco in his mouth. "You're living under the roof of one of the best bootleggers in town."

Patrick had to think a moment. "Jack?"

Real Joe nodded. "If he's staying in town, he'll be mining."

"But Mary said—" Patrick hesitated in revealing how many questions about Jack he'd asked, but then plunged ahead anyway. "Mary said he never went back in a mine."

Real Joe's eyes twinkled. "Mining's in his blood. If he's back in town, he's battled whatever demon he needed to."

Patrick had his doubts about that, given Jack's drunken state. He pressed his lips into an expressionless line and stayed silent.

Real Joe nodded slightly. "Well, Steel Man, you can try him. You'd have to have balls to ask Jack after—well, everything he has going on." He avoided Patrick's eye, making Patrick wonder just how bad these rumors about he and Ruth were getting. "Think what you will of Jack, but he's a good miner. If he stays sober, he's a hard, fast worker. He expects the same of those he works with, which is why he works with Rhys and Hamy." He met Patrick's eye. "I've told you before, you're smart like him. You think like him, like a leader. So do you think you can work *with* him?" His eyes drifted to Ruth's front porch, where she sat crocheting while the girls played hopscotch on the street in rust-tinted squares.

Patrick caught the implication, though Real Joe didn't have to voice it. He met Real Joe's eye again. "I'm just a tenant. I can work with anyone, so long as they pay me." He thought back to the mine. "Besides, isn't Roger back to work now?" The man's knee was still smashed, but rumor had it he'd also been hired on to guard the entrance at night. "Won't be long before I lose my temporary place in the mine. I'll still need work."

"Fine, Steel Man. Then try asking him. Best to do it when he's sober."

Patrick and Isaac were just about done cleaning up when Jack walked into the basement, as black as they'd been just thirty minutes before. Ruth called the children in for dinner, which also served as the boarders' dinner bell. Bogie hadn't bothered to clean up, much to his mother's protestations, and instead had been up there complaining about his lost job for the past half hour. Patrick had suspicions she'd made him strip down to his underclothes and wash in the sink, for her complaints on his cleanliness had ceased while his tirade had not. Jack's eyes flashed to the ceiling above, where Bogie could still be heard railing on, and he smiled.

Patrick hadn't seen Jack in the mine. Yesterday's debacle made it clear they wouldn't hire him, so he must have been bootlegging. Real Joe was right, and he was working. Isaac headed up the stairs. Patrick lingered, hoping to talk to Jack. He would have gone right into his question, but the look Jack gave him was so vehement, he lost all words. What had he done wrong?

Jack continued to strip out of his mining clothes as he glared. "I hear they call you Steel Man."

"So it seems," Patrick shrugged.

"I hear, too, that you've taken a fancy to my wife."

"Yes. I mean no." Patrick gritted his teeth, now knowing what this was about and wanting to both defend Ruth's honor and warn the drunk that Ruth wasn't alone if she needed help in the future. "She's a good woman. She deserves a man who's going to provide for her."

"Like you?" Tension radiated through Jack's torso, and Patrick noted how muscled the man was. Not one he wanted to fight with.

"I can hardly say after only a few weeks in town that I'm a stable option. She does deserve it, though, from someone. She deserves to be loved."

"I do love her!"

"Swell. Then hopefully you're that man. You are her husband."

Jack seemed to quiet a bit. "I'm going to give you one chance to come clean before I throw you into the deepest stripping hole in the county and leave you there, Kane. Did you touch my wife while I was away?"

Patrick shook his head, meeting Jack's eye. "I promise you, Mr. Flannigan, I did not. Your wife is an honorable lady. I'm a mere tenant, following her rules and crawling into my lonely twin bed at night, falling asleep to Isaac's snoring. That doesn't mean I don't appreciate who she is and how hard she works. I don't want to see her hurt again. Nobody does. There is *nothing* more than that between us."

Jack watched him for a long moment, then turned into the bathroom, shutting the door behind himself. Patrick went up to the kitchen, right into Bogie's raving about his father. Having exhausted his mother's listening ear, he was now explaining to Isaac all the unfairness of not being allowed to work. Isaac listened, just the slightest of smiles playing on his lips. True to Patrick's suspicion, Bogie was sitting shirtless and barefoot, only clad in his dusty pants. His face was still black with coal dirt, but it appeared his mother had scrubbed his hands clean and freshly bandaged his blistered fingertips. He was just about ready to list all the candies and new things his friends could get with their breaker earnings when Jack came upstairs. The room went silent. Ruth set the last dinner platter on the table.

Bogie, for all his words earlier, didn't seem to have the muster to complain to his father. Or perhaps he'd simply blown himself out. Jack beelined straight for his son, pulled out the chair next to him, and leaned over, his elbows resting on his thighs to be level with the boy's gaze, which was currently averted.

"Son, I think you were brave and honorable in wanting to support your mother and sisters while I was away. I appreciate that. Your heart is in the right place."

Bogie raised his eyes to meet his father as the rest of the people in the room watched. Hope seemed to spark in his eyes.

"Why won't you let me work then, Dad?"

"Because it's not your place. It's my place to take care of this family, and I intend to do so. The breaker is dangerous. I don't want you there."

The hope in Bogie started to fade.

"Since you want to work, though, I have an idea. Babba Belinski down the road needs her lawn mowed. So does Mrs. Gerhard. And I can give you a ride down into Brockton on the weekends when we take the coal truck to the breaker. I'm sure you can talk yourself into some more customers there. How does that sound?"

"So I can work...just not in the breaker?"

Jack nodded, a smile playing on his lips.

"Alright then." Slowly, Bogie's face lit into a smile.

"Now let me see your hands." Jack took Bogie's palm, and the rest of the table helped themselves to one of Ruth's fabulous dinners.

Patrick shoveled down his food with a bit less decorum than usual. He was tired of having to play witness to family matters. It was like rubbing salt in a wound. Staying in a widow's home with her children was one thing, but watching all five of them—a big happy family—brought up emotions he'd been running from for years. Maybe Jack was facing his demons, but Patrick's were still eating him with guilt one bite at a time.

CHAPTER 25

Friday, June 10, 1938

Ruth yawned as she slipped downstairs in the early morning light. Though the worst of her morning sickness had passed weeks ago, every now and then she still woke up queasy. Today was one of those days. On the bottom stair, she hesitated, watching Jack as he snored faintly on the couch. He lay sprawled on his back, one arm dangling to the floor. His afghan hung precariously over one leg, the rest already succumbing to gravity as a puddle of yarn on the floor. His torso and legs were bare, his hair askew in tufts. It had been a humid night, and despite all the windows being open, the room was balmy. Ruth tucked flyaways of hair back into her bandana, her eyes still locked on Jack. It was strange to have him home. It was comforting. It was stressful. How could it be everything all at once? She stepped down into the living room, and for a moment, she hovered over him, reached a hand out, longing to caress him. Then she drew her hand back, clasped it to her chest. No, not yet. That simple motion would wake him, and that would lead…elsewhere.

She wasn't ready to forgive that much yet.

Ruth heard the faint sound of a screen door slap and walked to the front door. Red was loading up a few tools as he readied to head to his mine. Ruth glanced back at Jack, and then quietly slipped out the door, making sure to hold back the screen door so that it didn't make a sound. Then she jogged across the street to Edna and Red's house.

"Morning, Ruth," Red said.

"Mornin'."

Red put his last box of dynamite in the bed of his truck, then turned to her. "Yes, they're on board." He smiled, then crossed his arms as he looked down at her. "I didn't tell anyone it was your idea, either. Just said, 'a few folks have been talking'."

Ruth breathed a sigh of relief and put a hand to her forehead. The town was going to rally. They were going to make sure change happened, protect their livelihoods, protect their homes. Then she brought her hand back down and rubbed her belly as the baby moved. "Thanks, Red."

"We've still got some folks to talk to, but Edna's working on that." He scuffed the dirt with his boot. "How's Jack?"

Ruth glanced back at the house. "He's working with Rhys and Hamy again. Says he's gonna stay sober."

"Good. If you ever need anything..."

"Thanks, Red." She stepped back towards her house and waved. "Hey, have a good day."

He tipped his hat to her and hopped into his truck.

An hour later, the boarders were seated at breakfast, finishing up, when they heard expletives come from outside. Ruth furrowed her brow, laid a hand on Dot's shoulder, then rose. She walked to the front of the house, with Isaac, Patrick, and all three children close behind, to watch the scene unfolding across the road. Edna stood on the porch with her youngest daughter on her hip, as Red gestured wildly and cursed as he paced in front of their front porch steps.

Ruth moved to head over there in Edna's defense, but then saw that Jack was already there, standing next to Red's truck, his arms crossed. He looked to Ruth, his expression grim. He said a few quiet words to Red, which led Red to put his hands on his hips and look heavenward. Then Red moved to his wife, who opened her free arm to embrace him, and then guided him inside. As Jack walked back across the street, he ran a hand through his wild hair, then tugged his coal-dirt blackened baseball hat down.

"What's going on?" Patrick asked, the concern in his tone making his voice rougher.

"His coal hole was blasted shut overnight."

"No!" Isaac exclaimed, stepping forward and putting a hand on the banister.

Jack nodded, then again took his hat off to rub his forehead, this time meeting Ruth's eyes. "Red thinks it was a bunch of company goons."

Ruth caught her breath. If that was true, and she found it likely, was the company out to shut down all the bootleg holes on their land? Or was it more sinister, their warning for the bootleggers to keep their heads down? The real question was, did they yet hear of Ruth's plan?

She wasn't ready to get fire-tempered Jack in on that just yet.

"I'm gonna go check my hole," Jack said.

Ruth nodded once. "Go."

The whistle down at the company mine sounded a warning, which got Isaac and Patrick running for the basement and down to the mine. Suddenly alone, Ruth turned to the children. All three of them looked at her with wide eyes. Ruth narrowed her gaze on Bogie.

"Bogie, can you run down to the general store and get today's paper?"

He nodded. "Mr. Moore won't give me that for free, though. Not till tomorrow."

"I know." She steered the girls back inside and found her purse. Then Bogie was off with enough money for a paper and some sweets, so long as he brought back something for his sisters, too. Ruth herded the girls back upstairs. "Dress quickly, ladies. We're going to go for a walk about town."

They were running out of time. While all the independent miners were buzzing about Red's coal hole, she had to know who was on board. Whoever Edna and Red hadn't talked to yet, she'd find herself. It was going to take the whole town to pull off. And if they backed out, if the blame fell solely on her, which she well deserved, then she very well may end up bringing this baby into the world in prison.

"Yo, Steel Man. Go home."

Patrick looked up abruptly. His boots were still untied, laces tucked in, and he was working on buttoning his shirt before he zipped up his coveralls all while jogging down the hill towards the mine. Isaac was a few paces behind, in much the same condition, except for his miner's cough.

Patrick's gaze focused on one of his fellow miners. The man was walking away from the mine, back into town. As was a staggered line of miners. A few expletives drifted on the breeze.

"What's going on?"

"Mine closed for the day," Monkey grumbled.

"Closed?" He felt anger and panic rising. It was pay day.

"Relax, Steel Man," Real Joe said as he walked past. He held up an envelope. "They've got our pay in the office still."

"This happen often?" Patrick asked, turning to walk backwards at a much slower pace than when he'd started down the hill.

"I sure hope not." Real Joe shook his head and continued home.

Patrick lengthened his stride and continued down to the mine office. Sure enough, there was a sign posted—mine closed through Monday, June twentieth. Roger was seated outside the mine tunnel, his bum leg stretched out before him on a crate. Patrick walked over, noting the man's wary gaze and the shotgun he held across his chest, arms crossed around it.

"Roger, what's going on?"

"Can't you read? The mine's closed for today into next week."

"But why? I gotta work."

Roger frowned. "So do I, but you took my job." He paused to spit a wad of tobacco to the side, then his posture softened slightly. "They don't tell me why. Mine boss doesn't feel like being open, I suppose." Roger chewed a moment, then added, "Last time they closed, they closed for six years."

Patrick sat down hard on a crate next to Roger. "I gotta work."

"Like I said, so do we all. Welcome to coal country. Where the coal kings call the shots, and we take what we can get."

They sat in silence for a bit, watching the miners express a range of emotions as they emerged with their pay. Frustration, wariness, anger. Patrick felt them all.

"How's the knee?" Patrick asked.

Roger grimaced. "Won't be getting down in the mine anytime soon. Doc says it ain't broken, but it sure don't feel right. Glad they're lettin' me sit guard here."

"They afraid we'll steal coal?"

Roger laughed. "You wanna steal coal, all you gotta do is go for a walk. It's free for the picking on the banks. No, I think they've got me here so some bootlegger doesn't come blow it all shut."

The hair on Patrick's neck prickled. "Did you hear Red's hole got blasted last night?"

Roger stared at the mine office, his face grim. "Thus why I'm sittin' here. Only a matter of time before the indies retaliate." Roger continued talking as if to himself. "I'm grateful to the company—I am—for givin' me a job. But I ain't standing in the way of dynamite, no sir." He hugged his shotgun tighter and shifted his weight on the crate. It groaned in protest.

Patrick didn't know what to say to that, so he tipped his hat, picked up his meager paycheck, and headed back to town. He was still in the middle of Main Street when he realized he had nothing to return "home" to. So he continued straight out of town, figuring it was as good a day as any to walk a few miles into the neighboring town of Brockton and see what he could see. The walk didn't take very long. The town was a little bit bigger than Maryd, with factories and a few restaurants and pretty girls that strode the street in neat dresses and red lipstick. It was nothing like Pittsburgh, but there was a certain buzz to the place that he'd missed. Solitude and quiet were good, but so was a bit more excitement.

He walked a few blocks, listening to the noise of the sewing machines and looms in the garment factories. There wasn't a whole lot to see, and most people were busy working. Contented with his adventure for the day, Patrick started walking back to Maryd. He got to the gas station on the edge of town and saw a familiar young face, Bogie. Bogie was sitting in the back of a coal truck, swinging his legs, pants lined with black dirt. Patrick's first thought was that the boy had disobeyed his parents and taken to mining again, which, if true, put him, Patrick, in a tight spot. Thankfully, he didn't have to debate the ethics of tattling versus meddling in his host family's affairs long, as Jack popped his head out from under the hood of the truck.

"Okay, Bogie, go turn the key."

Bogie hopped down from the truck bed and ran around to the driver's seat. Only the top of his head was visible over the dash, but a few seconds later, Patrick heard the engine try to turn over. It sputtered and went quiet again. Patrick could keep on walking. Or this could be his big opportunity to befriend his landlord and maybe get a new job.

"Need any help?"

Jack and Bogie looked up at him. Jack hesitated, then waved a hand at the engine while he wiped grease off his fingers with a rag.

"I thought it was just low on oil, but even with new oil in it, this engine's just not right."

Patrick looked under the hood, checked a few things. "You going for a load of coal or coming from delivery?"

"We got it delivered. But we have more runs to make."

Patrick saw the issue and tweaked a few things. "Alright, Bogie, go try again."

Bogie scooted back into the truck and turned the key. The engine sputtered, then caught, then roared to life.

Jack frowned at the engine. "So what'd you do?"

Patrick explained, and Jack listened intently, nodding. Some people quickly got lost when he talked about mechanics, but he had a feeling Jack not only understood the difference between an inlet manifold and an exhaust pipe but would be able to replicate the repair in the future.

"Thanks," Jack said, and shut the hood. "You heading back to the house? Need a ride?"

Patrick was enjoying the walk, but he couldn't pass up the opportunity. "Sure." He climbed into the cab, with Bogie between them. He turned to Bogie. "So how was your new job?"

"I helped Dad shovel coal, and I have two lawns to mow next week. It was great." He was like a different kid. The spark was back in his eyes, and he sat on the edge of the bench seat of the truck with eagerness. "We're gonna take loads this weekend, too, aren't we, Dad?"

Jack smiled. "As many as you want to help with."

Patrick leaned back and smiled as the truck pulled into Maryd. He was glad the family was getting itself back together. He also noted his opportunity. "You getting a lot of coal out of your mine?"

Jack turned wary, pursing his lips and hesitating as he turned left up North Main Street.

Patrick started talking faster. "The company isn't enough for me. I want to work more, build up some savings. I'm a good mechanic. I'm learning how to be a good miner. If you need help at all, please let me know."

"You want to be a bootlegger?"

"I want to make an honest living."

"Coal companies say bootlegging isn't honest. It's illegal."

"Well, then, I just want to work. Mine closed from today through next week. How am I supposed to make anything if I can't work?"

Jack chuckled without mirth. "Welcome to coal country. We've been saying that for six years."

Patrick frowned out the window as they pulled into Jack's driveway. Ruth was along the side of the house doing laundry with a new Maytag washer with an automatic ringer.

"I'll think about it," Jack said, then hopped out of the truck. Bogie followed behind him and Patrick slipped out his own door.

CHAPTER 26

Jack walked right up to Ruth and kissed her on the forehead. She was so startled she didn't even complain about the coal dirt on his hands as he caressed her belly. "Hi."

"Hi," he said back, a seductive note to his tone.

"Mom, I've got two customers in Brockton now," Bogie interjected. He jogged up and peered at the spinning squeeze rollers on the washer. "And Baba says hi."

Ruth ruffled his hair. "So you had a good time?"

"Yup." He pointed to the rollers. "Hey, you think I could try that?"

"Sure," Ruth said. "I just rinsed everything." She showed him how to take the clothes out of the washer, which continually swished back and forth with the agitator. She fed a shirt through the rollers, careful to keep the buttons flat. The water dripped onto the ground. The shirt came out damp, but not dripping wet. "Just watch your fingers."

Bogie took over, the wrung clothes dropping into the tub behind the roller.

Jack laced his fingers into hers. "So you like the washer?"

"You know I hate laundry. So yes, I like the washer. It makes everything quite a bit easier." She hesitated, then stood on her tiptoes to kiss him lightly on the lips. It was the first time she'd taken the initiative. In part she felt she owed him. For the washer. In part she just missed him. He seemed to really be back, physically and emotionally, just like he used to be. She tried not to think about what would happen if he started drinking again. Maybe, just maybe, she could trust that he would stay.

Jack smiled as she settled back on her feet, caressed her cheek with his thumb. She leaned into his hand, closed her eyes for a second, then opened them again and pulled his hand away.

"You're going to get coal dirt all over me." She smiled, though.

"Uh-oh. Mom! Mo—mmmm!"

Ruth turned to Bogie amidst the sound of something pinging off the wooden siding of the house and across the ground. He was desperately trying to straighten a shirt in the rollers, which were all but eating the shirt. Buttons popped off and pinged against the side of the house. Jack ducked as one sailed towards his head.

"Mom!"

Ruth took two steps and turned the machine off, then popped the top of the rollers so they swung apart. Half the shirt was missing buttons.

Bogie looked at her in horror. "I'm sorry. I thought it was flat and then it twisted and I couldn't straighten it and then it just kept going and going—"

Ruth held up the mutilated shirt and started laughing.

Jack and Bogie exchanged a look and stared at her.

"Ruth?" Jack asked.

It never failed. Even with the best technological advances, she still managed to ruin the laundry. Even with a brand new washer and wringer. All she could do was laugh. No housewife should be this bad at laundry.

"Oh, geez." She laid a hand on Bogie's shoulder. "It's fine, dear. Look." She pointed to a wash basket next to the washer, full of shirts with missing buttons. She tossed the one Bogie had ruined with the rest. "I haven't quite gotten the knack for the rollers either." She rubbed her forehead. "You think you could round up the girls and have them help look for buttons?"

Bogie stared at the pile of shirts, then slowly smiled. He nodded and ran down the back to find the girls, who had last been seen building a fairy fort under the lilac bush.

Ruth turned back to Jack and shrugged with a weak smile. "Sorry?"

Jack plucked one of his shirts out of the basket. "Are there any left?" he asked timidly.

She laughed again, the sound musical even to her own ears. It'd been a while since she laughed. She kissed him lightly again. "Yes. And you're in luck, because I can sew better than I can wash clothes."

He caught her waist. "I'm make a deal with you."

"Hmm?"

"You kiss me proper, and I'll wash the clothes from now on. Or at least run them through the wringer."

Ruth bit her lip, then cupped his face in her hands, and kissed him like she meant it for the first time in over five months. Her heart pounded, her mind went blank with pleasure, and the baby in her womb turned.

It wasn't until she heard the slap of the screen door that she realized Patrick had been watching.

CHAPTER 27

Saturday, June 11, 1938

"Yo, Kane."

Patrick woke to his foot being shaken through his covers. He sat bolt upright in bed, every nerve on guard.

"Hamy's working with Red, trying to get his hole open again. We need help on ours. You up for it?" Jack stood at the foot of his bed, arms crossed. The man might be his same age and height, but somehow Jack had the persona of a general.

Patrick nodded his head and blinked. "Uh, yeah, sure."

"Hurry up and get dressed then." Jack left the room.

Patrick glanced over at Isaac, who still snored. It was still dark outside. Lord only knew what hour it was. He still had some saving to do before he could afford a pocket watch. He swung his legs out of bed and grabbed a shirt, pants, and clean socks, then went downstairs. Jack was already in the basement pulling on his coveralls. He sized Patrick up. Patrick knew full well this was a test. If he complained, he wouldn't get the job. If he showed weakness, they'd laugh him out of town, and he wouldn't get the job. If he lacked skill, they'd simply send him home.

He dressed quickly and followed Jack out of the basement door and around the side of the house to the coal truck. They hopped in, and the old GMC turned over easily.

"How far is it?"

"Just up the mountain." Sure enough, within a few short minutes, Jack pulled off the main road and onto a forest road, bouncing through the rough terrain. The truck barely fit through the thick brush and mountain laurels. When Jack stopped the truck, there wasn't a clearing. There certainly wasn't a mine.

Patrick suddenly had the suspicion he was going to be murdered. Maybe Jack didn't believe that he'd kept his hands off Ruth. Maybe he was listening to all the rumors. Patrick's nerves tingled. He might not know this land as well as Jack, but he could run. He could fight, just like any good city boy. He tensed, his hand on the truck door.

But Jack didn't say anything. He got out of the truck, turned on his headlamp, and then walked a few yards away and reached into the brush. He dragged away the pile in two or three trips, revealing a giant winch on a dirt mound a few yards high. Below it was another pile of brush, which Jack also moved to the side.

"Well, you gonna get out of the truck or not?" Jack asked.

Patrick scurried out, clicking on his headlamp. He eyed the dark pit that had appeared. It seemed as if the hole dropped down into nothing.

"We follow the vein via a shaft, not a drift mine," Jack explained. He glanced at his pocket watch. "Rhys should be here any minute." They heard a rumble in the distance and then saw the glow of headlights.

"How do we get down?" Patrick asked, peering into the darkness.

"Winch and bucket. That's also how we get the coal up."

As if to prove his point, Jack started walking around the apparatus, which was built out of several solid timbers. A steel cable wrapped around a large metal drum, to which a hand crank was attached. The handle locked into a wooden groove, which Patrick assumed was the brake. The cable attached to a giant bucket, big enough for a man to stand in and deep enough to haul about a quarter ton of coal. It was the most basic of machines. It looked to be a very labor-intensive operation.

Jack unloaded a few boxes as the second truck pulled up, and Rhys got out.

Jack turned to Patrick. "We try to always mine with three of us. One topside, two digging. Of course, it depends on which phase of mining we're at. Sometimes there's only room for one down there." He studied Patrick's face, which despite his best efforts at a poker face, must have belied his bewilderment. "You'll see." He reached into the bed of the truck and pulled on rubber hip boots. Patrick looked at his own new, scuffed, very not-waterproof work boots. He had a feeling he was going to be in for a cold, wet day.

Rhys came over, hands in his pockets, mining helmet and headlamp already on his head. "Mornin', Jack. This the Steel Man, eh?" He looked Patrick up and down like a prize horse.

"Yup. Patrick, meet Rhys. He's our winch man."

The two men exchanged greetings and shook hands. Though no stranger to strong grips and in possession of one of his own, Patrick felt like his hand was in a vice until Rhys let go. Rhys was the one who should have been named Steel Man. The man stood a full head taller than he and Jack and was built like an ox.

Within a few more minutes, all three men were ready to go to work. Jack descended into the mine first, his headlamp blazing and a safety lamp tied to his belt. Patrick watched the first rays of dawn stretch over the horizon through the trees. They were pretty high up on the mountain, high enough to have a good view if the leaves weren't full. A few minutes later, the bucket returned, and Patrick climbed in. Rhys eyed Patrick's boots but shook his head in silence.

Hopefully, Jack didn't intend to bury him at the bottom of the coal hole.

The bootleg hole was barely wide enough for Patrick to slip down. He stood on the bucket, hands clutching the cable, as he was lowered down the hole. He watched Rhys crank the winch, arms pumping each rotation, until he was enclosed on all sides by damp rock. Thankfully, his time in the main mine had gotten him used to small spaces. Still, he resisted the urge to hold his breath. If he tipped his headlamp just right, he could see down into the recess below him. They'd told him this wasn't a deep mine. Maybe fifty feet. Still, in the narrow space, fifty feet seemed like an eternity. The swaying, bumping descent of the bucket unnerved him, so he leaned his helmet against the cable and closed his eyes. Only when the flash of Jack's headlamp illuminated his face did he open them again.

"All right there?" Jack gave him a look that promised he would be the laughing stock of the bootleg community if he said anything other than "Fine."

"Fine." He stepped out of the bucket into a foot of cold water. He winced as his socks and boots soaked through.

Jack already had buckets of coal on hand, which he tipped into the conveyor bucket. He gave the cable a solid shake. The bucket went up. Patrick was now trapped down in the shaft with his landlady's alcoholic husband. And wet feet.

"Come down this way with me," Jack ordered, then ducked low to crawl through a narrow tunnel. It must have taken them weeks of digging to shape this shaft, and when they hit coal at the bottom, they'd started working the vein laterally. Both men had to duck their heads, and both of Patrick's shoulders brushed the walls. It was much tighter confines down here than the main mine. "You're going to fill buckets and haul them to the big bucket. I'm going to start prepping for another blast."

The tunnel had opened into a small room where the loose coal lay, already fractured from the rock around it and ready to shovel. There were no supports anywhere in the tunnel or room. They had dug into the vein itself, and once the coal was gone from the walls, they moved deeper. There was no sign of wasted work in here. There was no pump for the water either, thus the foot of water that now froze Patrick's feet. Thankfully, the room with the coal was slightly elevated, so he could see what he was expected to shovel. He doubted his feet would dry at all, though.

Jack tapped the ceiling ahead of Patrick with a pry bar, testing for any loose coal. "We just blasted yesterday, so we've got plenty of product to move. Watch!" Jack grabbed his arm and yanked Patrick back.

Patrick scanned for what had alarmed Jack. He'd watched the company miners as they pushed the tunnel into the mountain, so he had an idea what to look for.

They often pried down the fissures in the rock that would lead to collapses. Right now, he saw nothing. Jack wedged a six-foot iron bar into an obscure crack in the ceiling and pressed down. A slab of shale fell from the ceiling, landing just feet away from them with a loud crash.

"Gotta watch for those widowmakers," Jack said, the sparkle in his eye flickering in the light of their headlamps.

Patrick scanned the rest of the room with an even more trained eye. He saw one other crack in the ceiling and pointed it out. Jack agreed they should leverage it, and together they made the shattered rock fall. The sound in the small space was loud enough to rattle his teeth. He stared at the pile of broken shale and coal that had piled up, grateful he had not been under it when it fell. Dirt swirled in front of his light.

"Alright," Jack said, scanning the little area of the mine. "Get to work."

Patrick didn't wait to be asked twice. Eager to prove himself to Jack, he shoveled as fast as his muscles would allow, then hauled the coal to the winch. Rhys made the bucket fly back up into the pinprick of daylight above. The bucket clanged its way back down at an even faster rate.

"Keep up with him!" Jack yelled over his shoulder. He had already drilled a hole into the bare rock face and had a quarter stick of dynamite ready to press into the void.

Patrick ducked his head into his shoveling, trying not to think about how he was in a small space with a whole box of explosives. Explosives that were in the hand of an alcoholic with no reason to befriend him. He stomped on the shovel, leveraged another scoop of coal into the bucket.

The bootleggers' goal was obviously to work fast and hard. Real Joe had told him they often only worked these holes for a few months, then started again somewhere else with easy-to-access coal. Rain could shut a hole. Or a cave-in.

Patrick was far more worried about the latter.

He hoped he wasn't digging his own grave.

CHAPTER 28

Jack came home in the late morning. He kissed Ruth on the cheek, then washed his hands, arms, and face in the sink. He was again shirtless, dressed just in his pants, which left a faint dusting of coal dirt across the floor.

She chose not to hassle him about it.

"You were gone early."

"The beauty of mining is you can work any time of day." He dried his face with a tea towel. "Truck's already full. Gonna take a run to the breaker and then try to load another this afternoon." He started rummaging in the cupboards. "We have any aspirin?"

She reached high up into a cabinet by the sink and produced a glass bottle of pills. That was good productivity. He had to be sore. He took them from her and popped two in his mouth and rinsed them down with water. Then he splashed water on his face again, which had already beaded with sweat.

"You haven't seen Mr. Kane, have you? He didn't come down for breakfast."

"He worked with us this morning."

If Ruth's eyebrows could have gone higher, they would have. "You let him join you? Isn't he working down at the company mine?"

"Hamy's helping Red, company mine is closed, and Kane wanted more work, so I figured we'd let him try." He scanned the kitchen, likely in search of breakfast. Ruth opened the icebox and gave him some cold creamed chipped beef and a slice of bread. "He's actually not a bad worker. He's smart enough to observe and apply."

Ruth watched Jack make the leftovers disappear. "Did he get anything to eat?"

Jack smiled into his food, his eyes sparkling with mischief. "Nope."

"What about his lunch?"

Jack shrugged.

"So you sent him into your mine on an empty stomach with no food?"

"He's got a canteen of water."

"Jack!"

Jack set his fork down with a little more force than necessary. "I'm not his mother. And quite frankly, that's what he gets for making eyes at my wife while I was away."

She stilled. "Nothing happened."

"Maybe it didn't. But the town's talking, Ruth. And I've got ears. I don't like it. And I'm gonna set it straight."

"How? By starving our boarder? Chasing him out of town?"

"I just gave him more work. I hardly think that indicates I'm running him out of town."

"Then what?" She put her hands on her hips.

Jack smiled and leaned back in his chair, cupping his hands behind his head. "If I believed he messed with my wife, I wouldn't hire him, would I? People will catch on to that soon enough, and your rumors will stop. Still, I want him to feel a little hungry for a day. I'm sure he'll learn to plan for his own food in the future." He caught her hand and pulled her over to him and onto his lap. "And I also want time alone with my wife. I've been gone a long time. And I think I've proven I'm loyal to you. I'm not drinking." He brushed her hair behind her ear. "Patrick says you need to be loved."

Ruth flushed. "He wouldn't say something like that."

"He would. And he also said I'm the one to do it." Jack cupped the back of her head and pulled her to his lips. He coaxed her into the kiss as gently as a caress, then deepened it. He needed her. She knew it as surely as she breathed. Her mind fought against the rationality that he hadn't been home long, that he could leave again, hurt them again. Her body felt only the passion, the longing, the surety of the touch of the man who knew her inside and out. Then she wasn't fighting anymore. She yielded to the wave, let Jack pull her along.

"The children..." she breathed.

"I caught them in the yard and sent them with Bogie to the post office. Then to the store. They each have ten cents in their pockets, so it'll be a while until they decide what they want."

He tasted like mint toothpaste.

She leaned into his ear and whispered, "Promise me something."

"Anything."

"Don't starve our poor boarder. I suspect the man doesn't have more to his name than the clothes on his back."

Jack's lips distracted her to oblivion. "Fine. I'll take him a sandwich." Then there was no more talking. As his hands began to roam up her sides, she whimpered, then lost all reason as he played her body to perfection, right there in the kitchen.

CHAPTER 29

Five minutes. That's what Jack had told Patrick before he left him on the mountain. He'd be back in *five minutes.* Patrick threw a chunk of coal against a tree. His aim was perfect, the bark chipping as the thud resounded through the woods. Like a dinner bell. Dang, was he hungry. Really, it was his own stupid fault. It took longer than five minutes just to get off the mountain, let alone go drop a load of coal and come back. In that respect, Patrick had expected Jack to be gone longer than five minutes. But hours? That's where he was stupid for agreeing to wait.

He'd been debating for a whole hour if he should start walking back to town. He was staying because he wanted a day's work. He wanted the cash Jack had promised at the end of that day. Wet, cold feet and all, he wasn't willing to break under Jack and Rhys' initiation to bootlegging. His wet socks were wrung out and drying on a laurel branch, the boots open with the tongues hanging out, not that they'd dry, but maybe they'd at least warm in the sunshine. His stomach growled. Apparently, this initiation also included starving.

The sun was heading towards the western part of the sky now, and Patrick again sent a rock flying at the tree, which was now decorated with pockmarks. Maybe they weren't coming back. Maybe he *should* start walking. Pity he couldn't be digging, working all this time. But Jack had been adamant that it wasn't safe to be alone down in the coal hole, not to mention if he was down there and no one showed up, who would work the winch? He didn't mind the dark confines underground, but he didn't want to be trapped down there as part of some joke. He brought his arm back to let another chunk of coal sail, then froze. Like a hum on the wind, the engine of a truck sounded from below the ridge.

Finally, one of the men was coming back.

Unless it wasn't them at all, and they'd turned him over to the police for bootlegging. He shook his head, letting the coal in his hand drop to the ground as he reached for his damp socks and boots. Jack and Rhys wouldn't do that. They wouldn't reveal their coal hole to the authorities or the company that owned the land it sat on. It was too much work to dig, and they had plenty more coal to pull out of the ground before they moved onto the next spot. He'd seen that coal with his own eyes, and he'd pulled more of it from the ground in a morning than he had working with the company over the past two weeks.

The truck pulled up to the hole, and Rhys hopped out, his brow furrowed. "You're still here?"

Patrick gritted his teeth. "We *are* still working this afternoon, aren't we?" Rhys had gone down the mountain a few minutes before Jack, so maybe there was some awful communication error.

"Well, yeah. But Jack didn't take you down? Did you bring a lunch up here?"

"No, I did not." Patrick tried to keep the frustration out of his voice, and it came out high-pitched, almost comically so, instead.

Rhys shook his head and smiled. "Well then. Let's get you working."

Patrick tightened the laces of his wet boots.

Rhys put his hands on his hips. "He didn't tell you there was water down there either, did he?"

"No. He neglected that warning."

Rhys shook his head and smirked. "He's got it out for you, Steel Man. He think you've been running with his wife?"

"Dunno."

"Did you?"

"Hell no." He felt the heat of anger flush his cheeks and was about to start defending Ruth's honor when Rhys nodded. Patrick bit his tongue.

"I believe you. Ruth ain't like that. Even when Jack doesn't deserve her."

"Right. She's a good woman."

"I've known her since grade school. Sweetest girl in the class. Never had eyes for anyone but Jack though." He reached into the bed of his truck and pulled out a pair of hip boots. "What size are you?"

"Honestly, at this point I'll take anything dry." Patrick took the boots with relief. At least he wouldn't have ice-cold feet for the rest of the day. The boots were a size or two too big, but that was better than too small. He was just straightening from attaching the ties that held them up to his waist when the rumble of Jack's truck sounded, and he pulled up.

Jack stepped out of the truck with a smirk on his face. "Looks like you two are ready to go."

Patrick folded his arms across his chest, debating if he should comment on Jack's timekeeping skills, but then decided it was better to bite his tongue. He headed towards the coal hole.

"Hey, Kane, you hungry?"

Patrick turned to glare at Jack.

Jack tossed a smashed sandwich into the mud at his feet. It had a strong resemblance to a pancake, indicative of being sat on.

Patrick looked down at it, then back up, his veins turning to ice. He didn't need a job this bad. There were plenty of other kinds of work.

Jack's arms were now folded across his chest, his own glare meeting Patrick's like a dog ready to fight.

Rhys looked from one man to the other as he waited at the winch. "Jack, you're as daft as a mule's backside. You want the man to work, he's gotta eat. Y'all are killing daylight, and I wanna get home for dinner."

"I want to know why the rumors still persist that 'Steel Man' here was more than a boarder to my wife. She seemed awfully keen to ensure your well-being. She cares about you."

Rhys rolled his eyes. "Jack, she cares about everyone. Get in the hole."

"No, I need to know if I can trust this vagabond. Where'd you come from, anyway? No one comes to coal mining from steel."

"I'm a mechanic." Patrick kept his expression neutral.

"That chose to slop underground instead of breathing fresh air and working on trucks? Couldn't find work in a factory?"

"Jack, you're wasting time," Rhys called.

"Answer me!" Jack screamed at Patrick.

Patrick noted the tremor in Jack's hands. His forehead shone with sweat, though it wasn't terribly hot or humid. He met Jack's eye and asked, "How long has it been since you had a drink?"

"Ain't had any all day! Not that it's any of your business."

Rhys came down from the winch and stood next to Patrick, his eyes full of concern for Jack as he too studied the signs. "You quit the booze, man?"

Jack leaned against the truck, then ran a hand over his face. "I promised Ruth. She thinks I need to get off it completely."

"How long?" Patrick asked again.

"Fifty-nine hours." Jack sighed and looked at his shaking hands.

Rhys ran a hand through his hair, pulling it back from his forehead. "Jeez, man."

"I expected the headache. Pushed through that like usual. This is new for me." Jack opened and closed his fist, watching his fingers tremble. "I've got to work. Promised her that, too." He pushed himself from the truck and popped open the front door. A bottle appeared in his hand. "One swig should get me through the day. Then I'll wean myself off more gradually."

Before he knew what he was doing, Patrick had snatched the bottle and thrown it against the tree he'd been throwing coal at. The bottle shattered, the brown liquor dripping down the bark as if the tree was crying. All three men stared at it, then Jack roared.

Jack charged at Patrick, his shoulder leveled like a lineman's tackle.

Patrick stepped into the charge with fists raised, eager to release his own frustrations, but the blow never came. Rhys had his muscled arms tight around Jack, wrestling to restrain the angry man.

"Knock it off!" Rhys shouted.

"It's none of his—" Jack thrashed against Rhys' bulk.

Patrick held his ground and pointed a finger at Jack. "She deserves better! I told you that. She deserves better than a drunk! And you can be better! You *must* be better! Because she wants *you*."

Rhys's eyes grew wide.

Jack spat in fury like a chained monster.

"You will lose your job, your family, your little unborn baby if you don't get it together. This is bigger than you. You are fighting the wrong monster. It's not me. It's that bottle." Patrick pointed to the tree with its liquor tears.

Jack stilled, staring at the tree. He roared, then shook off Rhys as if he were a burlap sack. He didn't come at Patrick, though. He walked off into the woods alone, the anger and frustration radiating off of him in waves.

Rhys and Patrick stared after him.

"I didn't know he had it that bad," Rhys said in awe. "I mean, we all drink."

Patrick pursed his lips, then looked at the ground. "In some people, it becomes more than just a drink. At first a habit, then an addiction, then a monster that eats their lives. If he doesn't find the will to beat this now, he's gonna lose everything."

Rhys looked sideways at him. For a moment, Patrick thought he was going to question how Patrick knew this, but he remained silent. After a while, Rhys ran his hand through his hair again and sighed. "I wanted to get another load up yet this afternoon. Dang it." He kicked an old tin can into the coal hole.

"I'll go down. The coal is down. The walls have already been checked. All I have to do is shovel."

"You okay down there by yourself?"

Patrick shrugged. "Rather be alone down there than with that man. At least right now." He looked towards the hole, well aware he sounded more confident than he felt. Real Joe had been right; Jack had an eye for safety in a mine. He'd spotted that widowmaker that Patrick couldn't see. And that was while battling the early signs of the withdrawal that had just hit him like a sledgehammer. Patrick could only hope he had been thorough before the symptoms hit. He himself would have to avoid those dynamite sticks that were already planted into the wall of the mine. He picked up his safety lamp and lit it.

"Well, let's get moving then," Rhys said, looking out in the direction Jack had disappeared. "We lost enough time."

Patrick reached down to the ground and picked up the smashed sandwich. He brushed off the dirt and had it eaten before he'd stepped into the coal bucket. "Do me a favor, Rhys. Don't let him come down here until I'm out of this hole."

Rhys chuckled. "Deal, Steel Man."

And the bucket went down.

CHAPTER 30

Jack walked into the house like a storm cloud. Ruth could feel the energy roll off of him like a lightning strike, building up. Where would it hit? Would he explode at her? At the children? At some random piece of furniture?

The basement door took the brunt of it, the walls of the house shaking as he slammed it behind himself. His heavy boots thudded on the stairs, and she knew she couldn't complain about the muddy tracks that ran from the kitchen door to the basement or things would only be worse. She bit her lip as tears threatened at the corners of her eyes. After this afternoon, she'd been on a rollercoaster of emotions. She wasn't sure if she regretted letting her guard down or not. Right now, the dial was pointing towards regret. And yet she hated that. For those few minutes, every reason she loved him had come roaring back, leaving her heart full with hope.

What had changed?

She headed to the closet for the broom. Out the window, she noted the figure of a man strolling along the side of the house. Patrick. And he wasn't strolling. He was pacing, arms crossed. The tension rolled off of him as it had Jack, even through the glass of the window pane. She got out the broom, swept up the mess.

The basement shower turned on, and it ran for a long while. She put a fresh pot of coffee on the stove despite the fact that it was now evening. He'd need something. Hopefully, coffee was enough. And dinner. Dinner was cooking, right on schedule. Less mouths to feed tonight. Isaac had taken Bogie down to the ball field to watch the baseball game: Maryd versus a rival patch town. Bogie had a few cents in his pocket for the concession stand. Just the girls and Jack tonight. And Patrick.

Ruth looked out the window again, but Patrick was gone.

She heard the shower in the basement turn off just as the coffee began to perk. She poured herself a cup and leaned against the sink, bracing for whatever mood Jack was in now. Thankfully, the girls were still playing in the living room. She could see them from the kitchen sink. Their dolls would hold them off for a few more minutes. She prayed that was all Jack needed to gather himself and appear as a father again.

The man who ascended the stairs was anything but. He was pale, with a sheen of sweat on his face that was out of place considering it wasn't terribly hot and he'd just showered. His hair, due for a trim, hung in damp curls across his forehead. He hadn't shaved, which wasn't unusual, but the bristle only added to the appearance that something was off. He stood in front of her shirtless, hands in the front pockets of clean pants, with his eyes down. There was something so completely broken in his stance that she pushed off the counter and came to him. Had someone else been hurt? Was he sick?

"Jack—"

"I'm gonna do it, Ruth. I swear this time. I'm gonna break through it this time if it kills me."

"If what kills you?" She froze, hands on his arms.

He pulled his hands from his pockets and stared at them. They trembled like the leaves of the birch tree down the back.

She looked up into his gaze. He met her eyes boldly, daring her to scold him. She didn't.

"The alcohol?" she breathed. "It's that bad?"

He nodded. "Every time."

Just how many times had he tried to quit? She inhaled. Still, his gaze held level with hers, daring her to show her disappointment. She pursed her lips. "Okay then. Now let's get through this."

The girls chose that moment to come scampering into the kitchen. They shrieked in delight when they saw Jack.

"Daddy!"

He winced, then forced a smile as he turned to them, wrapping his arms around them as they barreled into his legs and clung on. He turned back to Ruth, tears in his eyes. She again took a deep breath and stepped towards him, then cupped his face in her hands. "You are still the strongest man I've ever known." She kissed him lightly, then turned to set dinner on the table. "Come, girls, let's eat." Her eyes flicked up to Jack. "Maybe try to eat some of the bread. I just made it. And drink a lot of water. Coffee's hot, but stick to one cup so you can sleep."

Jack nodded and slipped into a seat next to her. He still looked miserable. She caught one of his shaking hands.

"I'm proud of you. It will get better."

She didn't dare ask why their boarder, a newly christened bootlegger, wasn't cleaned up and eating dinner with them.

Patrick was walking. He wasn't sure where or how far he'd go, or even if he'd stop to get cleaned up, but he was walking. He shoved his hands deeper into his pockets, fingering the lint and pieces of dirt that had accumulated there since the last washing. He didn't feel the itch of the coal dirt on his face or arms tonight, such was his frame of mind. He walked around the mud puddle that had once been a swimmable stripping hole. He caught a trail on the other side that led up a decades-old culm bank and began to climb, his calves burning as each step in the loose gravel made him slide another foot backwards. But eventually, he crested the bank and broke into virgin timber on top of the mountain, which was like a whole other world after being down in the coal dirt around town for so many weeks.

He followed the ridge, still lost in his thoughts. He cursed Jack, cursed himself for showing up in Maryd with the wild idea that he'd be able to stay. He strategized where to go next, then pitied himself for never having a home. All that took him back to cursing himself for screwing up the life he'd had in Pittsburgh to start with.

Jack didn't know what he had. And it was making Patrick realize what he'd lost. And that made him hate Jack—pity Jack. No, that wasn't quite right either. Patrick wanted to go back in time and fix his own errors. He wanted to stop Jack from making the same mistake.

A loud crash sounded in the woods next to him, and he flinched and looked up. A doe leaped away, spooked out of its bed mere feet away. Patrick inhaled and calmed his heartbeat, then spun in a circle to get his bearings. He was deep in the woods. The sun was setting, which meant he'd walked for hours, and it was well past dinner. He'd have a good hike to get back to town.

He sighed. Just as he was about to step back in the direction of town, he glanced down. There, not ten feet from him, a great black hole yawned up towards him. He stepped closer to the edge and leaned to look down. It was maybe three or four feet wide, with a pile of tailings creating just a slight bump on the hill below. The pile was covered in a thick coating of leaves, blending with the ground around it. It was an old hole, likely an air shaft. Patrick tossed a small rock down and didn't hear it hit bottom for a good long while.

His knees suddenly felt shaky, and he sank down to the ground. A few more of those absent steps, and he would have fallen in, never to be found again. That deer had just saved his life. Crazy, how sometimes the briefest encounter with another living thing could change your life. He inhaled. Maybe that was why he was in Maryd. Out of all the patch towns he'd come through, he'd wondered for weeks why Maryd had attracted him. Maybe he needed to be that encounter for someone else.

Maybe, if he could be, it would make his own past worth surviving.

CHAPTER 31

Jack was sitting on the front porch, still sweating off the tremors and nursing a cup of coffee, when Patrick got home. It was dark; their figures were outlined by the porch light. Ruth watched the encounter from the kitchen. Whatever they said was brief, terse, and yet the handshake that followed seemed to mend whatever wrongs were between them. Patrick headed down the back, and a while later, she heard the basement door open and close. She opened the ice chest and got out Patrick's plate. There was no way to warm it up except to put it back on the stove, but she'd let him do that, just in case he'd eaten elsewhere or wasn't hungry.

She went out to Jack and put a hand on his shoulder. He caught it with his own.

"Girls asleep?"

"Yes," she said quietly. It was a peaceful night. The cicadas sang in the background as the fireflies lit the yard. "Bogie should be getting ready for bed. He said it was a good game." The rest of the town was filtering home from the game, both on foot and by car. She could tell from the laughter that sang from front porches that the team from Maryd must have had another victory.

"Sit with me?" Jack pulled her hand ever so slightly.

She slipped into the seat next to him.

"Do you want to know where I got the money?"

She pursed her lips.

"I won it, Ruth. Playing cards."

She held her breath. So her suspicion was true then. "We gonna have gamblers running down our door now?"

"No. I only played enough to win, only in games where I knew the count."

Ruth inhaled. Behind the drunken façade of a barely making ends meet coal miner, there was a brilliant mind. Only those in their closest circle knew he could keep the count in any card game, from Poker to Pinochle. He could be cocky with his skill and prone to gambling. Though he'd never—yet—taken them into debt with it. It was more hobby than an addiction for him, unlike his drinking. Still, taking other gamblers' money didn't create friends. "And no one knew?"

"No." His eyes flashed up to hers. "Give me some credit, Ruthie."

She didn't yield, her lips in a thin line. "Don't do it again."

Jack's knuckles tightened on the armrests of the porch chair, then softened. "Fine. I won't drink and I won't gamble. I'll just dig tunnels like a groundhog, waiting for someone to shoot me as soon as I pop my head out into the daylight."

"Jack, that's not what I—"

He turned to glare at her. "You don't know what it's like!"

She flinched back, eyes wide. She'd hoped this side of Jack was gone. But no, it was always just lingering under the surface. All those regrets from earlier in the day roared back, now coupled with a loneliness that barely left her upright. She stood, flashing him a glare of her own. "I'm going to bed." She had to move while she still could.

He snatched her wrist as she moved to walk by, and she struggled to yank it out of his grip. "Let go," she hissed through clenched teeth.

"I gave up everything for you!" His voice carried across the yard. She envisioned every house in Maryd listening in.

"Shh," she pleaded. "Don't cause a scene."

He was on his feet now. "A scene? You think it's not a scene when you bring other men into my house?"

"We've been through this. They're *boarders*. I needed money to pay the mortgage after you left—"

"Oh that again!"

She finally twisted her arm out of his grip and clutched her wrist to her chest as the skin burned. She spun on her heel and burst back into the house. She'd get the girls and Bogie and go. Leave Jack to figure out the mortgage. She'd go to her mother's. Ask Edna or Real Joe for a ride into Brockton. Bogie met her on the stairs. His pajama bottoms rose well above his ankles, proof of his childhood growth, and yet his eyes met hers with a maturity she was now going to rely on.

"Bogie, dear, go wake your sisters. We're going for a little ride."

"Like Hell you are!" Jack followed her into the house.

"Mommy?" Addy asked from the top of the stairs, her hand in her little sister's.

Bogie was the only one who could move, and he took the hands of both little girls and pulled them along down the stairs and towards the kitchen door, away from the storm of a man who blocked the front door. Ruth spun on Jack, wishing to delay him enough for the children to escape. They knew where to go.

"How dare you raise your voice at me? You're worse sober than you are drunk tonight! You could tell me what's wrong, but instead, you're on the offensive, like I'm the enemy. I'm not your enemy, Jack! I'm your wife!"

Patrick burst from the basement door, shirtless and fresh from the shower. "What's going on?"

The sight of him pushed Ruth's emotions over the edge. She was too embarrassed to speak, and then she was mad at herself for feeling embarrassed because she'd done nothing wrong. Though she couldn't control her own husband. Was that even her responsibility? She wiped a tear and ducked past Patrick, out the back door, and up the street. She caught up to the kids as they ducked under the tin roof of the shed in the back of the post office, just as the sky unleashed a flurry of raindrops the size of marbles. Pennsylvania's fickle weather had changed its mind again. She held the three of them tight and turned her eyes to the heavens, praying for a miracle that would change the only man she'd ever loved. The girls cried softly, and Bogie, too old for emotion and too young to process this drama, just let her hold him like he was still her little boy.

CHAPTER 32

Sunday, June 12, 1938

"Morning Patrick. You're here early."

Patrick blinked his eyes open, then flinched as Rhys slammed the door of his pickup. He stretched and untangled himself from the green army tarp that usually covered the winch. He was still wet from the short downpour the night before, but at least it had stayed fairly warm overnight. He pulled himself to his feet and dusted off the dead leaves and pine needles that clung to his pants.

"Morning."

Rhys hesitated, a fresh box of dynamite posed on his hip. He cocked his head. "You sleep out here?"

"Apparently." He hadn't slept too poorly either. It was better than a concrete sidewalk in the middle of a dirty city, which he'd done enough times. Or the coal-filled back of a railroad car as the train whistled and rattled all night long. He glanced at the coal hole. He wondered how his prisoner had slept.

As if reading his mind, Rhys set the dynamite box at his feet and looked at the hole. Anyone could notice that the bucket was still down there, but Rhys, as the winchman, had a particular eye for it. "Patrick...who's down there?"

As if the man below could hear their conversation, the winch cable started shaking with vigor, the cue for the bucket to raise. It had been doing that all night, at least what Patrick had been awake for. This time, though, they could hear a voice echoing from down below. And the man didn't seem too happy.

"Jeez, Steel Man. What'd you do?" Rhys beelined for the winch.

Patrick jogged after him. "Just give him a few more minutes." Well, maybe a few more hours.

"Who's down there? Jack?" Rhys leaned over the edge of the hole, as if he could see down. "You okay down there?" he shouted down.

A muffled voice echoed up, incoherent.

"You're a frickin' ass, Patrick." The cable shook hard, and Rhys started winching it.

"Hear me out! He was mean enough last night that Ruth and the kids had to run and hide!"

The winch came to a stop. "Drunk?"

"Dry drunk." Patrick sighed. "He's still going through withdrawal. He needed some time without temptation."

"So you put him underground?"

"Yes."

The man down the hole shouted something.

Rhys eyed the hole warily. "How'd you get him down there?"

"Wasn't easy." It had taken a false threat on the coal hole, Jack's truck, an old belt, all of Patrick's muscle, and bribery with a now-broken bottle of booze to get him to go down. "He has his safety lamp," he added, as if that made all the difference. He held a glimmer of inner satisfaction that Jack's headlamp was still in the front seat of his truck. Had to be awful dark down there with just the flicker of a candle flame.

"Jeez of Pete's sacred heart," Rhys swore, then winched as fast as his arm could handle. Patrick sighed and readied himself for the onslaught about to come. If Rhys and Jack decided to turn against him, he could easily end up being the one thrown down the coal hole. Or worse. His family had no idea he was even near little Maryd, and no one would go looking for him if he just disappeared. That had been the point of traveling the state, but now Patrick saw the downside.

"I was just trying to protect Ruth."

Rhys still cranked, a sheen of sweat now decorating his brow.

"Dang it," Patrick said, tossing his hat on the ground. "I thought this town cared about her. And yet you'll all turn your backs on her while her husband drinks their money away, negates her hard work, and makes her and her kids run out into a rainstorm out of fear."

Rhys shot Patrick a glare, his arm still pumping. "You assume a lot for an outsider."

"Well, explain it to me then. Why am I, the outsider, the one who finally noticed that Jack had a problem? Why am *I* the one who wants to step in and help that family? Dang it, I'm trying to help Jack himself. He needs to *get* sober before he can *stay* sober. Why am I the only one who sees that?"

"Why indeed," Rhys mused. Then, to Patrick's surprise, he stopped winching just as Jack's head cleared the rim of the coal hole. Jack looked like a tiger, ready to claw his way out into the daylight and devour whoever he saw first. Rhys called over to him, "It true you sent Ruth and the kids running last night?"

"I didn't lay a hand on her!" Jack moved to stand on the rim of the bucket so he could leap the last few feet out of the hole.

Rhys let the bucket drop a few feet, which threw Jack off balance and made him swear. Jack kept his feet in the bucket. "That ain't what I asked. Did you send them running?"

"I don't know why she ran. We were just talking."

"Ruth ain't no sissy. You had to have done or said something."

Jack mumbled something under his breath that Patrick couldn't make out. He was pretty confident he didn't want to.

Rhys wasn't pleased. "Well, maybe Steel Man here's got the right idea. Get yourself in a fatherly state of mind and start acting like you've got a family to take care of." With that, Rhys dropped the bucket, sending Jack back down into the hole.

Patrick stared wide-eyed.

Rhys shot him a look. "I like Ruth. And yes, the folks of this town look after each other. Even when it's hard." He sighed. "We'll let Jack out after he's ready to own up to his actions." He locked the winch back in place and eyed the few gears it consisted of. "Might as well grease this thing while I have the time," he mumbled and went to his truck, where he pulled out a toolbox.

A few hours later, Patrick and Rhys were sitting back enjoying lunch. They'd done all the work topside around the bootleg hole that they could for the day, and they figured it was soon time to let Jack out of the hole, for better or worse. Patrick closed his eyes to the sun filtering through the trees around them. The humidity had baked off, and now it was a warm day with a slight breeze. It was good to be above the ground.

Rhys seemed to be enjoying the day as well. He'd stretched out against a tree, his long legs crossed at the ankle in front of him with his hands behind his head. He looked intently down the hill, but a frown graced his face.

"What's wrong?" Patrick ventured.

Rhys shook his head. "Just trying to picture what this will look like after it's all bulldozed away."

"What do you mean?"

Rhys sighed and scratched the back of his head. "You heard about how they're proposing a strip mining operation?"

"Well, yeah, a little."

"By definition, a strip mine takes everything off the surface of the mountain to get down at the coal. What we underground miners do isn't without a mark." He gestured towards the growing tailings pile below the coal hole. "But it's hard to imagine this whole mountaintop just...gone. No trees. No topsoil. Just barren piles of black dirt. I mean, even the shape of the mountain is gonna change if they go through with it."

Patrick looked at the forest around them and pictured it as desolate as some of the mines he'd seen on the way from Pittsburgh. "Seems like an awful lot of earth to move."

"It is. But have you seen the size of those shovels? You could fit my entire pickup in the bucket. A few dozen of those scoops an hour and moving mountains isn't impossible anymore."

Patrick whistled. "I guess that is easier than going underground. It's got to be safer at least."

"Yeah. But the men who do this job know it well." Rhys picked up a blade of grass and twirled it between his fingers. "We were begging for work all through the Depression these past years. And now they think they can just park a shovel here, one man, one machine, and obliterate our source of income. It won't be just the company mine that shuts down this time. They'll ruin every single bootleg hole. Dozens of livelihoods, gone to one man operating a shovel."

Patrick thought for a moment. "I've never seen a town so at war with the company mine like Maryd. When they tunnel underground, people complain that it jeopardizes their houses. When they offer to strip mine, it threatens the entire landscape and your jobs. And when they're closed, you blame them for the lack of jobs. What *does* this town want?"

Rhys sat forward, his elbows on his knees. "I think the problem is we've changed. We've been forced to. Back in 1929, the town loved the coal company. And they were more exploited than ever. The town was still owned by the mine company—everyone rented. That general store was a company store where people used their script to buy overpriced necessities. And yet there was work. So much work. The men went down the mine shafts almost every day. You know how much coal they pulled out of those tunnels? Two hundred fifty thousand tons. A year. There were three hundred fifty men working—the whole town. Then one day in '32, they hung a sign out and closed it all. Even had the nerve to dump all the coal that had already been dug *back down the shaft*. Can you imagine?" Rhys smiled to himself. "What they didn't account for is the ingenuity of the people of this town. It wasn't long before we took to the hills ourselves and started independent mining." His smile grew wider. "When they opened that old mine shaft this past spring, that pile they'd discarded back into the earth was much smaller than it had been. And the tunnel systems were quite a bit more complex."

Patrick smiled. "The independent miners stole the coal that was already blasted?"

Rhys shrugged. "I don't know nothing about it. I just—"

A loud boom echoed from the coal hole in front of them, the ground vibrating beneath their feet. Both men jumped to their feet as a plume of dust rose from below.

"Jack, you alright?" Rhys shouted down. He jogged to the winch. "You sent him down with a lamp, right?"

"Yes!" Patrick leaped up the last few feet of the bank that braced the winch. His heart pounded. Had he killed a man again? All to prove a stupid point to a stupid man who had a stupidly pleasant wife?

"Come help me!" Rhys begged, not that he had to ask at all.

Between the two men, they worked the winch at double the pace. Patrick's arms strained. Rhys sweated as his thick arms worked. This bucket was heavy. Finally, they had it to the top, and much to their surprise, the bucket was full of coal with the lid of an empty dynamite box on top. Rhys locked the winch, plucked the sign off the bucket, then laughed. He tossed it to Patrick, then went about unloading the bucket. Patrick looked down at the words scratched into the wood.

SEND MORE DYNAMITE YOU BUMS

Then in smaller letters, he'd written:
AND MY DAMN HEADLAMP

Patrick laughed, too, and went to get the headlamp and dynamite from the back of Rhys's truck. When the coal was emptied, they sent the newly loaded bucket down. A few minutes later, the cable shook, and Patrick cranked up another fresh load of coal. He had to admit, he was surprised. Jack was loading down there faster than they could unload topside.

"Isn't he hungry?" he asked Rhys as he again lowered the bucket.

Rhys smiled. "You're about to see Jack at his finest, Steel Man. You better get moving. Our day just got much busier."

If Patrick had any doubts as to what that meant, they were soon erased. As fast as he and Rhys could unload and send the bucket down the hole, that's how fast Jack was refilling it. All the while, there were two more blasts that came from below. Jack was doing the work of two men down there, moving at a breakneck pace. It wasn't even dinner time when Rhys finally sent the bucket down with a new sign.

TRUCKS FULL

When they winched Jack to the surface, he had the look of a man who was physically steamed out and yet in a much better headspace. His skin and clothes were black with coal dirt. Only the whites of his eyes showed their flash of color. He climbed out of the bucket to a friendly cheer and a slap on the back from Rhys. Jack's focus immediately turned to Patrick, his focus laser sharp. Before Patrick could see it coming, a fist slammed into his jawbone. He staggered. Jack pulled him back to his feet, then pulled him into a bear hug.

"Thank you. Now don't ever do that to me again." Jack abruptly broke away and climbed into his truck, leaving Patrick rubbing his jaw. "Y'all coming or what? I'm starving."

CHAPTER 33

Ruth had not spent the night out in the elements. When the rain had passed, she and the kids had walked home to find the house vacant of everyone other than a snoring Isaac. She had tucked the kids into bed, gotten a few restless hours of sleep herself. When she was done straining for the sounds of Jack and Patrick coming home, she pulled herself out of bed while it was still dark and started breakfast. When Isaac and the kids woke up, she had a veritable feast laid out for them with creamed chipped venison and fresh biscuits. The kitchen was sweltering, and the food was cold. Isaac was polite enough not to complain. The girls never ate creamed chipped meat anyway—Addy, and by default, Dot, hated the texture—and Bogie was too glum to do more than pick at his food, so she got them all dressed and herded them across the street to Edna's, intent on hitching a ride to Brockton. Edna and the girls always went to church on Sundays, with or without Red, so they were going right past Ruth's mother's.

Thus, with Edna driving, Ruth found herself riding shotgun with five kids crammed into the big back seat of the Ford. Ruth wasn't sure she ever wanted to go back.

"Wanna talk about it?" Edna said quietly.

"Nothing more to say." Ruth glanced over her shoulder as the girls shrieked with dramatics over a fly that flew in the window. Bogie, pressed against the left window seat, stared out the window with his chin on his fist. Ruth's heart ached for him.

"What are you gonna do?"

"See what my Mama says, I suppose."

Edna pulled into the short driveway of Ruth's mother's Brockton townhome. Mama came out on the porch, dish towel in her hands and apron around her waist. The girls piled out of the car and barreled over to her widespread arms. Edna's girls waved from the car with an easy familiarity. Bogie was a bit slower to approach, but Mama softened his expression with a knuckle under his chin and a two-armed hug exclusively for him. Ruth shielded her eyes from the sun and rubbed the small of her back as the baby kicked.

"I'll pick you up in a couple of hours," Edna called out from the car, then drove away.

Ruth turned to face Mama.

"Well, I've got a fresh batch of sugar cookies just out of the oven. They're all on the counter." Mama threw her hands up as the girls cheered and rushed past her into the house.

"Mint tea, too?" Bogie asked.

"Just for you." She managed to get a smile out of him as he followed Addy and Dot into the kitchen.

Mama turned to Ruth, and just the expression she gave her—pure love and worry—was enough to make Ruth want to cry. When Mama's arms wrapped around her, she did cry, though she wiped the tears quickly, lest she make a scene.

"Oh, love, my heart's breaking with yours. He's a stupid man. And yet what you two have has always had the potential to be the stuff of fairytales."

Ruth dabbed a last tear away. "But fairytales don't exist in the real world."

Mama rubbed the tops of Ruth's arms and cocked her head to the side. "Maybe not, but true love does. Doesn't mean it's easy." She wrapped an arm around Ruth's shoulders and steered her toward the house. "You know, the fairytales might have the happy ending, but that doesn't mean they had it easy either. Those lovers are always fighting dragons, riding to battle, or climbing towers to find each other. They have their hard all at once. You just have it spread out over time." They were now in the kitchen, and Mama turned to Ruth, cookie in hand. "Now, sugar helps."

The kids were already well into the big saucer-sized, fluffy sugar cookies, with glasses of cold mint tea all around. Ruth bit into her cookie, letting the crunch of the sugar on top melt into the sweet, buttery texture of the cookie itself. Mama knew these were her favorite. And with the sugar scarcities of the last few years, she hadn't been able to make them often.

The kids, even Bogie, chattered on for a while as they ate their cookies. Mama wanted a full update from each and every one of them on everything they had done since they'd last seen each other. When at last the children were tired of talking, Mama set them to work on the back porch in the breezy shade sorting, of all things, quilting squares. Even little Dot could match the colored fabrics, though the entire project took about ten times longer than it would have taken Ruth.

As if she read her mind, Mama said, "You've got to give them something to accomplish. Even if they're slow. Even if they fail. They need something to try and do. And when they do succeed, boy, can they be proud when they look at their work." Already, the mess of tangled fabric was turning into neat piles of colored squares.

Ruth just stared at the children, too tired to argue.

Mama leaned back in her rocking chair. "I heard you have your own project going."

Ruth stiffened. Now, where had she heard that?

Mama's voice dropped to a whisper. "You need to be careful, Ruth. You're walking a fine line between the law and right."

"Who told you?"

"Multiple people. Women talk. People around these patch towns talk."

Ruth frowned.

"They support you. And I think your cause is noble." She hesitated, and her voice wavered. "Your Daddy would be proud."

Ruth blinked away a tear. "You really think so?" she breathed.

"I know so," Mama nodded. "He would have loved to be part of it. He fought a long time for independent miners' rights." She reached over and patted Ruth's hand. "I'm just telling you—be careful."

"Yes, Mama."

Sometime after one o'clock, they walked back to Maryd, enjoying the sunshine. Bogie ran down the street to play with some friends as Ruth and the girls worked their way up the hill to home. They were still a few houses down when Real Joe jogged toward her.

"Ruth!"

She waited for him to catch up. For a moment, she wondered if he had news on Jack. Was he gone again? Instead, Real Joe stared at her, bright-eyed with excitement.

"Is it true? You have enough people to go through with it?"

"How the heck does everyone know?" Ruth clutched her daughters' hands tighter. Real Joe, though a friend, was second in command down at the company mine. If word of the plan got to the mine boss through him, it was all over. She felt her pulse race and, for a moment, became lightheaded.

"Because we want it as bad as you do. Say the word, and I'll join you."

The lightheaded feeling cleared. He was with them. "How many miners are willing?"

"I know at least two dozen. But there are more. And if I talk to the company men, they'll be on board." He didn't have to say it; the company men respected him. "I bet every man in town will help."

"And half the women," she whispered to herself. Everyone she'd talked to had agreed that action was necessary. Edna was worried about her husband's bootleg hole up on the mountain. Three other wives down the street also had men independent mining on leased land within a few miles of town. Their tunnels were at risk if blasting continued in Maryd. Then there were the widows who were worried about the foundations of their houses. They'd spent their life savings for the privilege of staying put near their friends. They'd have nowhere else to go if their houses started falling into the earth like some were in Gilberton. Even the wives of the company miners she'd spoken with had sounded like their men would be supportive. They didn't like the minimal salary their men were earning for the back-breaking work they were doing. Yes, the town was a fuse that was already lit. It was only a matter of time.

Ruth took a steadying breath and glanced down at her girls. "Well then, soon. And what should the signal be?"

"Everyone loves your bread, Ruth. I think if you deliver some to Edna, she'll get it delivered to the next wife." He smiled, and Ruth couldn't help but let a flicker of the same hope light her face.

Then let the resistance begin with bread.

As if her poor heart needed any more strain that day, Jack was in the driveway with a full truck of coal when they got back to the house. He was waiting on the top step of the porch, wringing his hat, still in his dirty clothes. He leapt to his feet when he saw her.

"Ruth," he breathed. "I am so sorry. Never again, Ruth. I'm straightened out now. Never again."

She so badly wanted to believe him. He meant it. He always did. But would it hold this time? She had no choice but to hope. She let him pull her into his arms and didn't even care that he got her clothes filthy with coal dirt. At least he was back. He was still sober. Maybe now, everything could turn around.

More than he knew.

The girls broke their embrace, demanding their own. Jack lifted one child in each arm and placed big kisses on each of their cheeks. The girls twined their arms around his neck and held on. Jack met her eye, then closed his own. She noted the damp tears that welled from deep within him. She cupped his cheek in her hand, and he again met her eye with a love so blazing hot that every doubt she'd fought against overnight evaporated. He was fighting for her. And she was going to keep fighting for him. Slowly, he let the girls slide to their feet.

"Girls, why don't you go get washed up for dinner? I'll be along shortly." They scampered off with glee. Ruth turned back to Jack and laced her fingers into his. "There's something I think you should know about."

CHAPTER 34

Monday, June 13, 1938

As soon as his feet hit the bottom of the coal hole, Patrick's skin prickled and his heart raced. Something didn't feel right. Maybe he was overtired. Maybe he was just tired of small spaces. Maybe it was because he feared Jack would play the same game he himself had the night before and leave him alone in the coal hole. He hesitated, a hand on the bucket, ready to shake the cable like he was supposed to, but the thought of being alone down in that space made his heart race even faster. He checked his safety lamp. The flame flickered but held. Was that normal? He sniffed the damp air, which held its usual notes of damp acidic earth. He turned his headlamp down each of the narrow corridors. No visible cave-ins or rock falls. Yet still, he couldn't shake the prickle on his neck. They had a ton of work to do. The guys were gonna kill him, but better dead in the sunlight than already in the grave. He climbed back in the bucket, then shook the cable. Slowly, he was winched back up.

He saw the looks of surprise from Rhys and Jack when his head emerged from the shaft. Embarrassed, he averted his eyes, jumped out of the bucket, and backed away from the mine shaft.

"What's wrong?" Jack asked. "Cave-in?"

Rhys latched the crank and joined them.

Patrick felt heat rise to his cheeks. Already, his chest felt better. Maybe he was getting claustrophobic. "Just didn't feel right down there." Trying to make light of it, he joked, "Don't we have a canary?"

Jack and Rhys looked at him with thin-lipped expressions, their concern quickly turning to anger.

Rhys crossed his arms across his bare chest. "You know, you're not exactly a feather. It takes a lot to work that crank. You either want to work or you don't."

"Kane, you wussing out on us? Or something actually wrong down there?" Jack asked.

He described the feeling he'd had to Jack. Jack checked the lamp on Patrick's hip, the tiny flame burning steady. "Your lamp says it's fine." Jack frowned.

"That sounds like the dark is getting to you," Rhys said. "Jeez, Jack. I'll frickin' go down there. Pansy toes can work the crank. Or do you just not want to work today? I thought we sat around enough yesterday for a whole week."

"I'll work the crank. I'm telling you, it just didn't feel right."

Rhys pulled a shirt over his head and rolled up the sleeves. "Send me down, Steel Man. Hope your arms are up to the task."

"Rhys, take the lamp." Jack took the safety lamp from Patrick's belt, but didn't hand it to Rhys. "Why don't I just go down?"

"Naw, I'm overdue to dig. Too hot up here anyhow. Let's see how Tin Man lasts on the crank."

"Fine. I'll be right behind you."

"Give me until he has cranked up the first bucket of coal to prove his muscle. I don't want both of us to be down there when his arms give out."

Patrick pursed his lips and crossed his arms at their mockery. Let them have their fun. He still didn't feel the mine was right. They'd soon see there was nothing wrong with his arms either. He moved to the crank.

Rhys climbed into the bucket. "Give me thirty minutes. Should be plenty of time to get a bucket together. Hell, I'll show you boys how it's done and do it in fifteen."

Patrick started pumping the crank. The bucket began to lower. Rhys saluted Jack.

"See you soon!"

There was a mark on the cable at the depth of the bottom of the shaft. Patrick latched the winch to lock it in place, then waited with Jack, watching for the telltale shake that would cue him to start cranking again.

"You really feel like something wasn't right?" Jack asked, his gaze locked on the shaft.

"Jack, I may be a rookie miner, but I ain't afraid of the dark. And I haven't been scared of tight spaces so long as I've been doing this. The feeling I got down there was like I was someplace I shouldn't be. Every instinct screamed to get out. I'll be your crank man if need be. Not sure what's wrong with me."

Jack pulled out a battered pocket watch and checked it, then slipped it back into his pocket. "If there were gases down there, your light would have gone out." He appeared to speak less to Patrick and more to reassure himself.

"You worked yesterday, and it was fine."

"Doesn't matter. Gases can seep in from cracks in the rock. Who knows how close we are to old mine workings? No way of knowing who's dug where. One crack that leads to a stale pocket of air…could be it. I'll work on getting a second ventilation shaft dug. Today." He pulled out his watch again. The cable still hadn't moved.

As the fifteen-minute mark passed, the men grew more tense. Jack stood over the shaft, listening. Patrick held the crank, watching the cable for any movement. Again, Jack checked his watch, then called down to Rhys. He shook the cable himself, then waited a few more minutes. As they ticked by, he started staring at the pocket watch. Finally, he turned to Patrick. "It's been thirty. He should have his bucket by now. I had plenty down yesterday. Get that bucket up here and get me down."

Patrick's heart pounded as he cranked the winch as fast as he could. The bucket could be heard banging around the shaft all the way to the surface. It was very empty. Jack jumped in before the bucket had even cleared the surface and waved at Patrick to lower him down. He clicked on his headlamp.

"No more than five minutes, Steel Man! If I'm longer than that, you don't come down here; you get help. Fast." Jack couldn't hide the panic in his voice.

Patrick nodded as he cranked, again rotating the winch as fast as his arms could allow. When the marker signified the bottom of the pit, he started counting to sixty. Five minutes flew by, and still the cable didn't shake. He debated waiting another minute or two, but recognized that Jack was right. If something was wrong, he was now powerless to help without others to work the winch. He started to jog to the trucks and then saw the cable shake. Hard.

He couldn't run back up the bank to the winch fast enough. As soon as he was in place, he started cranking, embracing the burn in his arms. The bucket flew up, heavy and steady. It was as if he pulled up the entire bottom of the mine. Finally, he saw Jack's head clear the top of the shaft. He was coughing, and Rhys was limp in his arms. Patrick locked the winch in place and leapt down the bank to the shaft in two strides, pulling Rhys over the edge of the shaft and out of the bucket. Jack stumbled after him, then fell to his hands and knees and vomited.

Patrick turned Rhys on his back and listened for a heartbeat. It was faint, but steady. The man barely breathed and was unconscious, but he did breathe. Patrick turned him on his side.

"He alive?" Jack gasped.

"Yes."

Jack breathed out a sigh of relief, then started coughing again, then sobbing. Patrick had never seen a grown man cry and had no idea what to do. He just sat with Rhys, whose breathing was gradually improving. Rhys stirred, then started gasping. As he gasped, his eyes flew open. Jack helped him sit up.

Rhys hunched forward, a hand to his head. "What the hell? Did I hit my head? Feels like it's gonna split in half."

Jack started to compose himself and crawled over to wrap his arms around Rhys. The big man's eyes went wide, but he didn't protest.

"What the hell happened?" Patrick asked.

"Black damp," was all Jack had to say. All three men sobered. Gazes dropped to the safety lamp on Rhys' hip.

The flame was out. Jack sat with his head in his hands and closed his eyes. "I thought you were dead. I thought I'd done it again, and you were dead."

CHAPTER 35

Ruth knew something was very wrong when Jack and Patrick pulled into the drive. Patrick got out and said something to Jack. Ruth stood on the porch, her eyes shielded from the midday sun.

"What happened?"

It was a way of life, knowing that something always happened in the mines. The real question was how bad and to who.

Patrick stepped back from the car. He nodded politely, though somberly to Ruth, then slipped around the back of the house to the basement. Jack stared at the steering wheel of the truck, hands at two and ten, eyes unfocused. She approached him and put a hand on his shoulder, gently turning him to face her. She looked him up and down for wounds. Nothing showed.

"Jack—"

"Rhys is in the hospital."

She put a hand to her lips in shock.

"Black damp almost got him. I pulled him out, but barely in time." He finally met her eye, his own showing the panic of a wild thing cornered, or a child that knew he'd made a terrible mistake. "Patrick warned us something wasn't right. Rhys laughed at him. We both did.

I should have known better. I should have checked the mine first."

"He's alive, though?" She clutched a hand to her heart.

"It was close, Ruth. So close."

"And are you okay? You pulled him out...you breathed that same bad air."

"I'll be fine." He sighed and pulled himself from the truck. She wrapped her arms around his waist and kissed his shoulder. The tension within him wasn't ebbing. "I almost did it again, Ruth. Killed someone. What if that gas had been fire damp and not the black damp? What if we'd both gone down and breathed it, and I was too weak to get him out? I know better."

"This is not your fault. And even then, sometimes things just happen."

"Yeah, just like with Ed, right? Only thing is, they keep happening around me."

"I support you if you want to get out of mining."

He scoffed. "And what would I do? Where would we go? Should I sweep factory floors? Or do you picture us moving south and turning into farmers?"

"You still have carpentry skills—"

"All I know is mining." He was too lost in his own thoughts to listen to her. "Just like my father." He spun to her, his face alive with a guilt she hadn't placed on him. "I thought I could bury that guilt from the other accident, but now today, I let the same greed eat at me. I sent Rhys down instead of myself—instead of telling the crew we should stop for a bit and figure out what Patrick was sensing. I thought that because of his inexperience, he was being a wimp. But he's not. He's more a man than I am. He saved us both." He pulled away from her, but she pulled him back. As Ruth held him, she felt the slightest tremor in his shoulders.

It terrified her.

"Maybe he is more deserving of you," Jack muttered, and then pulled away. He pulled on his cap, took a wistful look at the house, then started walking across the street.

Ruth was stunned for a moment, then bolted after him. "Jack! Jack!"

He hesitated in the middle of the street, his back to her, already halfway to the bar.

"Don't do it." She took a few steps towards him, the baby within her suddenly heavy. She was almost to him when he jogged the rest of the way across the street. A car drove between them, the driver giving a short honk and a friendly wave, as if nothing was wrong. "Jack!"

He disappeared into the bar.

Ruth put a hand to her forehead and spun in a circle, uncertain of what to do. She could go across the street, make a big scene. Odds were it wouldn't change anything. She could retreat back to the house, go back to her chores. The girls were waiting for her to play dolls in the living room. She pressed her hand to her lips, holding back a sob. Then, with one last look at the bar, she slowly returned to the house.

She couldn't fight his demons for him.

No matter how Patrick had tried to assure Jack that the incident wasn't his fault, he wasn't sure any words were getting through. The man was worried about his friend, rightly so. Patrick hadn't seen a man so close to death in a long time. Rhys was pale as a ghost when he reached the surface. Only by some miracle was his heart still beating. By equal miracle, the truck started on the first try, and the three of them were able to rush Rhys to Pottsville for further care. The doctors may have taken over from there, but it still fell to Jack to tell Rhys' wife what had happened.

She hadn't taken it well.

If he was honest with himself, Patrick wasn't taking it well either. It didn't matter the industry; there was danger everywhere. It didn't matter how much you talked about safety; mistakes still happened. He was glad he'd trusted his gut and gotten out of the mine when he did, or that would have been him.

That feeling settled in his gut.

How many times would he skirt around death? At least this time, the men he was with had avoided it, too. That moment of panic when Jack didn't return to the cable bucket felt as if it had just happened, relived again and again. Could he have acted in time to save both of them? He knew now he wouldn't have. It had been so close. Only by Jack's heroic rescue had the two men gotten out alive. He'd have to point that out to Jack. Maybe that would make him feel better.

He closed his eyes to the spray of the shower. His shoulder still burned from turning the windlass. He flexed it, trying to stretch. Rhys was certainly a beast to crank that all day, every day, with tons of coal. Maybe that's why seeing Rhys powerless in a hospital bed had been so nerve-racking to both of them.

He turned the shower to ice cold, then off. When he returned to the living room, Ruth was sitting on the floor with the girls, a pile of doll clothes spread out among them. The girls were deep into their play, picking new outfits for their dolls as Addy dictated what adventure the dolls would go on next. But Ruth sat staring at the pile in a daze, her eyes glazed, expression blank.

"What's wrong?"

Ruth shook her head, tried to wave him off. She straightened the ruffle on a doll's dress. But Patrick knew her better than that by now.

"Was it Jack? What did he do?"

"Nothing," she said, but her voice cracked.

"Where is he?"

Her lips pressed into a thin line.

Patrick laid a gentle hand on her shoulder. Again he asked, his tone quiet and soft, "Where is he?"

She avoided his eye but waved her hand towards the front of the house. Instantly, Patrick understood. Jack had gone to drown his guilt. Patrick gritted his teeth, knowing what this meant to Ruth and the family. They'd only just started repairing the damage to their relationship. If Jack went back to alcohol now, could he turn away again? Or would he run, hide from his family life to drift across the state?

Like Patrick.

Patrick gave Ruth's shoulder a squeeze. "I'll talk to him."

She shook her head. "It won't stop anything. He can't help himself."

But Patrick didn't believe that. He'd been in Jack's shoes. Maybe it was finally time to tell someone why he wasn't in Pittsburgh anymore.

CHAPTER 36

The bar was nearly empty this early on a sunny Monday afternoon. The lighting was dim, with streaks of sunlight cutting through worn curtains to highlight the swirls of smoke that lingered in the air from two retirees in a corner by the radio. The patches the light made on the floor highlighted years of hard wear by booted, working men's feet. Mary kept her distance down the far end of the bar, washing glasses. Jack was seated on a stool, staring into a glass of whiskey.

Patrick slipped onto the stool next to him.

"It's just one glass," Jack whispered. The pain in his voice told Patrick that he hadn't yet taken a sip. That meant there was still hope.

"Mary, two Cokes please." He'd be broke again until they took the next truckload of bootlegged coal to the breaker, but this was necessary. Maybe he could add washing dishes to his job list.

Patrick waited until both Cokes were uncapped and Jack had taken a small sip, then he started talking. "You know, it's dangerous work we do."

Jack snorted.

"And we're human. We do our best, and we still make mistakes. In our line of work, those can turn deadly.

Or, sometimes work turns deadly when it isn't our fault at all. Today, there was nothing you could have done differently. Neither of us knew what was in that shaft today."

Jack shook his head. "You did. And I should have listened to you."

"I was lucky."

Jack again shook his head. "No, you trusted your gut. I got lazy."

Patrick hesitated. "Why didn't my lamp go out?"

Jack took another swallow of Coke. "The damp can follow you. Rhys was maybe fifty feet down the tunnel when I found him. His lamp *had* gone out. Maybe just you going down and up disturbed the pocket and pulled the bad air through the mine." He looked at his whiskey again. "I should have been the one down there."

"But you weren't. He was. You can't regret surviving. That's not fair." Patrick took a drink of his soda. "You saved Rhys' life today, Jack. You braved the damp yourself. You were strong enough—and he's a big man—to get him out so fast you didn't collapse yourself." He took a deep breath. "Imagine if the damp had been down there the other night. I ignored your request to come up. I could have killed you." Patrick twisted his Coke bottle, then took a long sip of the cold, sweet fluid. He took a fortifying breath, then committed. "It wouldn't be the first time I got a friend killed."

Jack's eyebrows raised, but he didn't look away from the whiskey.

Patrick stared into the mirror that hung behind the bar. It was hard to face himself as he relived his tale, but maybe it was better this way. He could watch that pain in his own eyes. That made it more real. Maybe when he was done, he'd feel less numb.

"It was in the steel mill, about two years ago. I was a mechanic. Fixed all sorts of equipment to keep things running. Lots of moving parts in a steel mill. Well, the one day I was eager to get home. Had a date with my fiancée. There was an ore cart that needed to be fixed. A bolt was sheared off. Well, I didn't have a three-quarter inch bolt, so I used a five-eighth. The wheel held, but I knew without the right size it would break again. I figured I'd go back the next day, make it right."

Patrick drank another swallow of Coke, wishing it were laced with all the things he'd sworn never to touch again. "I went on my date. We went to the movies and then drank at a bar most of the night. I made it to work the next morning, but I was barely on time. The cart I'd 'repaired' was already in service. I didn't say anything. Knew I'd get in trouble. Figured I'd just fix it that afternoon." He hesitated, that familiar pit of guilt twisting in his stomach. He hadn't told anyone this yet. The pain hurt as if it were yesterday. He met his own eyes in the mirror behind the bar. "Car didn't make it until the afternoon. The wheel gave out. The car tipped. My best friend was crushed underneath several tons of ore. He didn't survive long enough to get to the hospital. The car set off a chain reaction that ended up knocking the molten ore bucket, which made quite the fireworks show. More people got hurt."

Patrick closed his eyes to the screams that echoed from his memory. He felt the hopelessness that had overwhelmed him as if he was watching it all over again. The blame for every one of those injuries, and his friend's death, lay squarely on his shoulders. He opened his eyes to stare at Jack's whiskey.

"I never went back to the mill. I knew if they investigated, they'd find it was my fault. My job was over. My career was over. Hell, they had a right to press criminal charges. So I've drifted ever since."

"What about your fiancée?"

That stone in his gut turned the old wound raw again. "Couldn't look her in the eye. The man killed, my friend—it was her brother."

"Damn," Jack breathed.

They sipped their Cokes in silence.

Patrick pointed to the whiskey. "We both could drown our pain in that, but it doesn't change the past. It only causes more pain. Believe me, for months after the accident, I tried. I left everything, tried to drown myself in a bottle, thinking that if I was numb, I wouldn't remember everything before." He had to pause a moment, remembering what it was like to wake up in places he didn't remember walking to, like dirty culverts or the beds of cheap prostitutes. Had Jack ever been that bad? He doubted it. But now was not the time to compare himself. This wasn't about his battle now. Patrick plunged ahead, intent on driving one more point home.

"I think all the time about Sally. I wonder if she knows it was my fault. Would she have forgiven me? Did I hurt her even more by abandoning her in her time of grief? Really, it was selfish of me. I only thought of my pain, not hers. She lost a brother *and* her fiancée, a man who had promised to stay by her side." Patrick shifted in his seat, aware how the guilt and blame when properly placed could paint a man in shades of the devil. Jack wasn't the worst man in town. It was he, the Steel Man. He nudged Jack with an elbow. "Rhys is going to be okay. This—" He nudged the whiskey with a fingertip as if it were venomous. "This isn't going to solve anything."

Jack watched the whiskey, a dazed expression on his face.

"You've got a mighty fine woman with Ruth. Beautiful kids. She needs you. More importantly, the woman is head over heels in love with you. You can't throw her away. Don't make my mistake."

Jack nodded slowly, then finished off his coke. "Mary..." he waved her over. He pushed the empty Coke bottle and the whiskey towards her. "I'm finished."

Mary gave him a wry smile and made it all disappear.

Jack turned to Patrick. "You know, I drug my feet for months, thinking that Ruth wouldn't want me back. Yet you tell me she still loves me. And I know you're right. Geez, imagine if I didn't come back, her so heavy with my child." He pointed at the bar, meeting Patrick's eye. "It wouldn't hurt to go back to Pittsburgh, find your Sally again. Maybe she's moved on. Maybe she's still waiting for you. You can't close that door until you find out. Then you can start healing."

Patrick frowned. He'd thought about going back a thousand times, mostly just to apologize before leaving again. Maybe going out west. He never considered that Sally might actually still want him, that they'd be able to repair the great damage he'd done.

Jack slapped a hand on his shoulder. "Think about it. After all, after tomorrow, no one in this town's going to have a job anyway."

Patrick's gaze narrowed. "What are you talking about?"

"Steel Man..." Jack pulled on his hat. "We're gonna need your help underground tonight."

CHAPTER 37

"Mom!" Bogie yelled as he came in the front door. "They're coming home!"

Ruth left her spoon on the counter and wiped her hands on her apron. She stopped at the front screen door, looking out as the two men crossed the street towards her. They didn't look inebriated, not even Jack. She pushed through the door, Bogie behind her, and the two of them watched the final approach. Jack stopped at the bottom of the steps. Patrick came up them, tipped his hat, and then slipped past her and Bogie into the house.

"Ruth..." Jack met her eye, the emotion within him visible.

She saved him the words. She took the stairs down to him in three big strides and threw her arms around his neck. He smelled of pine and coal dirt and tobacco smoke from the bar. But not alcohol. Not even a trace. As his arms closed around her, she felt her own emotions tremble, then erupt. She sobbed into his shoulder. His hands rubbed her back as he held her.

"I'm so sorry," he breathed.

She pulled back only long enough to kiss him, then buried her head in his shoulder again, her tears wetting his shirt. "You can't leave us again."

"I won't."

"Promise?" Her voice cracked, which she hated, but she didn't regret pleading. He needed to know how much she loved him, needed him.

"Promise."

Ruth heard the screen door softly tap shut as Bogie retreated into the house. The couple separated enough for another lingering kiss, not caring who looked over at their front porch. Let that put the rumors to rest once and for all. When their lips finally parted, Jack caressed Ruth's cheek.

"When we were on the way to the hospital, Rhys told me to tell you it should be tonight."

She shut her mouth again, stunned.

"If I hadn't been so wrapped up in my own issues, I'd have helped you. But it sounds like your women friends have all convinced the men."

"They're gonna do it?"

He nodded.

Bogie burst through the screen door. His voice full of excitement, he asked, "When?"

Ruth winced. Of course her son knew all about this secret plan. If it wasn't his friends that told him, it could have been Mama herself. Her lips began to turn into a smile at that thought. Mama secretly prying all the boys in town with cookies and knowledge of a secret rebellion so that they'd tell their parents. Word got around fast.

Jack smiled, his eyes lingering on Ruth. "Can you signal the rest of the town?"

She already had bread baking, though she hadn't expected it to be *that* bread. Was she ready to start a revolution? There would be no going back. And who knew how the county would end up prosecuting those involved. "Yes," she breathed. She only had to say the word. Or—bake the word.

Jack kissed her forehead. "Then let's do it. For Rhys. For your father and all the other miners who've given their lives to this industry. For the whole town."

CHAPTER 38

Ruth's heart pounded as she peered from behind the curtain like some fugitive. She reminded herself over and over that all she had done was take a loaf of bread to Edna's house. That was not an offence that would put her in jail. And yet as she watched one housewife after another crisscross the street with that basket and loaf, she couldn't help but think of what their men were going to do. What would the cost of that be? Jail? Worse?

Maybe, just maybe, it would solve all the town's problems and give their descendants a future. The company would stop threatening their houses with giant shovels and dynamite. The independent miners could keep their coal holes. The bootleggers could work. Maybe it would, at the very least, force the company to sit down and discuss the town's opinions and make concessions for the residents' quality of life. Not everything in this world could be about profit.

Ruth felt a man come behind her and instinctively knew it wasn't Jack. The fresh smell of his soap gave it away. Patrick reached an arm past her to push the curtain a little wider. Ruth didn't move, didn't feel threatened or uncomfortable. It was like standing next to her brother, God rest his soul. How could a man live in her home only two weeks and have such a profound effect on her entire family?

"Crazy how such a big thing can start with such a little one," Patrick said.

It took Ruth a moment to remember he was talking about their plans for the evening.

They watched Mrs. Krajnak jog across the street with her shuffle-limp stride. It was the fastest Ruth had ever seen the laundress move. She disappeared onto another neighbor's porch, basket in hand.

"Are we doing the right thing, Steel Man?"

"Right is complicated. The company won't think this is right. From what I've seen, what they want to do to Maryd isn't right either."

"I want something to be left of this place when my children are grown."

"I suspect there will be. With residents like you voicing their opinions, there will be."

She turned to face him, looking him in the eye. "Thank you, Mr. Kane. For whatever it is you said to my husband. A few nights ago and again today. I feel like we're finally starting to get him back." Fragile as their relationship may be, if they both kept trying, there was hope for healing there.

Patrick's gaze met hers without wavering. "You are welcome, ma'am." His gaze flicked to her lips, then back to her eyes. "I may as well tell you that I'll be leaving tonight."

Her eyebrows shot up. "Because of all this?" She gestured out the window.

Patrick shook his head. "No. I'm definitely going to stay for this. But your husband is back now. He's a hard worker, and I expect he'll make sure you don't need us boarders from now on. I feel it's time for me to move on."

She couldn't help but smile lightly. "You never stay anywhere long, do you?"

"Maybe one day I'll find my place." He reached into his pocket and pulled out a wad of bills. "This is all I've got. It's not the full amount we agreed to, but since I'm leaving short of the end of the month and Jack owes me two and a half days of labor—"

She closed his fingers around the money and pushed his fist back towards him. "You've given me far more, Mr. Kane." She turned to the window, where Jack was walking up the hill from the general store with a new box of dynamite on his shoulder. She could hear him whistling. She turned back to Patrick. "Thank you."

He stared at his fist a moment, then slowly put the bills back into his pocket. "That's not why I did it."

"I know. That's why it means so much more. To both of us." She smiled up at him. "Stay in touch, won't you? The girls like postcards. When you can send them."

Patrick nodded. "Right. That I can do."

Ruth thought she heard a waver in his voice. He stepped back from her. "Gonna miss your cooking." His face lit into a smile.

She smoothed her hands down her apron. "Well, tonight we're gonna have a feast. Let's do halupkis, mashed potatoes, and I think I can pull together a strawberry shortcake by nightfall. I hope you're hungry." She went to the cupboards and started moving, her hands flying as fast as hummingbirds. Cooking, yes, that could quell her anxiety until dark. And if they all ended up in jail tomorrow, let tonight be the most memorable meal any of them had ever had.

The vase that had fallen off the windowsill during the last blasting caught Ruth's eye. She carefully lifted it and ran a finger over the cracks where she'd glued the glass back together. They sparkled in the light like gems. It would never hold water, but still, the deep blue gave the kitchen a pop of color she craved. She gently placed it in one of the cupboards, where it couldn't fall again. Then she moved around the house and did the same with every other glass or fragile item, securing them away. Things might have shaken a little bit before. Tonight, the trees themselves were going to wonder if their roots grew deep enough to hold on.

CHAPTER 39

It was eleven o'clock when the miners filed out of town under the light of the moon. Their picks and shovels rested over their shoulders; free hands clutched dark lanterns. The women walked with them, their hands full of explosives or children that couldn't be left at home. Only the crunch of gravel and the swish of clothing could be heard. After they had passed the mine boss's house at the bottom of Main Street, they lit their lanterns and filed towards the mine.

Ruth walked between Jack and Patrick at the front of the column. Bogie walked just ahead of them, purposefully carrying his father's long hand drill over his bony shoulder. The girls were under Edna's watchful eye back at home, likely as wide awake as the rest of the town. Knowing Edna, she probably had them set up with chairs at the window that overlooked the mine, watching. Even the baby in Ruth's womb churned tonight, as if he or she could feel the excitement and danger in the air. There was so much that could go wrong. For once, she wanted to witness every last bit of it.

They spotted Roger's shadow at the mine entrance. He was already on his feet, shotgun in hand. "Back off! Back off, I say!" The man had grit to stand up to so great a mob.

Jack called out, "Roger, our trouble isn't with you! You're outnumbered. Just come away from there so no one gets hurt."

"I've got a job to do," Roger insisted. He didn't raise the gun to his shoulder, though. "You take up your issues with the mine boss tomorrow, the right way."

"That's been done. And he ain't listened!" a man from the back of the crowd yelled.

It was Patrick who advanced, much to Ruth's heart-pounding chagrin. He spoke quietly to Roger, and then when they were level with each other, quieter words were exchanged. More gesturing. Then Patrick calmly took the shotgun from Roger's hands and led him away from the mine.

"All yours, boys," Jack shouted out.

The miners around them clicked on headlamps and filed down into the mine. Two men stayed back with Roger as guards, steering him toward the mine office. Roger went willingly, watching over his shoulder and shaking his head. Ruth thought she heard him mutter, "Ain't worth dying for."

Jack appeared in front of her, his face alive.

"You be careful," she warned.

"Always." As if to prove his point, he lit his safety lamp and hung it on his hip. He kissed her forehead and went to turn, but she caught his shirt and pulled him back.

"Kiss me proper."

And he did. His lips pressed into hers with a passion and urgency that made her heart pound. His body pressed against her, accentuating the curve of her breast and belly.

His hands went to her face, gently and firmly locking her deep into the kiss, which radiated through her body like a sparking fuse. Then he pulled away, a mischievous glint in his eye, not unlike the expression he'd passed to his children.

"See you in a bit, my love," he said, then hurried down into the mine.

Then the men of the town were underground.

Patrick had never seen so many miners move so fast. Dynamite was being tossed through the air like it was baseballs. Drills whirred in every corner of the mine, and when the noise of one went quiet, the calls of "Need a stick!" and "Toss a blasting cap!" echoed through the tunnels. He did his best to stay out of the way, shuttling tools back and forth as fast as they were demanded.

He looked at the big timbers above his head, and at one point let his gaze linger on the chute he'd worked so hard to rebuild. These tunnels had taken so much effort to dig. It was somewhat sad to destroy them.

"You're gonna blast it all?"

"Yes," Real Joe smiled, then spit a wad of tobacco. He handed Patrick a stick of dynamite.

Patrick held it at arm's length.

Real Joe motioned towards the chute. "Time you learned how to blast, my friend. Figure out a way to attach that there. Oh, and here." He handed Patrick a blasting cap. "Press it in, nice and gentle."

Patrick felt his adrenaline surge as he held the explosive and thought back to all the times he'd watched the other miners in the past few weeks. It took him a minute longer, but he had the cap in place and then the stick wedged under the troublesome chute in no time.

Real Joe inspected his work. "Now you're thinking like a miner." He gave Patrick a slap on the back and started heading towards the mine entrance, checking explosives and sweeping men along with him as he went. The mine train, loaded now with every piece of movable mining equipment instead of men, chugged ahead of them.

From what Patrick saw, the mine was wired red hot.

"Where's Jack?" Real Joe called out at the tunnel intersection.

"Here!" Jack called, jogging from the depths of the mine. "We got everyone from Number Two."

"Number One clear!" shouted Red, emerging from the opposite direction.

"Then let's get topside for the show." Real Joe clapped a broad hand on Jack's shoulder.

A cluster of women gathered to the side of the mine office building, arms crossed, anxiously waiting for the men to come back to the surface. What if the mine boss woke? What if someone had leaked their plan and called the police? The women were tense, their voices hushed in the moonlight. After what seemed an eternity but was likely only an hour, they heard the mine train returning, and they streamed towards the mine entrance.

Crates of dynamite, blasting caps, and tools were unloaded from the mine cars. The women and most of the boys of the town, like Bogie, moved it all to the side, far from the mine entrance. Some of the crates were heavy, but Ruth relished the burn in her arms. She lifted whatever she could that the awkwardness of her bump didn't impede. Then the men started to appear, their coal-dirt-etched faces alight with excitement. They found their women, and everyone started to pull back from the mine entrance.

The last men out of the mine were Jack, Patrick, Real Joe, and Red.

"Confirm all topside," Real Joe shouted to the foreman.

The mine foreman, who'd also been helping, had kept a good handle on who was in the mine, as he always did. Instead of using miner tags, which could have been incriminating for all involved, the men had left their hats in a long line next to the mine train tracks. All hats were now claimed. "All here!"

"Hey. Hey!" The mine owner came running down the hill in his pajamas. "What are you doing?"

"All clear!" Jack shouted, ignoring the man.

"Clear!" "Clear!" Echoed around the coal yard. Everyone stepped even further from the mine entrance. Hands clenched each other in anticipation. Children hung on their mother's skirts, their fingers pressed into their ears, waiting.

The mine boss tried to run to the mine, his arms waving. His face was red and breath puffing as he leveled with Jack and Ruth. "Stop, stop!"

Jack caught him by the belt of his bathrobe before he could get too close to the drift.

"You're gonna wanna stay back. You're just in time for the fireworks." Jack smiled, his headlamp illuminating the boss's look of horror.

"I'll call the police. They'll arrest all of you!" The mine boss ran for the office.

Someone pressed the ignition switch into Ruth's hand. "It's only right." Before she could see who it was, they were gone. She looked at Jack, her eyes wide.

"Go for it," he said.

She smiled then, life pulsing through her body like she was a teenage girl again. "Fire in the hole!" Then she turned the switch, and the click echoed across the suddenly quiet mine site.

The coal boss stopped halfway to the office and stared. "No..."

At first, nothing happened. Jack twined his fingers with Ruth's. She squeezed onto him tight. She let the ignition box fall from her fingers into the black dust at her feet.

Then the first charge went off. The earth shook. That set off a chain reaction, and soon the ground shook as if there was an earthquake. It was far enough underground that the noise wasn't unbearable, yet still Ruth flinched away. Finally, a great shower of dirt and smoke exploded out from the mouth of the tunnel, forcing those closest to the shaft to turn their backs and retreat even further. The plume seemed to rise into the heavens, taller than any building Ruth had ever seen. The workings at the entrance to the mine collapsed, splintering. Small pieces of burning wood scattered around the mine entrance like sputtering torches to fallen miners.

As the dust settled, all headlamps turned towards the mine entrance. The mine boss approached first, each step tentative. There, where the outer mine workings had been, there was now just a pit of rock and debris. The mine was no more. The train tracks leading down dead-ended into a wall of earth that would be nearly impossible to dig out.

"No," the mine boss said in shock.

The townspeople didn't cheer. They stood watching the dust and smoke rise against the starry sky, their faces somber. Ruth turned to look up at Jack, his eyes glassy with a mix of emotions. He looked down at her, their eyes meeting. He turned off his headlamp, letting the moonlight illuminate the space between them. Then he raised her hand to his lips and kissed her fingers.

Sirens sounded in the distance, and soon a police car pulled up, siren blaring and flashers spinning, coating the people of Maryd in a secondary firework display of red, white, and blue light. Sheriff Fred Holman got out slowly and put his cap on his head. He scanned the scene, his eyes lingering on Jack just a second longer than the rest. Ruth squeezed Jack's hand.

The mine boss stormed over to Fred, bathrobe fluttering in the breeze. "Did you see what they did? Arrest them! Arrest them all. Look at this," he gestured to the group as a whole, "These are the perpetrators, right here!"

The crowd of four hundred residents faced Sheriff Holman. Fred pursed his lips and looked to Jack. "Anyone down there?"

"No, sir," Jack promised. "And no damage to the company's equipment either." He gestured towards the pile that had been unloaded haphazardly next to the mine train. Then he smirked. "At least not any equipment that could be moved."

Sheriff Holman took off his hat, scratched the top of his head, and then replaced it. "Well, good night then." To the dismay of the mine boss, he slipped back into his car.

The boss ran to the window, the belt of his bathrobe trailing behind him. "Wait a second, this mob just destroyed my mine! Arrest them!"

The sheriff looked at the crowd, then shook his head. "What do you want me to do? Arrest the whole town?" The police car turned over, and the sheriff slowly pulled away from the scene.

Ruth couldn't help but smile as she watched the boss's theatrics. He looked like he was torn on whether to storm the crowd, run to the smoking mine, or cry. He settled for locking himself in the mine office. She looked up at Jack, whose gaze lingered over the site of the mine.

"Amazing how something that can take so long to create can be destroyed so quickly. It's as if it was never even there."

"Kind of like us," Ruth mused. Jack looked down on her, brow furrowed. She explained. "We only have a short time on this earth. The mark we make is so small." She looked over to Bogie, who stood off to one side with his friends, throwing rocks at the dust plume still rising from where the mine entrance had been. "We can leave scars, or we can build something that lasts."

Jack raised her hand to his lips and kissed her knuckles. "I want us to last, Ruth."

She smiled, feeling the last chords of pain fall away. "Good. Because I do too. I chose you on our wedding day, Jack Flannigan. And I choose you again now."

He twined his arm around her waist and kissed her temple. "I promise to continue to choose you from here on out, Ruth. Every day."

Patrick scanned the group of townsfolk, all at once feeling part of something while also feeling like a total outsider. They stood with their families, with their friends, while he stood off to the side alone. Ruth and Jack were hand in hand like the reunited lovers they were. Bogie had his friends. Isaac had the other old timers. The women had their husbands, friends, and church members. The bootleggers had their union. The colliery miners had their coworkers. The town had united for a common goal, and they had accomplished that goal. Patrick, though, stood off by himself, alone. He was the owl sitting on top of the tree, watching all the other animals play.

The mine company was going to have a heck of a mess to figure out.

Real Joe strode over to Patrick, hands in his pockets. "I guess you're gonna have to bootleg for real, huh? Sorry about your job."

Patrick shrugged. "I'm not much worse off than anyone else in this town."

"Heard about Rhys. That has to throw your mind for a loop."

"Yeah, it does. But I think I was missing the sun before all this, anyway." He squinted up at the moon, which even then, compared to the dark of the mines, seemed to shine with living light.

Real Joe furrowed his brow. "You aren't gonna keep working with Jack's crew?"

Patrick looked back to Ruth, who seemed to glow with happiness in the moonlight. "Nope, I think I'm done. I've got some unfinished business of my own to attend to." Like finding Sally and apologizing. Maybe.

"What will you do?"

Patrick shrugged. "Dunno. Maybe be a mechanic. Seems to be a growing need for trucks in this state. Maybe I'll go further west, see what I can find." Either way, it was time to move on again.

Real Joe spat a stream of tobacco juice onto the ground. They watched the crowd in silence for a while. Now that the dust had settled, the townspeople were slowly beginning to disperse. "Well, nice knowing you, Mr. Kane. If you're ever in the area again..." He stuck out his hand, and they shook.

Patrick smiled. "I'll keep in touch somehow. You've got a small town. If I send a letter, they'll find you."

"Right you are."

"Stay safe down there, my friend."

"Always." Real Joe tipped his hat and joined the townsfolk returning to their homes.

Patrick picked up his rucksack from where he'd stashed it alongside the road. Heaving the bag over his shoulder, he caught Ruth's eye. He raised one hand in farewell. She raised hers and mouthed goodbye. She pointed him out to Jack, but Patrick was already moving into the night. He wasn't sure where he'd go. Maybe into Tamaqua, then catch a coal train back to Pittsburgh. He could sleep on the train. Maybe he'd find a new kind of work along the way. Either way, he wasn't going to stick around to see what the judge and jury did about this town.

The world was ever changing, and there was adventure in the air. He'd move as he wished until he found someone, something, that held on to him as tightly as Ruth held on to Jack.

Epilogue

Friday June 17, 1938

"Mama, hurry up!" Bogie shouted and honked the horn of Jack's pickup. Beep, beep.

Ruth ushered Dot and Addy ahead of her. "Dot, your doll does not have to come on this adventure."

"But she wants to!" Dot whined. "Besides, I want Mr. Patrick's postcard! I wanna show Daddy."

"We'll show him when he gets home." The card was the girls' new pride and joy. Already it hung prominently on the icebox. The black and white picture of a Pittsburgh steel mill fascinated Dot for hours. The words on the back were cryptic, saying "Tell Jack he was right." Ruth wasn't sure what that referred to, but clearly their boarder had returned home.

"Mama!" Bogie shouted again.

"Oh for heaven's sake." Ruth scooped Dot onto her hip, despite the little girl's whining. "Addy, climb in."

Addy bit her lip and climbed into the truck like she was climbing a mountain. Bogie reached across the seat and grabbed her hand, pulling her in. Then Ruth set Dot on the seat next to her and pulled herself into the driver's seat with a wince. Her belly seemed to get bigger every week now. She turned the key and the truck fired to life.

"Everyone ready?"

The children perched on the edge of the seat, their hands reaching for the dash eagerly. Even Dot had already forgotten her doll. Ruth smiled, then pulled out of the drive, joining the line of cars and trucks that filed out of Maryd.

"Bogie, you might as well open the window and start waving that flag."

Bogie beamed as he rolled the window down and leaned into the sunny summer air. He let out a whoop as he leaned partway out, waving a small American flag. The children in the other vehicles did the same. A bystander would think it was the Fourth of July, but it was not the Fourth. No, this was another motorcade entirely.

Every vehicle in town joined their line, each laden with residents waving flags and honking horns. Their line wove through the hills and all the way to the jail in Pottsville, where twenty-six of the town's men were being held. When the cars began to fill the lot and the streets around, the eyes of the police inside went wide. They watched the crowd with nervousness, knowing full well what this town was capable of.

"We're here to post bail!" Pal, former foreman of the company mine, yelled out.

"For who?" an officer asked.

"All of them!"

The officer stared at Pal, then scanned the crowd now surrounding the complex, some three hundred residents strong, cheering and waving their flags. Ruth heard Bogie and the girls add their voices to the mix, and she couldn't help but raise her own fist into the air and let out a shout of her own.

The officer went into the office for a moment, then emerged with a list. One by one he read the names of the twenty-four men who had been arrested. As each name was called, that man's wife or a family member came forth with the five hundred dollars of bail money. It was nearly a year's salary per man, a sum no one family had on hand. But together, the town had pooled the money to release every last one of them.

"Jack Flannigan, five hundred dollars!"

Ruth handed the envelope to Bogie and gave him a slight push forward. The boy squared his shoulders and marched forward, offering the money to the officer. The man counted it, nodded, and the town cheered. A few minutes later, Jack emerged from the jail. His eyes lit up as he took in the crowd, and then they settled on his family. His face lit up in a smile, and he jogged over to them, scooped Addy and Dot into a twirling hug, and then pressed a kiss onto Ruth's lips. When he set the girls down, he turned to Bogie and laid a hand on each of the boy's shoulders.

"Thank you for taking care of our girls, son."

"Sure, Dad." Bogie smiled, but his back was still ramrod straight, as if he was afraid to show any weakness that would disappoint his father.

Then Jack pulled Bogie into a hug, pressing the boy's head into his chest. "I am so proud of you, Bogie."

The emotion broke through the boy's resolve, and he turned into just a boy again, burying his face into Jack's shirt to hide his tears. He clung to his father, and Jack held him, rubbing his back. He lifted his eyes to Ruth, and they glistened with emotion. She pulled the girls into her, her own lips quivering with emotion as the last names on the list were read out, and the men's bail was posted. A cheer echoed through the crowd.

"Yo, Jack, you gonna come get a drink to celebrate?" one of his friends asked.

Ruth involuntarily tensed.

Jack looked down at her and shook his head. "Not today." The miner moved on, and still Jack's eyes were locked with Ruth's. "We're gonna be alright," Jack whispered.

She nodded, then let her smile break through, and laughed. Yes, they were going to be quite all right.

Sometime late in July, Patrick leaned back against a pile of coal as the train under him rattled and chugged up the tracks, winding through the picturesque Appalachian Mountains. He took out a newspaper he'd found on a discard pile in the last city and shook it. The woman next to him shifted, rattling coal beneath the worn blanket they shared. She laid her head on his chest and sighed with contentment.

"Whatcha reading?"

"Oh, nothing much."

"Planning our next adventure?"

He kissed the top of her head. "Maybe." His eyes locked on an article. "Well ain't that something. That little patch town pulled it off."

"Pulled what off?"

Patrick read, his smile brightening with every word in the short article tucked into the *Pottsville Republican*. Maryd had done it. With the help of the Independent

Miners, the attention of the governor, and some good legal counsel, all charges had been dropped for the residents charged with malicious mischief. He snorted. Blowing up a coal mine only counted as "malicious mischief". Better yet, the miners got what they wanted. The company was restricted to where they could strip mine and even had to offer any jobs that came available to independent miners. He folded the paper and tucked it behind his head, wrapping his arm around the woman next to him.

"They created change, that's what. Maybe there's hope for the rest of us after all."

Historical Note

This novel is a lesson in not taking our elders for granted. It would not exist if it were not for the memories of my grandparents, father, aunts, uncles, and other Maryd residents whose stories I have collected throughout my lifetime. Most of what I have gleaned has never been written down. Some of it was embellished by the storyteller or distorted by memory. The records of mine inspectors and old newspapers helped fill a lot of blanks. I believe the list of where I took creative license is shorter than the truths held within, so let me begin there.

WHAT I IMAGINED

As I said in my author's note, all of my characters and their families are my own creation. The exception being Sheriff Fred Holman, whom I kept in name only, since he was the one quoted in the newspaper article that inspired this tale.

I do not know if Maryd had a mine train, so that was my creation, as was the depth of the 1938 drift mine. Records are very sparse. I did learn from a resident that there used to be a small-gauge railroad in town, much like the train ride that runs in Knobel's Amusement Park in Elysburg. I do not know when exactly that rail line ran or if it entered the mine, but I used it and pictured the train that runs into the Ashland Pioneer Coal Tunnel as my inspiration. We know from newspaper articles that the Maryd Mine Company dug a brand new drift mine into the mountain in May of 1938, but I don't know how deep they were. The first hundred feet were blasted shut, but was that the entire working or was that just the entrance? To my knowledge, no maps of the underground workings exist. If anyone knows of any, I'd love to hear from you.

I also relocated the breaker and mine entrance from the top of the hill above Main Street to down in the valley below the town, where I remember seeing an old breaker out my grandparents' window. I'm not sure if that was the actual Maryd breaker or another one, nor if that was where the mine entrance was, but the story flowed with the mine down there, so I kept it. The block building that I describe as the mine office still stands just below the town intersection, and a resident told me that it was in fact the pay office. He is still working to have the ruin preserved as a historical site.

MINING HISTORY IN MARY D

This leads to the factual side of this tale.

The town of Maryd was founded in 1904 by colliery owner Truman M. Dodson, who named the town for his wife Mary Delores Dodson. The area was being mined prior to those years by the Kaska Williams Coal Company, going back as early as 1875. Once Dodson got his mine going, the town quickly filled up, with workers living in company housing. Most of the homes in Maryd are half doubles, with a few freestanding houses. The old mine boss's house really does stand at the bottom of

Main Street, and the modern-day post office was once the company store turned general store. The old post office was up on the top of the hill to the south. The original coal breaker was up on the north hill. The concrete ruins of the pump house can still be seen in the woods, just barely out of eyesight of the townhouses that line North Main.

I remember my dad taking me down to the old breaker that could be seen from my grandparents' window when the leaves were off the trees, warning me never to venture inside. It was a rusty, crumbling ruin. It has since been torn down, and the site is now the Maryd ballfield complex, which was part of a federal and state clean-up project. More on that in a bit. I assumed there was just this one breaker in Mary D, but after conversations with residents who didn't remember it being located where I remember it, I began to think I was losing my mind. That said, I think I've rounded up enough old photographs to prove it existed, though if it was considered by locals to be the Maryd breaker or the Bell Colliery breaker remains a mystery. I think it's safe to say there were several breakers in the area.

The Maryd Colliery of Dodson's era was running drift, shaft, and slope mines into several different veins. The records of the mine inspectors from 1906 to 1919 are incredibly detailed, right down to how many feet they were digging into which vein and when they built new mule stables. The breaker burned in 1908. In 1915 there was a disaster in which six men were killed when the cage lifting them from the bottom of the mine was overwound, tipped, and the men fell to their deaths. Production peaked in 1915 and 1916 when they were pulling

370,000 tons of coal or more out of the mountain. It was a very profitable mine.

When the Depression hit in 1929, Dodson supposedly lost his fortune in the stock market and had to sell the mine. Hazel Brook Coal Company ran the Maryd mine for a few more years until their lease ran out in 1932. There was hope someone else would step in to renew the lease, even General Electric from New York considered it, but alas, there were no takers. The company "robbed the pillars" as they left, leaving the mine highly unstable. The mine equipment was sold off, right down to the pumps in the pump house and the machinery in the breaker. The mine was closed, and without the pumps pumping, the tunnels quickly filled with water. The residents of Maryd lost their primary source of income, and to make matters worse, most of the other mines in the area had also closed, by the dozens. Hundreds of men were now unemployed.

My uncle heard the story of the company dumping coal back into the mine shaft from my great-grandfather, who claimed to have linked his bootleg hole down into the old workings and took advantage of that easy coal. How much of that story is true we'll never know.

On the plus side, 1932 was the year the town was privatized. Residents were given the option to buy their houses, and most of them accepted. The town was no longer owned by the company. But the miners still needed work. And the cities still needed coal. Thus, many turned to bootlegging.

BOOTLEGGING

I grew up hearing how my great-grandfathers were bootleggers, and I knew they were running coal, not alcohol, as is commonly associated with the term. It wasn't until I started researching this novel that I learned about the third category of miner, the Independent Miner. These were men who legally leased land from the coal companies and then ran their own mining operations. The bootleggers dug wherever they felt like it, including out of their basements (like my great-grandfather) or off of company land (with no lease). I tried to showcase the variety of miners in this story. There was a great deal of friction between the companies and the bootleggers at this time, as the companies, with their expensive leases, saw this as theft. The bootleggers saw it as a natural resource owned by those who did the work to take it. Things did get violent. There are several articles about coal holes being blown shut by the company, and finally, Maryd residents did get their revenge.

The land around Maryd is unique in that the coal was and is very easy to access. The way the veins buckled underground, they actually set just below the surface of the ground in places. No deep mine was required, particularly back in the old days. It was a bootlegger's heaven, as these miners, who often had already gotten experience in the company mines, could easily dig good coal without a lot of workings. When it got too hard or unstable, they moved on to the next spot. Because of the shallow, simple nature of these "coal holes", they could use hand-powered equipment, even though mechanical drills and winches were available by the 1930s. I made Jack's bootlegging operation very small and simple, though some of the teams could have a dozen men and would power their winches off the engines of old Model T's. And yes, dynamite could be purchased at the store.

For more information on bootlegging in the anthracite region, I recommend Mitch Troutman's *The Bootleg Coal Rebellion*.

THE 1938 CONFLICT

It wasn't until 1938, when Lehigh Coal and Navigation Company renewed its lease of the land to the newly formed Maryd Coal Company, which was made up of a few out-of-town owners. The new company immediately began pushing a new drift mine into the mountain, blasting perilously close to the residents' homes. When residents protested, the company announced that it would begin strip mining.

It must have been clear to residents early on that both of these operations threatened their homes and businesses. They now owned their homes; they knew the dangers of mine subsidence, as other patch towns watched their houses crumble. Most residents also had established bootleg holes in their "backyards", which, though technically on company land, they had put a lot of work into. They relied on these coal holes for their livelihoods. Digging a bootleg hole to a profitable depth could take months of unpaid labor. The strip mining operation threatened to plow it all under in days. The residents also complained that strip mining would take all the "easy" coal close to the surface. They must have felt a high degree of betrayal by the company. They'd lost their jobs in the 1932 close, been forced to scratch out their own income by going independent, only to have the company come back at a much smaller, more destructive scale and threaten to take away that livelihood as well.

Eventually, the residents had had enough. In the dark of the evening of Monday, June 13, some 300-400 residents marched down to the company mine, escorted the watchman out of the mine, took out all the equipment, then set thirty-six charges. Boom, the ground shook, and the mine was blasted shut for a solid hundred feet. The sheriff, Fred Holman, didn't know who to arrest, as the whole town had been involved.

Eventually, twenty-four men were arrested. From here, the story gets even better. As the men sat in jail waiting for bail to be posted, the town formed a motorcade, complete with flags flying, and drove to the jail. Some 300 residents stood by as every single man's bail was posted to the sum of $500 per person. They also got the governor's attention, until finally the coal company sat down with representatives of the Independent Anthracite Miners Association and came to an agreement. There would be no more blasting under the town. They could only strip mine 1000 yards from the village (which still doesn't seem like much). And best of all, when company jobs became available, they first had to be offered to the independent miners of the town.

These men just wanted honest work.

Every single man arrested was released from all charges. My great-uncle was among them.

THE LAND AROUND MARY D

When I was little, just getting to the age of exploration, my dad gave me a pretty firm talk about wandering around the woods of Mary D. You have to understand, I grew up in the woods. It was nothing for me to take off wandering the mountain with my pocket knife, a walking stick, and sometimes a dog. I still picture him explaining to me the dangers of coal country. "You stay out of any depressions you see. They're the remnants of old mines. You never know which ones are just barely covered over by a thin layer of leaves, and if that layer gives way, you'll fall in and we'll never find you. And just so you know, stay out of the stripping holes. You had an uncle drown in one (I found out later that the uncle actually died in a flood) when a whirlpool sucked him to the bottom."

My dad was a great storyteller.

The reality is the land around Mary D and much of the northern tier of Schuylkill County is pockmarked with mines. Between remnants of bootleg holes, air shafts, and sinkholes from mine subsidence, my dad's advice holds true even today. There are still water-filled strippings with unknown depths. Just a few years ago, a kayaker drowned, and they were unable to find his body in the hundreds of feet of water.

That said, things are much better now than they were back in the 1930s and 1940s, when the town first voiced its concerns. Back then, there were culm banks right up to people's property lines. These banks occasionally collapsed or caught fire. A fire was burning just outside of Maryd in the 1960s. There were water-filled stripping holes as close as fifteen feet to the houses, and yes, in 1935, a little boy did drown in one. He slipped while trying to grab his friend's ball. As I mentioned in my story, the whole town came out to watch the recovery and support his family. For decades, the creek ran orange with acid mine drainage, and the Schuylkill River was dead from the breakers and factories dumping into it.

RECLAMATION

We (yes, you if you are a U.S. taxpayer) have spent millions reclaiming the land around Mary D. The old breaker area is now a beautiful ballfield. The old ballfield just outside of town is now a revolutionary acid mine drainage filtration area. A massive desilting program in the 1940s and 1950s cleaned up the Schuylkill River, and it is now one of the most scenic rivers in the state and is full of life. Today, the culm banks are shrinking as they continue to strip mine, only now the "waste" that the old underground miners left behind is being used. The landscape around Mary D continues to change as reclamation efforts continue to heal the land's scars.

Acknowledgements

This book was tough to write. Not only did I have to get the research just right, but I wrote the bulk of this when I was nine months pregnant with all the delightful pregnancy symptoms in full force. I then finished it throughout my son's first year of life, through the sleepless nights, the short naps, the oh-my-God-thank-you-for-two-hours naps, the love and adventure and awe that is new parenthood. It was interesting. And yet here we are. Thankfully I had a heck of a team to keep me pushing ahead, so here is to them, with thanks from the bottom of my heart.

Thank you to my beta readers and fellow authors, Melissa Roos and Lavada Martin, who put up with the rawest draft of this novel and gave me the feedback my sleep-deprived brain needed to make it stronger.

Thank you to my amazing family from Mary D. I can't wait for you to play the game of how many of the plot points within this novel are inspired by true events and stories you've told me over the years. I used you as a sounding board on so many things, and you helped me reconstruct what the town was like in 1938 and separate legend from truth. I wish Granny could have read this one. I know she'd get a kick out of it. Pop, you might be famous now. Thanks for letting me use your pictures for the cover!

Thank you to Ed, who supplied me with some interesting Mary D tales from beyond my family. And thank you to the research librarian at the Pottsville Library for helping me access microfilm and old mine records with an eight-week-old in tow. I appreciate you not kicking us out of the library.

My grandfather and his 2 youngest sisters circa 1938 in Maryd

To my editor, Gail Delaney, I am so glad I found you. It has been a pleasure to work with you through these novels. And to my cover designer, Laura Schaeffer of Venom Co, it always amazes me how you can bring my vague ideas to life and provide the visual for my story. Thank you both!

Thank you to my husband, who chased a baby in circles around a hotel room during our vacation so I could crunch the last draft of this out.

Then of course there is my giant THANK YOU to my readers. You asked for another book and without your support and encouragement, I might have just sat on this one (twenty years like *Knightess* maybe? haha). You challenged me to keep telling the stories that swirl in my head. I appreciate you taking the time to read my work *so much*. I hope you enjoyed *Patch Town*.

About the author

J.A. Stein grew up exploring the woods surrounding her Pennsylvania home. It was there that she learned to let her imagination run wild. Love of the outdoors led to a career training horses, now shared with her passion for writing, for which she has a bachelor degree. Her debut novel *Knightess* is a winner of a 2023 Royal Dragonfly Book Award. Her contemporary Schuylkill County novel, *The Last Farm*, received a 2024 Royal Dragonfly Book Award. She runs a horse farm by day and currently attempts to write during her young son's naps.

Stein spent a great deal of time in Mary D as a child at her grandparent's house and grew up hearing the stories of her dad's adventures around the town, some of which inspired this novel.

Want to connect? Please subscribe to her blog and newsletter at www.authorjastein.com. Free short stories and bonus chapters await! You can also follow her on Goodreads, BookBub, or YouTube under @AuthorJAStein.

Also by J.A. Stein

Need more Schuylkill County tales? Read the story of a farmer debating if he wants to sell to a warehouse developer, a story unfolding in real life right before our eyes. Winner of a Royal Dragonfly Book Award.

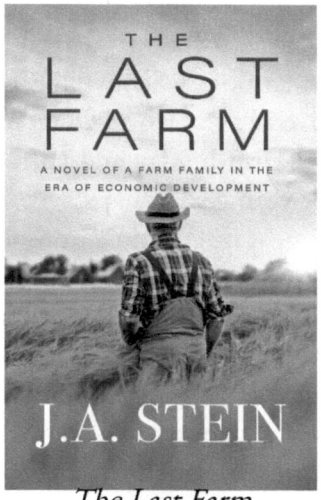

The Last Farm

Need more historical action? Jump back in time with J.A. Stein's first novel *Knightess*, part of an epic medieval trilogy. This series follows Eleanor, a woman hiding from her past, as she steps forward into her inheritance, her strength, and her independence by becoming a knight. The tale of an incredibly strong, resilient woman, with enough drama and romance to keep you turning pages late into the night. The series only gets better as you go, with *Lady of the Tournament* and *English Winter*. Winner of a Royal Dragonfly Book Award.

Knightess, Book 1 of *Swords of Resilience*

www.ingramcontent.com/pod-product-compliance
Lightning Source LLC
LaVergne TN
LVHW041219080526
838199LV00082B/963